BRIDEGROOM

BRIDEGROOM

The Cryptonym of a Spy

JAMES ZAFRIS

Merrimack Media
Boston, Massachusetts

Published by Merrimack Media, Boston, Massachusetts
September 2016

This does not constitute an official release of CIA information. All
statements of fact, opinion, or analysis expressed are those of the
author and do not reflect the official positions or views of the Central
Intelligence Agency (CIA) or any other U.S. Government agency.
Nothing in the contents should be construed as asserting or implying
U.S. Government authentication of information or CIA endorsement
of the author's views. This material has been reviewed solely for
classification.

CHAPTER ONE

Wagner waited until the other passengers had crowded toward the exit before he unfastened his seat belt. It felt good to stretch again after the long TWA flight from Paris. And it was a relief finally to be rid of the smelly man who had occupied the seat next to him.

Now that the door was open, a wave of heat began to fill the cabin and outside the window he could see the sun's rays shimmying along the silver wing. His friends had warned him to expect a strong dose of Greek heat even in early May.

Almost unconsciously he touched the inside of his jacket pocket to make sure his passport was still there. Then he pulled a piece of hand luggage from the overhead rack and stepped into the aisle, giving a friendly nod as he passed the young French stewardess who stood smiling as he approached the exit door. Wagner had one of those faces that seemed to invite warm smiles from attractive young women.

A nervous little man wearing the sweat-stained uniform of a minor official was standing at the bottom of the stairs directing passengers to the area where they eventually would recover their luggage and have their passports stamped. Wagner fell in behind the straggling procession and followed it inside the main terminal building. The room was filled with a cacophony of voices and confusion. He decided to put down his bag and have a smoke until things began to get sorted out. But before he had a chance to take the first long drag, he felt someone's hand on his sleeve.

"Mr. Wagner?"

When Wagner turned, he was facing a dark-haired young man, slightly in need of a shave but clearly quite self-impressed. "Yes," answered Wagner skeptically.

"Good. Give me your passport." When Wagner hesitated, the stranger laughed re-assuredly. "No, it is all right. I'll take care of it for you. Mr. Swasey sent me."

"Where is he?" asked Wagner. The stranger pointed his thumb and Wagner looked across the room. Swasey was leaning nonchalantly against a wall just inside the door as though completely bored with the proceedings. As Wagner looked over, Swasey nodded and started toward him.

"How are you, Jack? Have a good trip?" he asked as he extended an unenthusiastic hand.

"Yuh, fine thanks," responded Wagner. "Who's your friend?"

"Him?" replied Swasey in a half-amused voice. "Just one of our liaison contacts. Don't worry...he's been cleared. He also happens to be on our own payroll."

"It beats standing in line," smiled Wagner.

"That yours?" asked Swasey referring to the bag at Wagner's feet.

"Yes."

"Well, grab it and let's go," said Swasey in a tone that suggested he had better things to do than meet a new arrival at the airport.

"What about my passport and my other stuff?"

"That's what our buddy over there gets paid for," replied Swasey gesturing toward his contact who already was signaling that everything was in order. "Don't worry. By the time I get you to your hotel, he'll be waiting for us with baggage, passport and outstretched palm." Swasey continued in an almost friendly voice, "But, if we leave now, we might have just about enough time for me to buy you a cold beer before you officially check in."

Wagner reached down and picked up his bag. "Sounds good to me. Lead the way."

Swasey, who was a couple of steps ahead of Wagner as they wove through a row of parked cars, turned and almost as an afterthought, said, "By the way, your old friend, Bob Foster, planned to be here but had to beg off. He wanted me to let you know that he'll be swinging by your hotel in the morning to give you a lift into town. He lives in Kifissia, not too far from the Pentelikon Hotel where you'll be staying."

"That's great. It will be good to see him again."

"Yuh, I'm sure,"responded Swasey indifferently as he pulled open the door of a tired looking 1952 Vauxall. "Well, this is it. Climb into my Greek sauna. If you play your cards right, you'll probably inherit this piece of junk when I leave. Now let's find that beer."

****

Ellis started to pick up the cable announcing Wagner's flight number and E.T.A. but he put it down when he again felt the sharp pain. Instead, he reached into his desk drawer, took out an aureomycin tablet and swallowed it without water. Then he glanced at his watch and tilted back in his swivel chair, his elbows resting lightly on the arms, his hands folded under his chin. By now they were heading back into the city.

Remembering Swasey's bitter reaction at being told Washington had decided to send Wagner out as his replacement, Ellis wondered how things had gone at the airport. These rotations of personnel never were easy but this was one of the most unpleasant he could recall, particularly since Swasey was convinced that Wagner somehow had personally engineered the transfer. But Ellis knew differently. He knew that Headquarters was concerned with Swasey's freewheeling methods and he had tried to convince him to tighten control over his operations which centered around the Greek-Romanian emigre community in Athens.

In the two months since he arrived to take over the job of Chief of External Operations, Ellis had become increasingly skeptical that any of Swasey's activities had much chance of paying off with the recruitment of field agents with any real value. Greece and Romania had not had formal diplomatic relations since before World War II, so the exchange of diplomatic or trade personnel didn't exist. Without personal access, how do you spot and recruit targets of interest? Ellis had no answer.

Maybe there was some justification for continuing Swasey's WEDDING PARTY operation, if only to keep a finger on the pulse of the local emigre community. Swasey's principal agent was the acknowledged Greek-Romanian emigre leader who had managed to enhance his influence by the occasional publication of an anti-Communist newspaper which included news on emigre meetings and activities as well as personal items listing births, deaths and weddings...all at Company expense. A more productive part of WEDDING PARTY was the monitoring of ship to shore radio traffic from Satellite vessels in the Black Sea and Mediterranean which Washington seemed to find useful.

The operation that troubled Ellis the most was the planned airdrop of three Romanian escapees who were living in a safe house outside of Athens where they were being given wireless training before their proposed re-entry. Swasey's reports on their progress were vague at best and Ellis knew the Company's success rate with cross-border airdrops was close to zero. But with the Dulles brothers running both State and C.I.A., the current mantra was "roll back the Iron Curtain", so a chosen few of Company personnel were wasting their time writing long-range operational plans to create an army of anti-Communist guerillas in the Transylvanian Alps.

Screw it, thought Ellis. The decision to replace Swasey was inevitable, so maybe it's best to say goodbye to him and see if Wagner can get a better handle on things. At the moment, his only regret was that he had invited both men to join him for drinks on this particular evening.

He felt as though a rat was gnawing his gut...dysentery again...probably from eating at a village taverna on his last trip out of the city. All of which meant that later in the day he would make a pilgrimage to the dispensary where he would stand around self-consciously with other discomforted Americans, a pint-sized container in hand, waiting for his turn to deposit a specimen of stool for microscopic analysis. He had been through it before. It was time-consuming and not a little embarrassing, but, he mused with a wry smile, it had its humorous side. He was certain that when the boys in green-carpeted Washington offices 5,000 miles away thought of their Chief of External Operations, they did not picture him squatting awkwardly over a tiny cardboard carton in a dingy dispensary men's room. The trick is to keep your bellyache out of operations and that is not easy thought Ellis as he again flicked his wrist and looked at his watch.

Slowly he cleared his desk, tossing the cable on Wagner's arrival into his "Out" box. Then he stood up. He decided it already was too late for the morning sick call. He might as well have something to eat. Plain rice and a cup of tea should be safe enough.

****

At two o'clock in the afternoon, the city dozed in the white heat. The shops were shuttered and barred and the streets were empty. The people of the country had eaten their noonday meal, undressed and gone to bed. It was a difficult time for foreigners...the English and the Americans and the Russians...who were unused to serious daytime sleeping. A few of them catnapped in preparation for late nights ahead, but most continued their normal activities in slow motion.

At the dispensary, Henry Ellis sat in the waiting room at last, his cardboard carton held loosely in his hands. With amusement he noted the young secretary on his right who was attempting to conceal her carton under a large red handbag and the Naval officer on his left who had neatly covered his with his cap. The fan throbbed overhead and the sweat trickled sweet and cool inside his pant legs.

****

And across the city a secretary handed a report from Moscow to a small man seated behind a large desk in the Russian Embassy. He read it carefully and when he put it down, he knew the letter had been mailed and that it was only a matter of time before he could expect a visitor.

****

It was eleven o'clock and Wagner was back at his hotel. The evening had gone well. Ellis was a gracious host and Wagner welcomed the chance for a low-key renewal of their brief Headquarters relationship before getting down to more formal business in the morning. He decided to order a tonic and sit outside on his small balcony for one last smoke before turning in.

The night air was clear and full of stars after late afternoon showers. Kifissia was halfway up Mount Pelion, which itself was surrounded by more mountains. He could see the lights of houses in the distant hills and the dark outline of mountaintops silhouetted against the sky by sporadic flashes of heat lightning.

In spite of the late hour, the street below was alive with activity. Horse drawn carriages, with their mustached drivers and their two kerosene side lanterns passed directly under his window. He could hear the clatter of horses' hoofs echoing off the cobblestone street and the dull ringing of the driver's bell, a warning to people walking in the shadows of the dimly lit streets. As they walked, they sang, either in groups, or couples, or alone. They were unexpectedly pleasant sounds to Wagner who ground out his cigarette and sat quietly to listen before slowly standing and stepping back into his room. His first day in the field was over.

CHAPTER TWO

Wagner nursed a cup of coffee as he watched as Foster came through the door, pausing briefly for a quick look around the lobby, before spotting him and raising his hand in friendly recognition.

"Hi, Jack. Great to see you again. What's it been . . . a couple of years?" smiled Foster as he gripped Wagner's hand. "You don't look any the worse for wear. That D.C. air must have agreed with you."

"I didn't know it was that obvious," laughed Wagner.

"Well, unless you want another jolt of that Greek coffee, I've got the stretch limo waiting outside.

"I'm ready when you are. It was dark when I drove out here last night, so I'm curious to see the daylight version of the road back to Athens."

Although Wagner was six feet tall, he had to cock his head and look up at Foster as they headed for the lobby exit. They were both about the same age, approaching thirty, but not quite there. They walked with the easy gait of athletes. Foster seemed to bend slightly forward in an unconscious effort to match Wagner's eye level. He wore no hat which exposed his thinning hair and receding hairline. He was already tanned from the Greek sun and his love of tennis. His face was quite unremarkable except for his eyes, one of which was artificial, the result of a childhood accident. He had a pleasantly rumpled look, the kind of appearance one might associate with an aspiring young faculty member crossing an Ivy League campus on his way to class, a route Foster had planned to travel before being approached by The Company.

Wagner matched his colleague, stride for stride. His hair was closely cropped and he had the broad shoulders of a running back, which combined with his strong jaw and broken nose, gave him a formidable look. But his personality was more accurately defined by his easy smile and friendly eyes.

"Sorry I wasn't at the airport to meet you yesterday," said Foster as he pulled away from the hotel. "The Cyprus issue has heated up again," he added. "The Greeks living in Cyprus and the Greek Government here in Athens are lobbying hard for union between Cyprus and Greece. The Greek word for all that is ENOSIS. You'll hear it everywhere. Archbishop Makarios has climbed back on his soapbox to whip up support and raise the passion level."

"The fact that Cyprus is not that far off the Turkish coast and that there are a few thousand Turks living on the island who have a different point of view doesn't matter to Greece. There is no love lost between Greece and Turkey. By the way, the Greeks aren't happy with us because we haven't come out in support of ENOSIS. We're worried that if things heat up, it could end up with the Greeks and Turks fighting each other with equipment we're supplying to both sides as part of the Greek/Turkish Aid Program which is supposed to stabilize this part of the world."

"To make a long story short, I'm part of a working group trying to keep tabs on what's happening from day to day while we use whatever limited leverage we have to dampen the inflammatory rhetoric and discourage street rioting."

"That's why I wasn't at the airport."

"No problem, Bob. Al Swasey drew the short straw and made sure I got through the lines without any problems."

"I hope you were properly impressed." said Foster wryly. "He usually saves himself exclusively for high priority events. Or, so I've been told. Anyway, I'm glad you made it. I know that once you've settled in, you're going to like it here . . . great people, great country. By the way, what took you so long to get here?"

"A couple of things . . . one Company business and the other personal," replied Wagner. "My bosses back home thought it would be a good idea for me to take a crash course in Romanian before launching my career in the field."

"Did you learn anything?" laughed Foster.

"I hope enough so I can muddle through most conversations without causing an international incident," replied Wagner, before adding quietly, "Working through my personal issues was the hard part."

"You and Joan?"

"Yes. We're divorced . . . not something either of us planned or wanted. It just slowly happened. I guess you could call it a case of mutual misjudgment. We met while I was winding down after a couple of years of grad school and she was finishing her senior year in college. We hit it off from the start. I proposed. She accepted and I suddenly needed to find a job. The Company recruiter came along and off we went to Washington."

"Looking back, I think I now know she was just being the good wife, letting me take a fling at playing spy until I got it out of my system and moved on to something with a little more stability and better pay. I don't think she ever imagined that I'd stick with this forlorn business, beginning as a GS-7 with the lofty salary of $4,250.00 a year."

"She had a point," observed Foster.

"I know she did. I was just too dumb or too self-indulgent to realize it until it was too late. I thought it would be just a matter of time before she got caught up in the romance of a life of intrigue and travel." Wagner paused before adding, "I sometimes think that if that recruiter had been from a New York bank or a major international company instead of the Agency, we might still be happily married."

"I'm sorry it didn't work out. Kathy and I didn't get to see much of the two of you before we headed for Greece, but we really liked her and thought she was a great person."

"She is a great person," responded Wagner. "On our second anniversary we decided to splurge and go out to dinner and dancing on the rooftop of the Roger Smith Hotel. We hadn't planned a serious conversation and I'm not sure how it happened, but before the evening was over, so was our marriage."

"There were no tears or anger . . . just a lot of sadness and although it might be hard for someone else to understand, a lot of love," said Wagner with a shrug of sadness.

"Life is full of knuckleballs," observed Foster.

"And knuckleheads," smiled Wagner in reply.

They drove quietly for several minutes as they edged out of Kifissia and began the slow descent from Mount Pelion along the road back to Athens. On either side of the highway there were modest houses built of brick or stone or stucco: most in various stages of construction or repair. Some were painted white but most were a faded pink, which Wagner quickly concluded was the color of choice for most Greeks.

It was common to see a goat or a donkey tethered to a stubby looking tree, or chickens running in the dusty yard of one of these houses. An occasional stonewall bore the red and black letters of a Greek advertisement, an improvised equivalent of an American billboard.

The landscape was dotted with small tavernas. It seemed to Wagner that wherever there was a shade tree, someone had set out a couple of small tables where Greek men sat with their coffee or beer. And it was not unusual to pass a house where a whole lamb was being roasted over an open fire.

As they neared Athens, the traffic became more congested and they quickly transitioned to a more urban atmosphere. These were the suburbs closest to the city where many American and foreign diplomats lived. It was only a matter of minutes before they were on Queen Sophia Avenue heading toward the heart of the city and Constitution Square. Foster took a quick right on to Venizelou Street as they passed the Parliament Building and another quick turn as he headed uphill toward Kolonaki before easing his way into an empty parking space.

"We lucked out. It isn't always so easy to find a space in this area. We are in the Kolonaki section which you could say is the Beacon Hill of Athens. It's also just a short walk downhill to where you'll be hanging your hat," said Foster as he stepped out of the car.

Foster led the way, pausing only long enough to dodge the

on-coming traffic that was beginning to clog the main streets. As they approached the elevators, Foster leaned toward Wagner and smiled. "Your crew is comfortably ensconced in the penthouse, but the elevators only go up to the fifth floor so it's a good thing you brought me along to show you how to get into the inner sanctum."

"Is there an extra charge for that?" laughed Wagner as they pushed into one of the crowded elevators. The smell of garlic filled Wagner's nostrils, which Foster observed with an amused smile.

"Pretty potent stuff," commented Foster as he led the way to the Company offices. "There are a lot of Greeks who consider garlic to be their number one defense against all forms of illness. They feed it to prisoners to prevent epidemics among inmates. Rumor has it that if you approach a Greek prison, you'll smell it before you'll see it." Foster paused before opening the door. "But that's enough local folklore for the morning. Let's go in and see if we can find a few of your old friends."

There was nothing plush about the office space, perhaps a slight upgrade over the dilapidated temporary buildings next to the Reflecting Pool that housed the C.I.A. Headquarters In Washington. Wagner stopped along the way whenever he spotted the familiar face of a former colleague.

Ellis' office was at the end of the corridor, guarded by his secretary who sat at a desk outside his door.

"You must remember Heidi," said Foster as they approached her desk.

"Of course I do. It's great to see you again, Heidi. It looks like Hank wouldn't let you get away. Good for him," responded Wagner with a friendly smile.

"It's nice to see you again, too," she replied. Henry has been looking forward to getting you out here."

"Is he in and accepting unannounced visitors?" asked Foster jokingly.

"Yes, he is in and yes, he has been expecting you. I'll let him know you're here," she replied as she opened the door to Ellis' office.

"So you finally decided to come to work," smiled Ellis as he leaned back in his chair, his hands cupped behind his head as he beckoned them in. He was wearing a dark blue business suit, white shirt and striped tie. Wagner could not recall a time when he had ever seen him casually dressed. Ellis had narrow features and an aquiline nose. His full black hair was set off by a meticulously trimmed, pencil-thin mustache. He was perhaps ten years their senior, but was clearly comfortable in his role as Chief of External Operations.

"Thanks for giving Jack a lift into town this morning. I know you've got your hands full in your own shop."

"Glad to be useful for a change," laughed Foster. "It gave us a chance to catch up on the last couple of years. You probably don't know that we came on board the Agency on the same day and worked together on the Greek Desk during our first few months, so we had a lot to talk about," replied Foster.

"I didn't know you had that much history together. That helps ease my conscience. With a little luck, we'll find Jack a set of wheels and you can turn in your chauffeur's hat." Ellis turned toward Wagner. "Is this the morning Swasey's supposed to introduce you to one of his principal agents?"

"That's what he told me when we were at your house last night."

""I'd like to sit in on that one," interjected Foster dryly.

"Let me know how it goes," said Ellis as he walked them to the door. "It would be nice to know what's happening on my watch," he smiled. "And thanks again, Bob, for lending a hand today."

CHAPTER THREE

Swasey sat on the edge of his desk and swung his feet with short studied strokes, as though he were kicking an invisible object suspended in space just above the floor. He stared across the room at Wagner, who was studying the operational case file. Swasey's face was taut with annoyance, an echo of the rage that had contorted it a month earlier when Ellis had called him into his office to tell him Headquarters was sending his replacement.

Now he slid off the desk and walked toward the window with his back toward Wagner, as though trying to forget his presence. Swasey was 31 years old. He had blond hair, a thin face and well-formed nose. He was not quite six feet tall but his slender frame gave the impression of greater height. Everything about his body seemed compact and needle-like, as though he had been built to slide through narrow slits.

For a few moments, Swasey stood looking down at the street below, already snarled with mid-morning traffic. He watched a pith-helmeted Gendarme in a blue and white traffic box gesturing impatiently as the driver of a giant yellow bus tugged at the two cords extending from the back of his vehicle which had slipped off the overhead electric cable. A cab driver hung halfway out the window of his 1940 Ford, shouting epithets and pounding with an open palm on the side of his taxi, as though expecting his personal exhortation to set the stalled lines of traffic in motion. The light tan uniform of the Gendarme already was dark with sweat in spite of the sun shield covering his stand. Today would be another scorcher.

He was still looking out the window when he spoke. "Let's

not keep the Old Man waiting. I told him we'd be there at ten o'clock."

"I'm ready whenever you want to get going." answered Wagner as he closed the file.

Swasey turned around, casually tapped a pack of cigarettes against his thumb and pulled out a smoke. "Have you decided what name you're going to use?" he asked.

"How do you usually handle it?"

Wagner had pushed back his chair and was standing beside his desk, nonchalantly fingering the file he had been reading. He felt like telling Swasey to go to hell. Instead, he replied, "Why don't you call me Mr. Rogers?"

"You're the boss," snapped Swasey.

Three years in the field hasn't done much to improve your personality, thought Wagner, recalling their last encounter in Washington. Even then, Swasey had regarded each of his contemporaries as an immediate rival for power and never passed up the chance to remind the "Headquarters types" of his army experience in Germany and of the fact that he had just completed his first tour with the "Company" and was already being briefed to begin his second. It was a little hard to stomach that much arrogance from someone only two years his senior but right now Wagner's only concern was taking charge as quickly and efficiently as possible. If he had to swallow a little bile to placate Swasey's ego, so be it.

"Look, Al, you got this operation started and I want the transition to go smoothly. I can understand that BRIDEGROOM is probably feeling pretty unhappy to see you leave and apprehensive about working with someone new. He knows you and trusts you and I think you're the guy who ought to decide how we should handle the turnover."

Swasey looked at Wagner with a patronizing smile and then walked over and jammed his cigarette into an ashtray. "All right, if you really want my opinion, I'll tell you what I think we ought to do." He hesitated as though to marshal his thoughts before continuing. "You're right," he said with a casual shrug, "the Old Man's very upset to have me leave. There's no question about it." He paused so that Wagner would fully understand the importance of what he was saying. "I've done as much as I could to build you up and ease his mind. I've told him you'll keep things going the same way I have. But you've got to realize that this thing has shaken him up. Most case officers never really learn that the most important thing in this business is the personal relationship you build up with an agent like BRIDEGROOM. You can call it mutual respect or confidence or anything else you want to. I've never bought into that 'don't fall in love with your agent' crap they feed you in training. I'm not exaggerating when I say it's not a hellova lot different than the relationship between a doctor and his patient." Swasey's eyes were pinned on Wagner as he spoke. "I'll tell you something, Jack. When you're running an operation like this, you're God to an agent like BRIDEGROOM."

The oppressive heat that filled the room and the drama of Swasey's words gave Wagner a heady feeling of unreality, as though he had too much to drink. A horsefly hummed overhead and Wagner could hear it vibrating against the ceiling as he replied. "I know you're right, Al. That's why I think it's important that this first meeting goes off smoothly."

"O.K. I think we see eye to eye on this thing, so let's settle on how we're going to move you in." Swasey walked slowly across the room, his hands lost in the back pockets of his trousers. "I don't know what they tried to teach you down on "The Farm," he continued, "but if I were you, I'd forget most of it. As far as I'm concerned, the best way to qualify as a training instructor is to screw up somewhere else."

"I think I know what you mean," laughed Wagner.

"Yuh. Well, what I can tell you is this," said Swasey decisively. "This operation will practically run itself. I'm not trying to say I'm the smartest guy that ever ran a show like this. That seems to be a matter of opinion," he added bitterly. "But I knew that sooner or later someone would be taking over from me. It just happened a lot sooner than I figured. Of course, I'm not blaming you for that," he said, his mouth twisting into a knowing smile.

"I know it must be tough to leave," answered Wagner.

"Well, to hell with it," responded Swasey. "I'm just trying to tell you that your big Job will be to reassure BRIDEGROOM and get him the support he needs. He knows what we're after and he knows how to get it. But I'll tell you this. You're going to have a lot of deskbound nitpickers on your back, asking for a notarized chit every time he spends five bucks. If I listened to those bastards, I'd be a bookkeeper instead of a case officer.

As Swasey stopped speaking, Wagner began cleaning a crusty-looking pipe he had pulled from his jacket pocket. "Look, Al, I understand where you're coming from. I know you haven't wanted to get bogged down in red tape. But not everyone sees things quite the same way." He paused and rapped the bowl of his pipe hard against the heel of his hand, knocking loose ashes into a green office wastebasket. "As a matter of fact, some of your friends back home are having a hard time getting approval for more funds and they asked me to give you a heads-up."

Swasey's neck reddened but he answered in a calm voice. "What's bothering them?"

"There's no problem with them. They understand what's going on and if they had their way, they'd give you all the leeway you need. But every time you ask for more money, they have to fight it through a half dozen staffs. The last time Bill Benson went looking for more funding, he was told it was the last dime they'd approve until you sent in a financial accounting and a few receipts from BRIDEGROOM. You'll know what I'm talking about when you get back and start fighting the battle of Headquarters."

"So what did they send you out here to do . . . balance the budget?"

"I hope that's not the only reason I'm here," answered Wagner with a patient smile. "I respect all you've accomplished, Al, and I want to build on it. Let's just say that they've let me know I won't be here very long if I don't account for operational expenses."

"I suppose that means the boys back in the ivory tower think I've let BRIDEGROOM get out of hand."

"No way," responded Wagner, trying hard to control his growing irritation. "It's no reflection on you at all. I can tell you without equivocation that you have a solid reputation back home. But from here on out, my marching orders are to tighten up on controls."

"Well, that's your headache. Just remember that BRIDEGROOM isn't someone you can buy and sell. I'm sure he depends on the Company stipend. But he's a proud man. This operation is just part of our job, but it's very personal with him. Put yourself in his shoes." Swasey slowly twisted a pencil between his fingers. "Here's a guy who was a successful businessman, the head of his own export company. Plenty of money. Big house. Servants. Before the war, he belonged to the business elite and had influential friends in government and commerce all over Europe. Then overnight the Communists come in and lower the boom. First they take over his house and confiscate his business. And finally he finds himself in prison until one of his friends greases the right palms and he gets an exit visa, leaving a sick mother behind. So what is he now? Just another middle-aged refugee with a firm hold on nothing and no prospect for improving his situation. I don't think we have to worry about what motivates him."

"Al, I understand what he's been through and I'm not about to forget that he's got problems if that's what's bothering you," answered Wagner calmly.

"O.K., Jack. I'm not trying to deliver a sermon. We're in the wrong racket for that stuff. All I'm trying to tell you is that you're going to get more mileage out of the guy if you remember to wipe his nose once in awhile." Swasey gave a nervous hitch to his trousers, which seemed to be perilously close to sliding off his narrow hips. "We might as well get going. I told the Old Man you'd be with me and he knows you'll be in charge after today."

"Is there anything special you want to talk over with him at the meeting?" asked Wagner.

"No. This is strictly for you to meet him. After this, I'm out and you'll have to set up the next contact."

"Where's the meeting today?"

"He'll be waiting on a bench in the National Garden. We'll walk past so that you'll get a chance to see each other. He'll wait until we've gone by and then he'll catch up with us long enough for introductions and for you to arrange a new meeting. That's all there will be to it."

"Do you use any signals?" asked Wagner.

"What do you mean?"

"I mean in case he thinks it wouldn't be secure to meet you."

"Look, he's no babe-in-the-woods. If he thinks anything is wrong, he'll shove off and get in touch with me later," answered Swasey who was annoyed by the question. "I don't play cops and robbers with him. But if you want him to start scratching his armpit every time he sees you, I'm sure he'll do it."

"No, Al, all I'm trying to do is get things straight before I meet him," responded Wagner coldly.

"All you have to remember is that I'm 'Fletcher' you're 'Rogers' and he's 'Victor'. Then decide when you want to see him again." Swasey moved slowly toward the door. "You ready."

"Sure."

****

Swasey pushed open the door leading from the grayly lit corridor to the sidewalk and squinted under the glare of the blinding hot sun. He stopped only long enough to put on his sunglasses and without waiting for Wagner, quickly began sliding and picking his way through the crowd of morning shoppers, peddlers and tourists which moved sluggishly along the pavement. Wagner kept pace a few yards behind Swasey. From time to time he lost sight of his colleague as Swasey's slender form plunged into and out of tight knots of people like a porpoise breaking and re-entering water.

Their route took them along one of the main avenues of the modern city but they were soon lost in the narrow streets and alleys of the old market place where it became increasingly difficult for Wagner to follow Swasey. The foot traffic was heavy and people spilled off the sidewalks and choked the ancient streets. Wagner quickly sensed that Swasey was taking a circuitous route to their meeting place. He couldn't decide whether it was to give him a fast walking tour of the old Plaka district or to prove he was still calling the shots.

Here in the market place the worlds of the East and the West scraped one against the other like abrasives, wrenching the air with a discordant chorus of shouting and haggling. Dark-complexioned street merchants, their eyes alive with excitement, stood in front of pushcarts, squeezing and testing succulent-looking fruits for skeptical old women.

The windows of the marble-fronted shops that lined the sidewalks were cluttered with huge brass and copper trays, china, old coins and cheap tourist trinkets. The more expensive antique stores exhibited quiet displays of rich artwork and brightly painted icons. Inside these shops haggling was conducted on a more subdued level and no shop owner would think of discussing a price until he had first offered his customer a demitasse of Turkish coffee.

As they proceeded further into the market area, the marble-fronted stores gave way to rows of wooden street stalls. Here one could rummage through piles of used clothing, second-hand books, bottles and tools; or even find a part for an outdated automobile. Itinerant peddlers, confidently balancing enormous straw trays of fish or bread on their heads, brushed easily through the crowd. A sweating carpet salesman, a brightly woven rug slung over his arm like the napkin of a head waiter, scanned faces for likely looking prospects.

The mid-morning heat was so intense that Wagner had shed his jacket and tossed it over his shoulder. A layer of dust blanketed the entire area, teasing his nostrils and puffing up over his shoe tops with each footstep.

The intriguing sounds and sights of the market had distracted his thoughts from the meeting with BRIDEGROOM so that he was momentarily caught off guard when Swasey suddenly turned into a dirty alley. The two men walked only a short distance over broken paving stones before they were crossing Constitution Square, Athens' main plaza, which during times of political unrest, served as a rallying point for student rioters. Their sudden emergence from the disordered confusion of the old market place to the relative calm of the square jolted Wagner's senses.

The square, which covered an area of about two blocks of the city, was flanked by two elegant Old World hotels, the King George and the Grande Bretagne. Across the wide boulevard opposite one end of the plaza was a cluster of government buildings, dominated by the drab, hulking frame of the Parliament Building. The farther end of the square was closed in by a row of fashionable shops, airline offices, tourist agencies and ice cream parlors.

Here in the coolness of late afternoon, hundreds of people gathered each day for animated conversation over sweets and coffee at the dozens of small tables set tightly together on a wide marble-paved area across the street from the ice cream parlors and coffee houses. Now only a few perspiring tourists waited impatiently for slow-moving busboys to weave through lanes of motor traffic to deliver their trays of lukewarm lemonade.

The sun's rays exploded off the marble pavement and made Wagner's eyes water. A few white-frocked sidewalk photographers already had fixed their black-curtained box cameras on tripods and were vainly seeking shade under the few palm trees that lined the footpaths. A cab driver, waiting for a fare, glanced listlessly at them as they passed the Grande Bretangne

As soon as they had rounded the corner and entered the square, Wagner noticed a squad of brightly uniformed Evzones stepping along the sidewalk toward the War Monument in front of the Parliament Building.

"We'll be right on time," said Swasey. "They change the guard every hour on the hour."

"How much farther is it?" asked Wagner.

''We ought to be there in a couple of minutes."

Swasey watched Wagner begin pulling on his jacket as they walked. "What the hell did you bring that for? No one wears a jacket in this heat."

There was no question he was right. Practically every man they passed was wearing a white open-necked cotton shirt and sunglasses, which gave them the appearance of straggling columns of green-eyed bugs. But Wagner was tense with anticipation and Swasey's remark about his jacket, with the implication that he was a greenhorn, rankled him and he didn't reply

They walked in silence for a short distance before turning into one of the crush-stone-covered paths leading through the park. On one side of the entrance there was a play yard with a few swings and slides and on the other side, a large open circular area surrounded by gray wooden benches. White-aproned nannies already were sitting in the morning sun gently rocking baby carriages and watching the older children play across the way. Two or three of the nursemaids were carrying on innocent flirtations with grinning soldiers who had sat down beside them.

Just beyond the entrance area, nearer the center of the park, Wagner saw an almost empty pavilion set among the green shrubs and trees. A couple of waiters were leaning against the railing chatting and a few people sat in the shade of the pavilion sipping coffee. A small barefoot boy, about eight years old, who had been sitting on the pavilion steps, saw them and suddenly dashed at them, carrying a basket of pistachios under his arm.

"Hey, mister, how about buying some pistachios?"

"Gowon, beat it," said Swasey in a sharp voice as he tried to wave him off. But the boy danced around them as though he were tied on a string.

"Aw, com'on, mister. Be a pal. Just one bag."

"Shove off. We don't want any of your goddam nuts," said Swasey with increasing irritation.

The boy continued to dog them and turned to Wagner. "Whatta you say, mister, buy some? They're good and they're cheap." Wagner reached into his pocket, pulled out a coin and handed it to the boy. "Thanks a lot, mister. See you tomorrow," said the boy as he headed back for the steps.

Wagner took the pistachios he didn't want and jammed them into the jacket he didn't need. "He looked like he could use the money," he said, half amused, half apologetically.

"I'll tell you something," said Swasey. "Sooner or later you'll find it out for yourself. But if you try to buy pistachios from every hungry kid in this country, you're gonna run out of dough. It's a fact of life you might begin getting used to."

"I suppose you're right, Al, but we've got him out of our hair anyway."

"Probably just as well," said Swasey. "The Old Man ought to be right around the bend."

Instinctively they slowed their pace like hunters sensing quarry nearby. The air was cool still. The only sound they heard was the hard crunching of their shoes grinding against the tiny stones underfoot. Green shrubs and hedges abounded and crowded to the edge of the footpaths that wound through the park. Everywhere around them eucalyptus, palm and pine trees shot skyward, shading this oasis in the sweating dusty city. A musky smell of geraniums from neatly manicured gardens clung to the air. Wooden slat benches were placed along the paths. When they rounded the turn, Swasey spotted BRIDEGROOM sitting on one of them.

"That's the Old Man," said Swasey. "We'll walk past him slow so that you can get a good look at each other. After we get by, I'll stop and light a cigarette and he'll catch up with us. Don't waste a lot of time. Just tell him when you want to see him again and we'll get going."

"Right," answered Wagner.

BRIDEGROOM had been sitting with his hands folded across his lap. A newspaper lay on the bench beside him. He glanced up when he heard their steps but gave no sign of recognition. When they walked past, Wagner could feel his eyes looking him over.

Swasey stopped and pulled out a smoke and Wagner could see BRIDEGROOM get off the bench and walk slowly toward them. "How are you, Victor?" Swasey asked casually.

"Quite hot," answered BRIDEGROOM with a friendly smile to Wagner.

"Victor," said Swasey, "this is Mr. Rogers."

BRIDEGROOM extended his hand as he turned to face Wagner. "Mr. Rogers," he said formally, almost as if he were clicking his heels. "Mr. Fletcher has spoken of you often and it is a great pleasure to meet you."

"I've been looking forward to meeting you, Victor," responded

Wagner in a relaxed manner that betrayed none of the tension that was clawing his chest. The voice was his and the perspiring flesh and hard knuckles of BRIDEGROOM's hand was genuine enough, but the situation seemed so unreal, that for just an instant, Wagner had the queer feeling that this drama in the park was in fact a vivid, but quite implausible dream.

It was Swasey who broke the spell. "Victor," he said with a trace of regret in his voice, "I think you and Mr. Rogers have a few things to talk over so I'm going to say goodbye for now." He paused and looked at BRIDEGROOM with a wistful half-smile but quickly caught himself and continued in a firm voice. "We've got something good going here and I know you'll keep it rolling. I'm only sorry I won't be around to see it through with you." He put his hand awkwardly on BRIDEGROOM's arm and said, "Keep up the good work. We'll meet again."

BRIDEGROOM, who had been listening solemnly to Swasey's words, took Swasey's hand in both of his. "Mr. Fletcher," he began as though there was something he wanted to say, but instead he released his grip. "Good luck."

They watched Swasey walk quickly out of sight. "He was a good man," said BRIDEGROOM as though speaking to himself.

They were standing on the edge of the footpath not far from a small lily pond. A gentle breeze stirred against the leaves of the shrubs and trees and they could hear water gurgle out of the fountain in the center of the pond.

Now that they were alone, Wagner suddenly was acutely conscious that he was at least a head taller than his agent. Normally he felt ill at ease when he towered over someone as he did BRIDEGROOM. But there was something in BRIDEGROOM's confidently erect manner that seemed to compensate for the disparity in their heights.

Although Wagner was sweating uncomfortably in his jacket, he had been relieved to see that BRIDEGROOM also had chosen to wear a suit and necktie. His trousers and jacket were badly frayed but they had been neatly pressed, and in spite of the dust, he somehow had managed to keep his shoes carefully polished. The suit, which still had an unmistakable look of quality, undoubtedly was a legacy from better days. Yet, BRIDEGROOM wore it with such assurance that, if anything, its frayed appearance enhanced rather than detracted from the overall impression of dignity and competence which he conveyed. BRIDEGROOM easily could have passed for a former member of the Board who was a bit down on his luck.

He was moonfaced and his shirt-collar seemed to bite into his stump neck; but his dark eyes, alert, animated and keenly intelligent, dispelled any thought that this was another indolent fat man. Wagner had the disquieting sensation that even as BRIDEGROOM waited politely on his pleasure, the quick mind behind those quick eyes had already recorded every detail of his person and much of his personality and character and even now had gone on to subtler points.

"Let's sit over her for a minute. It looks a little cooler," said Wagner leading BRIDEGROOM to a nearby bench. Until this meeting, Wagner had never met an agent and BRIDEGROOM himself had been nothing more than a name in cables. He had wondered apprehensively whether he would know what to do and what to say when they met face-to-face. But now that they were together, he realized that there was no magic to this business and he had no trouble organizing either his thoughts or his words.

As they sat down, Wagner said, "I don't want to keep you very long this morning and this probably isn't the best place to do much talking but I do want to get together with you within the next two or three days."

"I'll be at your service," replied BRIDEGROOM agreeably.

"One thing I would like to have you understand is that everyone is very pleased with the work you've been doing and I certainly wasn't sent out here to make any drastic changes," said Wagner.

"I'm happy to know our people are satisfied," BRIDEGROOM replied with a smile.

"Naturally, I suppose I might do some things a little differently than Mr. Fletcher but I don't imagine any two men operate exactly the same way," continued Wagner.

"You just give the orders and tell me what you want," answered BRIDEGROOM in impeccable English.

"Well, I think the best way for me to get started would be for me to meet your two people here in town. Can you arrange that for the next time?" asked Wagner.

BRIDEGROOM seemed surprised by Wagner's sudden request to meet the other two agents in OPERATION WEDDING PARTY and he hesitated a few seconds before replying. Certainly, if you like, but Mr. Fletcher did not meet them directly."

"I understand," said Wagner, "but he was familiar with every detail of the operation. I think it would be helpful for me to get to know them."

"All right," said BRIDEGROOM. "Where do you want to meet them . . . and when?"

"Are they still living in the safe house?" asked Wagner.

"Yes."

"Is there any reason why we can't meet there?"

"No. I don't think so," said BRIDEGROOM.

"O.K. Let's make it next Thursday night at nine o'clock if that's agreeable with you," said Wagner.,

"I'll be there," replied BRIDEGROOM.

"Good." Wagner reached into his pocket and took out his pipe. "I don't think we should try to cover anything else today." They eased themselves up off the bench and shook hands.

"Perhaps it would be just as well if we didn't leave here together," said Wagner. "I'll let you get on with your business and I'll wait here a few minutes and have a smoke."

BRIDEGROOM took his sunglasses out of his pocket and put them on. "Thursday night," he said and started down the path.

CHAPTER FOUR

BRIDEGROOM stood on the sidewalk outside the entrance to the gardens and looked automatically in both directions before he began walking slowly toward the bus stop where five or six people were waiting. It wasn't long before a dilapidated motor-driven bus, already crowded with passengers, pulled to a stop. Two faded-blue fenders hung loosely from the long old-fashioned snout of a hood and the tires were worn smooth to brown corded patches. The door was suddenly swelled open by a dozen bundle-carrying passengers, all trying to get off at the same time. Before the last passenger had alighted, people on the sidewalk began jamming and pushing in the opposite direction trying to get on. BRIDEGROOM was shoved involuntarily forward until he felt his weight on the bottom step which sagged like a lifeless springboard. The door squeezed shut behind him.

His movements since he left the park had been responses to reflex rather than to conscious direction. His mind had been so completely focused on the implications and possible consequences of his meeting with Wagner that he scarcely noticed the awkward position into which he was now uncomfortably wedged. The bus reeked with the familiar smell of garlic and body sweat. One of BRIDEGROOM's arms was locked closely to his side but he had freed a hand and managed to steady himself by holding a pipe-rail attached to the dashboard. It was not until he felt the bus lurch, backfire and then speed recklessly forward through the congested streets of the city that he was snapped back into an awareness of his immediate surroundings.

BRIDEGROOM looked across at the driver, who was maneuvering the vehicle with the fearless abandon of a charioteer at a Roman carnival, and watched him with a certain detached fascination, observing at the same time the not uncharacteristic personal touches adorning the driver's tiny cubicle. Fresh wild flowers filled a cone-shaped vase that was screwed on the wall next to the driver's seat and a crucifix and a small framed photograph of three children had been attached just above the speedometer. A sandwich was jammed between the sun visor and the roof of the bus.

In a few minutes they had made their way through the worst of the traffic and were passing the factories and tavernas that lined the broad pockmarked avenue leading toward the waterfront. The bus was so cramped that BRIDEGROOM had trouble breathing the stifling air. And every few seconds, great gusts of dust swept through the open windows, stinging his eyes and coating his face and hands with a thin gritty layer of brown. He was relieved when he finally climbed down at his stop.

The street ascended sharply from the main artery next to the bay where he had gotten off the bus and the uphill climb was tiring for a man BRIDEGROOM's age. His ankles were twisted uncomfortably by deep ruts in the unpaved side street but he could see the red-roofed stucco house only a short distance away. He slowly mounted the chalk-white marble stairs, crossed the wide veranda that fronted the house and pressed the doorbell three times. While he waited, he noted that the wooden shutters around the one-story building had been closed tightly against the morning heat and the flowers in the red window boxes were burnt brown from lack of water.

The door was opened by an enormous man wearing tortoise-shell glasses. "Hello, Victor," said the big man laying a friendly hand on BRIDEGROOM's shoulder. "A little hot, eh?"

"Hello, Nick," answered BRIDEGROOM as he walked through the entrance hall into the shutter-darkened living room.

The big man followed him. His wrinkled brown shirt was unbuttoned in front and his hairy belly sagged in loose folds over the top of un-pressed beltless trousers. The zipper on his fly had slid down a little. He shuffled across the floor in badly worn slippers that were broken open at the toes exposing large yellow bunions. He looked like a man who slept in his clothes and had just woken up.

Yet there was something disarmingly pleasant about the big man who was standing trying to brush his sparse graying hair into place with his hands. He had a full face, big ears and a powerful jaw but his eyes sparkled with good humor and he was quick to smile.

BRIDEGROOM slumped wearily on the sofa and wiped a handkerchief across his forehead.

"Well," asked Nick, "how is the new man?"

"I'm not sure yet," replied BRIDEGROOM.

"What's the matter," laughed Nick, "did they send another boy?"

"He's young . . . I think younger than 'Fletcher,' but it isn't the age that matters," continued BRIDEGROOM, "'Fletcher' had his good points . . . a little brash perhaps . . . but not hard to handle."

"And this one?" asked Nick.

"We'll find out soon enough," replied BRIDEGROOM.

"What does this one call himself?" asked Nick.

"Mr. Rogers."

"Mr. Rogers," repeated Nick, pursing his lips and grinning, "not bad." Then he looked at BRIDEGROOM who seemed unusually grim and said jokingly, "but why be so sad?"

BRIDEGROOM had learned not to expect too much from Nick but he was tired from worry and Nick's inability to comprehend the seriousness of their situation frustrated him. "Nick," he said in a slow irritated voice, "you have a thick skull."

"Oh, ho," responded Nick still grinning and now pounding the side of his head with his fist, "so you found out too."

BRIDEGROOM ignored the joke and said in a deliberates tone, "He wants to come out here and meet you."

BRIDEGROOM's remark struck home and Nick sat down before he replied. "I see," he said slowly, "new man . . . new ideas."

Neither man spoke as Nick lit a cigarette. "When do we have our little meeting?"

"Thursday night at nine" answered BRIDEGROOM. Then he asked, "Where is Tina?"

"She's in back cleaning up," answered Nick.

"Go get her and bring her in," ordered BRIDEGROOM.

Nick stood up and lumbered toward the back of the house while BRIDEGROOM sat with his eyes closed, rubbing his fingers slowly back and forth across this brow.

In a minute a short dark-haired woman, still wiping her hands on the front of her cotton housedress, came through the door of the living room. "Hello, Victor," she said, extending her hand as he rose to greet her. "Nick just told me you were here and wanted to see me."

"Hello, Tina," said BRIDEGROOM. "Yes, I want to talk with you. Sit down."

At one time in her life she might have been a beautiful woman. She still had clear blue eyes and small well-formed features but her face was wrinkled and she apparently made little effort to improve her appearance. She wore no makeup and although her hair had been tinted brown, it was showing gray near the roots where it was growing out. The blue housedress she was wearing was soiled in front and hung shapeless on her plump body and her bare arms were heavy with fat and her hands were red from work. But one had only to hear her speak to know that she was an alert intelligent woman.

"Is something the matter, Victor?" she asked as she sat down in the chair next to where Nick was standing.

"No, nothing is the matter," replied BRIDEGROOM, "but I thought I should tell you that I met the new man today and he wants to come out here Thursday night to meet you and Nick."

"Oh . . . do you think he is planning to change things?" she asked.

"Don't be silly," chided Nick, "he just wants to come out and have a cup of free coffee. You know they don't pay him very much."

"Be quiet, Nick," Tina said sharply, "and listen to what Victor is saying."

BRIDEGROOM was grateful for Tina's attention. "No, Tina," he said, "I don't think that he is planning any changes. I feel quite sure that he is just curious to meet you and see what the house looks like but I think we should be prepared for him."

"Of course, Victor," responded Tina, "what do you want us to do?"

"There is nothing special," answered BRIDEGROOM. "After he meets you and Nick, he'll probably ask some questions about the house, which I can take care of. What he really wants to know is whether or not what we do has any value to him. We have to convince him that it does. Just remember, the Americans and the Russians are competitors. They both want to control events. For them it's an endless game of political chess, where even the slightest move matters. We are just pawns in their game, but because we can influence the political direction of the Greek/Romanian community, we give Mr. Rogers a small advantage. He'll understand that."

BRIDEGROOM paused before continuing. "Nick, I know he'll want to know more about your work. I got the impression from 'Mr. Fletcher' that his people value those reports on ship movements. Show him your equipment and how you monitor the ship to shore traffic that goes into your reports. Remind him that you are an experienced radio operator with years of work in Constanta before you met me and that you still have a lot of friends you left behind. Just don't exaggerate," he concluded with a knowing smile.

"Don't worry about it, Victor. Before we're through, I'll have him eating out of my hand," replied Nick with an amused shrug.

Tina listened soberly while BRIDEGROOM spoke. It wasn't necessary for him to explain to her the possible meaning for them all of this change in the American command. The memories of her life in the refugee center had been sharply imprinted: they might fade with time but they could not be erased. And although she tried to make herself accept her present situation for what it was . . . a temporary bit of good fortune that could end without notice . . . she was no longer certain that she possessed the moral strength to return to the privations she and Nick had endured together in the years before BRIDEGROOM introduced them to his work and persuaded 'Mr. Fletcher' that they should be moved into a house where they could operate securely.

As these thoughts passed through her head, she suddenly remembered the letter she was holding for BRIDEGROOM. She quickly stood up and took the envelope off the mantle of the blocked-off fireplace and handed it to him. "Victor," she said, "I'm very sorry. I almost forget that your cousin was here early this morning and left this letter for you from home. Perhaps it has some news from your mother."

"That's all right, Tina," said BRIDEGROOM. "Here, let me see it."

They watched him tear open the envelope and read the message inside. "Is it news from your mother?" asked Tina in a concerned voice.

"Yes."

"I hope she is well."

"It seems she is worse," replied BRIDEGROOM calmly, "but perhaps that is to be expected of someone her age."

He was re-reading the section of the letter that had disturbed him more than he dared show. "My Dear Victor . . . My heart bothers me more each day and I believe I shall die soon without proper medicine. Your letters tell me you have mailed packages . . . but they do not arrive . . . We are told by friends that there is another way . . . that packages are being received by the Russian Embassy and delivered here. My son, if your conscience lets you ask this favor from your enemies . . . if not . . . I understand . . . "

BRIDEGROOM handed them the letter. "Will you try it, Victor?" asked Nick sympathetically "Why not ask a favor from the devil?"

"I don't know," answered BRIDEGROOM solemnly. "I will think about it." Then, as though dismissing thoughts of the letter completely from his mind, he said, "For now, all we have to worry about is our new friend 'Mr. Rogers',"

"We'll take care of everything," assured Tina.

"I know I can rely on you, Tina. Thank you."

BRIDEGROOM started toward the front door, but he stopped and looking down at Nick's ugly feet, he said, "Nick, when 'Mr. Rogers' comes . . . wear your shoes." And then he stepped closer to Nick who was standing in the hallway and added in a quieter voice that Tina could not overhear, " . . . and zip your fly."

Nick reached quickly for the front of his trousers and grinned as BRIDEGROOM closed the door.

❀❀❀❀

BRIDEGROOM walked pensively away from the safe house in the direction of the wide cement promenade that circled the bay. The sun reflected with white brightness off the surface of the water and the coarse pebbly sand of the beach was washed wet and dark brown by softly lapping ripplets. The sky was cloudless blue. He walked slowly, only half noticing the barefoot children who were sitting on the sand below, their backs propped against the base of the promenade, mending the large fish nets that were spread across their legs.

Almost without thinking, he descended some stairs that led from the sidewalk to a small taverna on the beach and sat down at one of the crude wooden tables that had been placed under an awning next to the water. It was peacefully quiet.

A busboy hurried over and put a glass of water on the table. "Yes, sir?" he asked.

"Coffee," answered BRIDEGROOM without looking up.

"Right away," responded the boy turning toward the kitchen.

After the boy had left, BRIDEGROOM reached into his pocket and took out the letter that Tina had given him and read it again. When he saw the boy returning, he carefully folded it and replaced it in his pocket.

He sipped his coffee slowly, putting down the cup several times to look out across the water. After a few minutes, he pushed back his chair, dropped one coin on the table for the coffee and pressed another into the hand of the boy, who thanked him with a broad smile.

CHAPTER FIVE

"How did the meeting go?" asked Ellis as he waved Wagner into his office.

"It went well," replied Wagner, pulling up a chair facing Ellis' desk.

"First impressions?"

"I'd say positive. I liked him. I had the feeling that he had the situation pretty well sized up before we got there. He has a few years under his belt so the transition from one case officer to another didn't seem to faze him. But I sensed that he understood that Al was miffed about being replaced and wanted to distance himself from that issue."

"I can't fault him for that," laughed Ellis.

"On the other hand, just watching their interaction, I think they had a pretty close working relationship," continued Wagner. "After Al introduced us, there wasn't a lot of small talk. No farewell speeches. But with a few words and gestures, BRIDEGROOM managed to make it clear that their relationship meant something to him and I think he was sincere. They shook hands, wished each other good luck and Al walked away, leaving the two of us to form our own first impressions."

"Who broke the ice?" asked Ellis.

"I suppose I did. We didn't spend a lot of time together, just long enough for me to re-assure him that we weren't going to make any major changes. That seemed to please him and he was quick to let me know he was ready to do whatever we needed. We set a time for our next meeting. I told him I wanted to visit the safe house and meet the other two agents."

"How did he react to that?" asked Ellis.

"A little surprised. Apparently that wasn't part of Al's modus operandi. But he agreed and I'll be taking a ride out there next Thursday night."

"Does that mean that the boys in the motor pool found you a set of wheels?" asked Ellis jokingly.

"It wouldn't have happened without your help. It pays to have influential friends," responded Wagner.

"Well, now that I know you've got a way to move around without calling a taxi, do me a favor and get out there and see what the hell is going on with those three guys we're supposed to be training for an air drop. The contract agent who's doing the W/T training gets rave reviews from everyone who knows him, but I have no idea how much progress he's making." Ellis paused before adding, "If any."

"What has Al been saying about it"

"You know Swasey. He has a problem with straight answers," smiled Ellis.

"Hank, if I'm not out of line, who dreams up these operations?" prodded Wagner.

"Do I detect a touch of cynicism?" laughed Ellis. "But you know the answer. You just left Washington. The Agency has been split down the middle from the day it was put together. Somewhere along the line we got away from concentrating on old-fashioned intelligence . . . doing the hard work of developing agent networks that could give us direct access to the kind of information that we're supposed to be providing to our users who make the tough policy decisions." Ellis paused to reach across his desk for a roll of lifesavers before adding wryly, "But it takes time and patience to identify, recruit and train potential agents who have that kind of access. Unfortunately, patience is not one of our strong suits."

"So I've noticed," agreed Wagner.

Ellis leaned back in his chair for a few moments and looked across at Wagner while trying to decide the wisdom of sharing his observations of the inner workings of The Company with his younger colleague before he continued. "Jack, there are a lot of people, both inside and outside the Agency, who are still sold on the idea that we can roll back the Iron Curtain if we mount enough cross-border operations and somehow create a resistance force inside Eastern Europe. Time will tell whether or not they're right but they lobbied hard to get The Company a broad mandate allowing it to take almost any action involving intelligence or national security. They must have made a convincing argument because we got handed a lot of power that a few people in the Agency are willing to stretch to the limit."

"I assume that includes political action," interjected Wagner.

"Sure. But I don't have any problem with that. If the Russians are bank rolling their candidates in elections in Greece or Italy, we better be ready to do the same for our political friends. That makes a lot more sense than firing howitzers at each other."

Ellis hesitated before continuing. "The problem with almost unlimited power is that there always will be a few people who don't know how to handle it. We have to keep an eye on them. I'm not concerned about infiltrating a few agents, by air if it makes sense, as long as they have a specific mission that they're qualified to execute. That's part of our job. But I think we'll be asking for trouble it we let that kind of activity morph into broader para-military operations that we ought to leave to the Marines or some of our friendly political proxies."

Ellis looked at Wagner with a whimsical smile before adding, "Of course, that's just one man's opinion."

"I happen to agree," responded Wagner.

"Well, back to my original point which was to take a real hard look at those three agents so we can decide whether to go ahead with their training or recommend pulling the plug before we stub our toe. Let me know what you find out and I'd like to know your impression of the contract agent who's doing the W/T training."

"Consider it done," laughed Wagner.

"By the way, Jack. You picked a great time to arrive. The political winds are shifting. There seems to be a little more dialogue between Greece and Romania and a few months ago who would have predicted that Marshal Tito would be coming to Athens on a five-day official visit?"

"I'll give him credit for having a big pair of brass balls. It takes a lot of bravado to make the leap from condoning border incursions and kidnapping Greek citizens to riding through the streets of Athens in a welcoming parade," mused Wagner. "But he thumbed his nose at Stalin so I suppose all is forgiven."

"I'm not sure all is forgiven but I think his defection is a plus for our side. It will be interesting to see what kind of reception he gets from the Greek man in the streets when he shows up," concluded Ellis before shifting focus and asking, "What do you have on your docket today?"

Wagner slowly stood up as he responded. "I'm having lunch with Bob Foster and then we're going to try to nail down a lease on a place for me to permanently hang my hat."

"I hope you pull it off. I know it will be a relief to get the housing issue out of the way. Let me know how you make out."

"You'll be the first to know," smiled Wagner as he stepped through the door into the annex where Ellis' secretary was working.

"Hi Heidi. It looks like you have your hands full. I don't want to interrupt," observed Wagner hesitantly.

Ellis' secretary looked up from her typewriter and responded with a warm smile. "It's a welcome interruption. I can use a break . . . just trying to finish this dispatch in time to make the next out-going pouch. But there's no rush. It can wait a few minutes." She pushed her chair back from her desk before continuing with a touch of motherly concern in her voice, "But it's more important to know how you are doing. Have you begun to settle in and have you had any luck in finding a place to live?"

By Agency standards she was an old pro with more than seven years of experience. She had watched case officers come and go, including a mixture of older OSS veterans hoping to re-ignite the spark of their WWII days and a collection of former Army Counter Intelligence agents for whom The Company represented a new safe haven. And there would always be a smattering of newly minted recruits, still wet behind the ears, who, like apprenticed tradesmen, were getting their first chance to practice their tradecraft in the field. Wagner didn't fit neatly into any of those categories. This might be his first field assignment but she knew he was no novice.

Wagner waited a few moments before responding to her questions about his search for permanent housing, aware that her voice reflected sincere interest rather than the customary obligatory inquiry that he was used to hearing. Apart from a few casual encounters in Washington and now here in Athens, she was a stranger to him, although he realized they were contemporaries. A wave of her blond hair had fallen just above her left eyebrow, highlighting inquisitive blue eyes and her soft, contemplative smile. She wore almost no makeup which somehow enhanced her attractiveness, an attractiveness not lost on Wagner, who now replied.

"I'm making progress. Not quite there yet, but I'm getting close. Hank found a car for me and it looks like before the end of the day, I may have found a place to call home."

"That's wonderful. Congratulations."

"Curb your enthusiasm," joked Wagner. "I'll give you fair warning that if it works out, I'll be knocking on your door asking for help in teaching me the ins and outs of shopping for groceries at the commissary."

"Grocery shopping is one area where I qualify as an expert, so don't hesitate to knock," she replied.

"I won't. It's been a long time since I've brewed my own cup of coffee in the morning, but first I've got to find the ingredients. It looks like I'll be setting up shop just down the hall so you'll have a hard time avoiding me," smiled Wagner as he turned to leave.

"Don't worry. I'll be ready whenever you are. Just send up a warning flare when you need help."

****

Foster waited until the waiter finished delivering their lunch before raising his glass in a good-natured toast. "Here's to closing the deal on that house you've been eye-balling for the last couple of days."

"It wouldn't be happening if I didn't have you as my interpreter. Lunch is on me," responded Wagner.

"And I thought this was going to be pro bono work," laughed

Foster. "But we'd better be on time. I stopped by to see your future landlord yesterday to confirm things for you and he greeted me in his pajamas so I think we should get there before we have to wake him up from his siesta."

"Is that why you suggested eating at Floca's, which is practically next door to my office . . . just to cut down on travel time?"

"No. This is a really good restaurant . . . very popular for people watching. When things begin to stir in the late afternoon, it's hard to find a seat at one of their sidewalk tables. Greeks like to watch good-looking girls on parade and apparently good-looking girls like to parade."

"Does that explain the real purpose of Tito's visit?" asked Wagner with a wry smile, before continuing, "Do you remember our first assignment on the Greek Desk when we officially came on board the Agency? I think we both showed up on the same day . . . took the mandatory trip to Building 13 for our welcoming polygraph and finally got handed a stack of messages that were taken from a Communist crypt in Glyfada. The guy on the other end was transmitting from Tito's Jugoslavia. But that was 1950 and times have changed."

"Sure. I remember," replied Foster. "As I recall the story, the Athens Station wasn't having much luck pinpointing the location of the transmissions with its DFing equipment and finally had to get some help from a ship in the Sixth Fleet that was anchored offshore and had a more efficient direction finder. When they raided the crypt, the W/T operator, who was still transmitting, put a gun in his mouth and pulled the trigger, leaving behind a treasure trove of messages filled with Communist Party pseudonyms that we spent the next few weeks trying to identify."

"It was pretty heady stuff for a couple of rookies. I think that's when I really got hooked into staying in this business and it was probably the beginning of the end of my marriage without my knowing it," said Wagner ruefully as he paid the check and they got up to leave.

CHAPTER SIX

BRIDEGROOM had seen the Soviet Embassy hundreds of times before but now he stood on the corner and contemplated it in detail. It was just one of several four-storied, marble-faced buildings that housed foreign embassies on this tree-shaded street a few blocks from the heart of the commercial section of the city; but perhaps because he knew what it represented, it looked foreboding. A short driveway arched in from the street and out again and he could see a chauffeur in black driver's cap polishing the Ambassador's limousine that was parked in front of the entrance.

He began walking toward the building, past the tall wrought iron fence that guarded it from the street, still not yet sure in his own mind that he would turn in when he reached the open gate. The chauffeur nodded without expression as BRIDEGROOM walked around the rear of the parked limousine and mounted the three steps leading to the door. He stopped for a moment on the top step and like a stranger not quite certain he was visiting the right house, read the engraving in Russian and in French that told him he had made no mistake. Then, without hesitating, he turned the knob of the heavy door and went in.

Once inside he realized as he had many times before that the anticipation of an event is far worse than reality. A pleasant-looking receptionist who was sitting at a desk just inside the alcove looked up from her work when he entered and asked, "May I help you?"

BRIDEGROOM smiled and walked over to where she was sitting. "Perhaps you can." He bent his body forward so that she might hear as he spoke in a lower tone. "I wonder if there is someone here who might help me arrange to send a package of medicine to my mother who is quite old and very ill. I know, of course, that this is an unusual request."

The girl smiled sympathetically as she answered, "Not at all. Would you give me your name please?"

"Victor Bergarsch."

"Thank you. Would you please sit over there," she said pointing to a leather chair next to a reading table. She got up from her desk and walked through a door leading off the office.

In a few minutes she returned in the doorway and motioned to BRIDEGROOM. "Won't you come this way," she asked politely.

BRIDEGROOM rose and followed her through the door into a handsome wood-paneled room. The receptionist went out closing the door behind her.

A man of about 40, who had been sitting at a desk in one corner of the room, stood up and came around toward BRIDEGROOM. "Mr. Bergarsch?" he said questioningly, "How do you do?"

The man had dark eyebrows and black hair. His head was small and the skin on his face seemed to have been pulled too tightly around his skull, giving his cheeks a sucked-in look. He was about the same height as BRIDEGROOM and was quite thin except for a round protruding belly like that of a woman in the last stages of pregnancy. But if the man was unimpressive physically, his inquisitive eyes told BRIDEGROOM that it would be unwise to dismiss him lightly.

BRIDEGROOM, who was not sure whether or not he should offer to shake hands, answered, "How do you do, sir."

The Russian said, "I understand there is something you think we might be able to do for you."

"I'm not sure that it will be possible, but I wanted to ask," replied BRIDEGROOM with a faint smile.

"Well," said the Russian in the congenial tone generally used by a person who has something to give away, "why don't we sit down and find out what your problem is." He motioned

BRIDEGROOM to a comfortable looking sofa and sat down beside him. BRIDEGROOM acknowledged to himself that this was a good place to talk. The room had been decorated with taste and had the informal intimacy one might expect to find in the drawing room of an exclusive men's club. The floor was covered with an expensive oriental rug and the sun's rays were softened by heavy drapes that covered the windows. There was a large open fireplace on one side of the room and two attractive oil paintings hung on the wall. Only the small desk lamp disturbed the subdued atmosphere created by the dark rich paneling.

The Russian pressed a buzzer and said, "I'll get us some coffee." Somehow BRIDEGROOM had the feeling that his visit was not entirely unexpected.

The Russian offered BRIDEGROOM a cigarette from the box on the coffee table in front of the sofa and then lit one himself, inhaling deeply. "Well, Mr. Bergarsch, you have courage coming here," he said with a smile. "Some of your countrymen seem to have the idea that we don't let anyone out once they come inside. You see," he said gesturing expansively with both hands, "we're really not as bad as that." He puffed again on his cigarette, waiting for BRIDEGROOM to answer.

"I was not worried," replied BRIDEGROOM, "and this is a personal matter that I have come about."

There was a knock and the door opened. The receptionist came in and put the coffee on the table in front of them, nodding to BRIDEGROOM as she left.

"You want to send some medicine to your mother," said the Russian, who already knew the purpose of BRIDEGROOM's visit. "My secretary has told me."

"Yes, if it is possible," replied BRIDEGROOM.

The Russian paused before answering. "It is not easy," he said and then he added slowly, "but it is possible."

"I shall be very grateful."

"There is no question about gratitude. It is simply a question of a sick woman. You should not forget, Mr. Bergarsch, that we all have mothers and although it may surprise you, we understand and sympathize with your predicament. Of course, if you had not left your country . . . but that is another matter," he said with a shrug.

"I have come here without pretense," said BRIDEGROOM. "You know my political feelings. I can't change them but I am not ashamed to ask your help for my mother."

"We admire personal honesty even in people who don't share our political philosophy," replied the Russian looking intently at BRIDEGROOM. "And I think you are a practical man, but please remember that you are asking me to arrange to deliver medicine in a foreign country."

"I understand," replied BRIDEGROOM without expression.

"It will take a little time," said the Russian, "but I suggest that you buy the medicine you want to send to your mother and bring it to me."

"I shall do it at once," said BRIDEGROOM.

"Good," said the Russian. "Let's consider the matter settled."

"My sincere thanks," said BRIDEGROOM starting to rise.

"It's nothing," replied the Russian with a wave of his hand. But instead of standing, the Russian reached for another cigarette. "You seem to be a very busy man, Mr. Bergarsch," he said quizzically.

"One has to keep busy to eat these days," replied BRIDEGROOM.

"Yes," said the Russian, "I suppose you are right. But of course the secret is to do the work that feeds the stomach best."

"One can only keep trying," responded BRIDEGROOM. "There is nothing else to do . . . and," he added thoughtfully, "there are others who need my help."

"You sound like an idealist," smiled the Russian.

"Perhaps," replied BRIDEGROOM, "but I have always considered myself to be a realist."

"Well then, maybe I should have said that you impress me as a resourceful man with ideals. At any rate, you seem to have done rather well since your arrival in this country," commented the Russian jocularly. "It is common knowledge that you are the accepted émigré leader in this city. Important officials of the local Government go to you for advice on émigré affairs. Your people look to you for help and direction and in spite of all these demands on your time, you manage a small but successful export company. That is, my friend, quite an achievement for a man who left his own country under . . . well . . . let us say . . . unfortunate circumstances." The Russian leaned back and rested arm on the back of the sofa, waiting for BRIDEGROOM's response.

"I am surprised that you know so much about me," said BRIDEGROOM. "I really don't think my activities are important enough to deserve so much attention."

"Ah, but it is my work to fill my head with information about this country and the men who influence its policy. I am sure you understand that my Government did not send me here to take a vacation with pay," laughed the Russian. "Only the Americans can afford that kind of luxury for their diplomats." The Russian sipped his coffee and added lightly, "You know, Mr. Bergarsch, my own work would be so much easier if you and I could by some bit of magic exchange our positions for a few days."

"I don't think I understand what you mean," answered BRIDEGROOM, who was growing suspicious as the conversation progressed.

"Oh, I really meant nothing . . . only that you apparently are on such friendly terms with so many people my Government would like to know more about. But, since there is no such magic, we unfortunately shall have to dismiss the idea." Then, the Russian, who had been watching BRIDEGROOM with what seemed like more than personal interest, looked at his watch and said, "I apologize, Mr. Bergarsch. I am keeping you from your work. But," he added, "when the conversation is interesting, the time flies the quickest." He stood up. "I hope we can continue our talk the next time we meet."

"I shall look forward to it with pleasure," replied BRIDEGROOM politely.

As they walked together toward the door, the Russian said, "By the way, Mr. Bergarsch, since this is an errand of mercy on your part, I would be sorry to see you jeopardize your standing in the community by coming here. You know," he added, "it is unfortunately true that one becomes politically suspect when he is seen visiting the Soviet Embassy."

"I am aware of that," replied BRIDEGROOM.

"I leave it to you and please don't misunderstand my intentions," said the Russian, "but perhaps it would be wiser for you to make your next visit in the evening."

"Thank you," said BRIDEGROOM. "I think you are probably right."

The Russian extended his hand and opened the door. BRIDEGROOM stepped out into the sunlight and walked past the limousine and chauffeur, who watched him turn out of the gate and quickly cross the street.

CHAPTER SEVEN

Wagner nursed a second cup of coffee and watched the waiter edging his way through the narrow opening between the rows of folding canvas chairs and small round-top tables that filled the sidewalk in front of the King George Hotel. It had grown dark since he first sat down but the sky glowed with the reflections of gaudy neon signs flashing eccentrically from the rooftops of the buildings encircling the plaza. He looked across the square and saw the electrically animated glass of beer begin to fill again, finally tilt toward the name of the only brewery in the country and then slowly drain. Almost automatically his eyes searched past the blinking advertisement of a German sewing machine manufacturer and came to rest on the emblazoned green initials of TWA Airline. From a slot just beneath these letters, a clock signaled the correct flying time . . . now 8:27. Wagner synchronized his watch and in the same motion ducked his head slightly to elude the raised elbow of the waiter who was carefully manipulating his tray to avoid striking anyone.

Plenty of time if I leave now he thought. His car was parked on a side street a block away and the drive to the safe house wouldn't take more than twenty minutes. He hesitated long enough to swallow the last of his coffee and then followed the waiter through the maze of chairs and tables. A steady murmur of voices rose and hummed evenly in his ears, broken now by the easy laughter of a young girl in a tight black dress who pushed her long dark hair back from her face and leaned smiling toward her balding companion.

Wagner stood on the sidewalk for a moment. There was a

peculiar sense of anticipation and excitement in the air that reminded him of Christmas Eve in the States. The heat of the day was passing. The city regaining its pulse . . . changing its mood. Impatient storeowners lowering protective metal grates over shop windows. Office workers with long loaves of bread clumsily wrapped in newspapers crowding toward the buses. Sun-bronzed laborers in cement-spattered shoes passing quickly before blending into night-darkened side-alleys. A motor scooter coughing away from the curb . . . dodging through traffic-clogged streets like a bug gone berserk. Overhead the orange spark of a trolley wire snapping like a live coal across a connector. A group of summer travelers waiting anxiously on the wide marble hotel steps to begin a tour of the city's nightlife.

Wagner glanced again at the airline clock and headed for his car.

❄❄❄❄

"Are you sure?" pressed BRIDEGROOM in a voice that reflected both concern and anticipation.

"I told you I am sure," replied Nick impatiently.

Tina was standing in the doorway between the living room and the hall. She was wearing a plain white blouse buttoned at the neck and her hair was combed back and tied neatly in a bun which gave her face an unusual appearance of gravity. "How can you be so certain?" she asked.

Nick slapped his head with the heel of his hand before replying. "How many times do I have to say that I can read his hand like a book? Trust me. I know the man. I know how he thinks. A radioman's hand is his fingerprint. I'm telling you he will be on that ship."

"Nick, if you are right and your old friend is on that ship," BRIDEGROOM paused, " . . . and if he hasn't changed his politics . . . we will have something important to tell Mr. Rogers when he arrives and it will be good news for him and I think even better news for us."

"Does that mean we change our original plans for the meeting?" asked Tina.

"No and yes," answered BRIDEGROOM in a more relaxed voice. "You can show Mr. Rogers the house just as we planned." He then turned to Nick. "But, Nick, it is more important than ever that you explain to Mr. Rogers exactly how you monitor the shipping traffic. He needs to feel confident that he can rely on our information."

"Don't worry, Victor, I'll have him dancing in the street," laughed Nick.

"Be serious," admonished Tina.

"After he has had a chance to look around, we'll sit down and I'm sure he'll have some routine questions. That's when I'll tell him about the ship's expected arrival. Once he hears that news, I think we know what we'll be discussing for the rest of his visit," concluded BRIDEGROOM with a smile of relief.

As BRIDEGROOM finished speaking, they heard the click of hard leather heels on the marble veranda followed by a short rasp of the doorbell.

"At least he is punctual," observed BRIDEGROOM getting quickly to his feet. Then, looking at Tina, who already was standing uncertainly in the center of the room, he added, "I will let him in this time." He hurried into the hallway and unlatched the door.

"Hello, Victor."

"Good evening, Mr. Rogers. Please come in. Nick and Tina are waiting in the next room." Wagner nodded and followed BRIDEGROOM into the living room.

"Mr. Rogers, may I introduce Tina and Nick."

"How do you do, Tina. Hello, Nick," said Wagner extending his hand. "I've heard about your good work and I've been looking forward to coming out and meeting you. You have a nice place here." Damn nice, he thought. I can't accuse Al of abusing his agents.

"Yes, it is a good place to work," answered Tina defensively.

"Before we sit down, I think Mr. Rogers might like to see the rest of the house," said BRIDEGROOM, addressing Tina while looking at Wagner for his approval. Still looking at Wagner, he added, " . . . and I am sure you will want Nick to show you his monitoring equipment and answer any questions you might have about his work."

"I think that will be a great way to start," replied Wagner with a friendly smile. "And then, perhaps we can sit down for a few minutes. I have one or two very basic questions that I'm sure you can help me with," concluded Wagner as he motioned to Tina to begin their house tour.

The satisfied expression on Nick's face when he and Wagner returned to the living room told BRIDEGROOM that his session with Wagner had gone well. Wagner nodded his thanks to Nick as he crossed back into the room and sat down beside BRIDEGROOM on the sofa. "You're right, Victor. This does seem to be a good place for your operation. But there is one thing that troubles me a little."

"Yes . . . what is that?"

"How do Nick and Tina explain being able to afford living in a house like this?" As he asked the question, Wagner noticed that Nick stopped fumbling with his cigarette paper and glanced nervously at BRIDEGROOM.

"It is quite a simple arrangement . . . one that Mr. Fletcher worked out," replied BRIDEGROOM with a slight smile. "You see, the house supposedly was hired by a wealthy American businessman who does extensive traveling. In his absence, Nick and Tina serve as caretakers. The rent was paid one year in advance and there are ten months remaining. Mr. Fletcher assured me that everything was in order but of course, if you feel we should make any changes . . . "

"No. We'll leave things as they are . . . at least for now. But I did want to confirm the story with you." What a hellova lousy cover . . . .no wonder he didn't bother to brief me on it before he left, mused Wagner as he pulled a pack of cigarettes out of his pocket and methodically tapped it against the side of his hand. "Here, Nick, why don't you try one of these?"

"With pleasure, Mr. Rogers. They are much better than mine."

"A little easier to handle anyway," said Wagner, accepting a light from the big fellow. He took a couple of slow drags and then asked casually, "What do you think about the house, Nick? Does anyone ever ask you about it?"

"No trouble at all," replied Nick, who was beginning to enjoy Wagner's attention. "And don't worry," he continued with a confident wave of his hand, "we understand all about security."

"I'm glad to hear that, Nick, because I have a few questions along that line that I wanted to talk over with all of you."

BRIDEGROOM, who had been following the conversation with mounting concern, shifted his position on the sofa and said, "Mr. Rogers, I apologize for interrupting. I know you have a lot to tell us tonight but there has been an important development since our last meeting that I think you should know about now."

"Don't apologize, Victor. If something significant has come up, I want to hear about it."

BRIDEGROOM spoke slowly, choosing his words carefully, "As you know, no Romanian ship has visited a Greek port since before the War. It now appears that is about to change." He waited, as though trying to measure Wagner's reaction before continuing. "Nick has learned that a Romanian vessel carrying a load of lumber will be docking in Piraeus within the next few days."

"When did you find that out, Nick?" inquired Wagner calmly.

"Today," responded Nick, clearly enjoying the spotlight. "For months I've been tracking Romanian ship traffic in the area and today I intercepted a message with that information. I hope it is useful," he added proudly.

"That kind of information is very useful. Good job," responded Wagner with a thumbs up to Nick before asking, "Do you know the date the ship will dock and how long it will be in port?"

"We should know within the next day or two when it will arrive," answered BRIDEGROOM. "And it usually takes two or three days to unload cargo. Isn't that right, Nick?" asked BRIDEGROOM , looking at Nick for confirmation.

"Yes, at least two or three days," answered Nick, obviously pleased to be consulted.

"Nick spent a number of years as a radioman in Constanta before he and Tina began working for me in Bucharest. So he knows their procedures very well," explained BRIDEGROOM.

Then, as though pondering the impact of what he was about

to reveal, BRIDEGROOM slowly stroked his brow before continuing. "I understand it is important for you to learn that direct maritime trade between the two countries is being resumed but there is something else that I think may be of even more interest to you."

"What is it?"

"Nick is almost certain that the radioman on that ship is an old friend of his and someone who strongly opposes what the Communists have done to our country."

"What Victor just said is right," said Nick, pounding his fist on the arm of his chair for emphasis. "He hates the Communists."

"How well did you know him?" asked Wagner, quickly becoming aware of the operational potential that had just been introduced.

"Like a brother," responded Nick emphatically.

"Perhaps not quite like a brother," interjected BRIDEGROOM tolerantly, "but Nick tells me they shared a very close friendship."

"Do you think he would recognize you if he saw you now?" asked Wagner.

"I told you. We were like brothers," answered Nick.

"Maybe more importantly, would you still be able to recognize him?" persisted Wagner.

"How much can a man change in seven years?" countered Nick. "I could pick him out of a crowd in a stadium," he added confidently.

"How certain are you that it really is your friend who is the radioman on that ship?" asked Wagner calmly.

For just a second, Nick closed his eyes as though in deep thought and began twisting his large nose between his thumb and forefinger as though kneading a small ball of putty. Then he replied. "Mr. Rogers, Victor and Tina have asked me the same question and I will give you the same answer I gave them." Wagner gave Nick a nod of encouragement to continue his explanation. "I can read his hand. His hand is his fingerprint and I can recognize it." He paused, "And if I am wrong, what will we have lost?"

"And if you are right," smiled Wagner, whose calm voice

concealed his mounting interest, "do you think we could arrange a meeting with him?"

BRIDEGROOM sat quietly watching the exchange between Nick and the young American case officer, his hands resting lightly on his knees. Nick brushed his hand back and forth across his chin as he contemplated his reply.

It was Tina who broke the tension, hurrying back from the kitchen with a tray containing three glasses of water. BRIDEGROOM watched her with a peculiar sense of nostalgia as she placed a glass beside each of the dishes she had set out before Wagner's arrival, reminded by her movements of a younger woman who years earlier had walked so often through his drawing room to serve tea to him and his mother. When she had finished arranging the dishes, she stepped back and smiled at Wagner. "Mr. Rogers, perhaps you would try one of our native sweets? It was a favorite of ours at home."

"Thank you, Tina. I'd like to very much," answered Wagner. Each of the small dishes contained a heaping spoonful of what appeared to be dark red jelly. As the thick syrupy-sweet substance slowly dissolved on his tongue and coated the inside of his mouth, Wagner understood why it was served by the spoonful. "It's delicious," he said politely after he had taken a couple of swallows of the water Tina had provided. He waited until the others had finished before he took out a cigarette and offered one to Nick. Then he lit a match, touched it to the end of his smoke, watched the flame flicker for a few seconds before he blew it out and turned back to Nick.

"Well, Nick, what do you think? Is a meeting possible?" he asked, as if there had been no interruption in their earlier discussion.

"Possible? Yes. Easy? No," answered Nick in a tone that reflected his increasing awareness of the risks involved in first making contact and then separating his old friend from other members of the ship's crew.

Wagner had sensed the subtle change in Nick's demeanor before he replied, "I know you're right, Nick. It won't be easy. We may not be able to arrange a meeting this time but if we can at least make personal contact without risking his security, we may be able to set up a meeting at some other port. I think it may be worth a try and who knows, we may get lucky."

"I agree that it's worth trying," said BRIDEGROOM before turning to Wagner and asking, "What can we do now to prepare for the ship's arrival?"

"What can you tell me about your friend, Nick?" was Wagner's response.

"His name is Alex Popescu," began Nick.

"Is he married?"

"Yes."

"Happily?" asked Wagner.

"I think so. He has two sons," replied Nick.

"How old is he?"

"Now?" responded Nick, as though asking himself the question, "Maybe he is almost fifty."

"Does he have many friends?"

"He is a good man. People like him." replied Nick.

"He has survived a long time for someone who has strong political beliefs," said Wagner, whose observation seemed more of a question.

"He is a private man. He is careful to share his feelings only with people he trusts."

"And you were one of the people he trusted?'

"Yes."

"Nick, it is important for me to know everything you can remember about your relationship with him. I want to know about his habits . . . good and bad . . . his strengths and weaknesses and your opinion of his willingness to take personal risks." Wagner turned to speak directly to BRIDEGROOM. "Victor, I want you to work with Nick and put together a complete report on everything we know about his friend. Ask Nick questions to help jog his memory. Write down every detail about Popescu that Nick can recall . . . even the smallest detail." Wagner paused and looked at Nick. "What we won't know is whether the man you remember is the same man today as he was then. We won't have the answer to that question until we meet him . . . if we do."

"Victor, how long will it take to prepare your report?" asked Wagner.

"One day, two days at the most," replied BRIDEGROOM.

"The sooner, the better. We have a lot of decisions to make and we won't have much time to make them."

"The ship is still in Constanta loading cargo," interjected Nick. "We have at least a week before it gets to Piraeus . . . maybe a little longer."

"Nick, how well do you know your way around Piraeus?" asked Wagner. "Do you know which gates we can expect the crew to use when they come ashore? And there must be a few coffee houses and tavernas that cater to seamen?"

"You don't have to worry, Mr. Rogers," assured Nick. "I have a lot of friends in Piraeus and I know every coffee house and taverna in the dock area. I go there often. Believe me, I'm no stranger to them," replied Nick, welcoming the chance to establish his credentials.

"That's good to know," responded Wagner with a friendly smile. "After you and Victor finish your report, I'd like to have you drive down to Piraeus with me and give me a personal tour by car."

"Whenever you say, Mr. Rogers. I'll be ready."

"I had intended to talk about other things tonight," continued Wagner speaking in a warm informal voice as he stood up and put his notebook in his pocket, "but they can wait a few days. For the time being, we'll concentrate on the ship's arrival and Nick's friend and I hope we have a little luck because you've all done a good job."

Then, turning to BRIDEGROOM, Wagner spoke to his principal agent. "Victor, I think it would be a good idea for us to meet and review where we stand and what we will need to do to arrange a secure contact with Popescu." Wagner paused before adding, "if, in fact, we decide to go ahead and try to make contact."

"Just tell my when and where," responded BRIDEGROOM.

"Let's make it Saturday night. That will give you a chance to finish your report and perhaps find out more about the ship's schedule. Be at the main entrance to the municipal cemetery at nine o'clock. When I drive by in my car, it's a small green Simca, get in. But don't wait more than five minutes. If we should miss each other, we'll try again at ten o'clock in front of the museum. By the way, you still have the telephone number Mr. Fletcher gave you, don't you?"

"Yes."

"Well, if we aren't able to meet, you can use the same number to contact me. But I prefer to use it as little as possible."

"I agree entirely," replied BRIDEGROOM seriously.

"Incidentally, Victor, I don't know how you've handled this in the past, but I think it would be a good idea for us to have some way to call off a meeting if you should feel there is any possibility that you are being watched. So I want you to carry a newspaper to every meeting. As long as you have the paper in your hand, I'll know everything is all right. But if you think it is better to avoid a meeting, put the paper in your coat pocket and I'll pass by."

"Ah, you know your business," exclaimed Nick approvingly.

Wagner gave him an amused nod of appreciation. Then, before he opened the door, he added, "I'm sure you all understand how important it is that nothing be said to anyone about Popescu or the ship's arrival."

"You will not have to worry about that, Mr. Rogers. We understand," replied BRIDEGROOM.

"I know you do, Victor. Goodnight. I'll see you Saturday."

For just a moment they could hear the distant hum of traffic along the waterfront. Then the door locked shut and the footsteps faded. BRIDEGROOM turned and faced the others. "Well?" he asked.

"He is a smart guy . . . a very smart guy," answered Nick soberly.

"Yes . . . he is," agreed BRIDEGROOM in a preoccupied voice. "Let us hope we can deliver Popescu."

****

Ellis was alone in his office. He had arrived early. After checking the incoming cable traffic, he was in the process of finishing a mid-year operational review which, as a recent dispatch had reminded him, already was a month overdue. It was a tedious irritating chore . . . nothing more than a rehash of stale information that had been forwarded to Washington in dozens of detailed reports over the past several weeks. But after a long career in this business, he knew that the machinery of government needed to be constantly lubricated with a never-ending flow of position papers, reviews and projected plans for the year 2000. He also knew that when his document arrived in Headquarters, it would be circulated and carefully read by the operational staffs. He could visualize the pink routing sheet filled with the astute observations of his Washington-based colleagues: the thoughtful "be sure Mac sees this;" the sharply critical "Bill, this paper is a sample of the fuzzy thinking out there that I've been talking to you about—particularly the last two pages. I think we ought to get together and kick this one around;" and the non-committal "interesting." Ultimately he knew his review would provide ample excuse for an operational staff meeting that would doubtless result in a lengthy critique requesting further clarification of these already outdated events.

He was in this frame of mind when he heard a short rap on his half-open office door and looked up to see Wagner standing on the threshold.

"Do you have a minute, Hank?"

"Sure. Come on in." Ellis welcomed the interruption in his paper work and stretched back in his leather swivel chair, his hands cupped behind his head, one foot resting informally on an open desk drawer. His friendly manner conveyed the pleasant, though not necessarily accurate impression that he had accepted Wagner as an equal. Yet, in spite of the warmth of his greeting, there was something quite awkward about his casual pose. Ellis simply was one of those men who look most uncomfortable when they are trying hardest to appear relaxed. "Well, Jack, what's new?" he inquired amiably.

"I do have something new to talk about," replied Wagner as he settled into his seat facing Ellis.

"I hope it's good news. It's too early in the morning for the other kind," smiled Ellis. "Fire away."

"Last night I went out to the safe house to see BRIDEGROOM and meet the other two agents."

"Any problems?"

"No problems. In fact it was a lot more productive than I had anticipated."

"In what way?" asked Ellis as he shifted his position and leaned toward Wagner, waiting to hear his response.

"For the past couple of years we've been using the safe house to monitor ship to shore radio traffic, particularly of Satellite vessels. That information has been getting passed along to Washington and apparently there are users there who have found it helpful. But we haven't gotten any direct benefit from it, at least until now," explained Wagner.

"I'm listening," responded Ellis calmly.

"The first Romanian ship to visit a Greek port since before the War is scheduled to arrive in Piraeus within the next few days to unload a cargo of lumber," said Wagner as he reached into his pocket and pulled out his pipe.

"That's interesting but not really a surprise," observed Ellis. "It confirms what we've all been thinking; that relations are loosening up and the first step in that process starts with a few normal trade exchanges. Next we'll probably see a trade mission arrive and eventually the beginning of negotiations for a resumption of more formal diplomatic ties. It's all a matter of timing but the end result is inevitable," commented Ellis, before adding, "But once all those deals have been made and people begin to travel back and forth, we should have a lot more opportunity to do a little of our own business . . . namely, identifying and recruiting potential agents with access to information that we can use."

"That's why I'm here, Hank. There's a chance that we may have a shot at recruiting one of the crew members on that ship."

Ellis leaned back in his chair and signaled to Wagner to finish his story.

"The agent who has been doing our monitoring is an experienced radioman who worked in Constanta for a number of years before he was hired by BRIDEGROOM. During those years he made some good friends. One of them was a guy named Alex Popescu who he claims is the radioman on the ship coming to Piraeus. Our guy, whose name is Nick, says that Popescu had strong anti-Communist feelings and he thinks Popescu will be approachable if we can figure out how to get to him," concluded Wagner.

"That opens up a lot of intriguing possibilities and just as many questions. For starters, how do we know it will be his friend who is on the ship?"

"I asked the same question. He claims he can identify him by his hand, by the way he transmits. And he's adamant about it, answered Wagner.

"What do you think?" asked Ellis.

"I think we ought to give it a try. If Nick is wrong, what do we have to lose? In fact, it will give us a chance for a dry run that we can use the next time we have a shot."

"You've got a point there," responded Ellis. "But let's assume that it is Nick's friend on the ship. We don't know whether his political position has changed since the last time they met. But if we operate on the theory that his political views haven't changed, how are we going to contact him without blowing our own hand and risking the poor devil's neck?"

"It won't be easy. I've asked Nick and BRIDEGROOM to put together a report with every detail Nick can remember about Popescu. I'll ask Headquarters to run a trace but there isn't much chance they'll come up with anything on an ordinary seaman about whom we can give them practically no information," replied Wagner who was methodically loading his pipe with tobacco. "Christ, I'm so new here I need a map to find Piraeus," laughed Wagner. "I'm not going to pretend that this thing is a piece of cake but I'm planning to take Nick to Piraeus to case the area and try to get a feel for where and how a contact might work. I guess you could say that on the plus side, Nick seems to be a familiar face in the area and shouldn't attract any special attention. He is just a big, gregarious, somewhat unkempt guy that you wouldn't connect with any form of intrigue."

"I hope he doesn't have an IQ to match," commented Ellis wryly.

"No. My impression is that he is no dumbbell. I think he's clever like a fox. If you ask me whether he can be controlled, I'm not sure. Give me a little more time to size him up and I'll tell you what I think. At the moment, he's the best means we have for reaching Popescu . . . far from perfect, but so innocuous looking that he isn't likely to attract attention." Wagner paused long enough to light his pipe before adding, "I think the real problem will be to overcome the surveillance we can expect from both the ship itself and Greek security that will probably be prowling around."

"If we're lucky, the ship's arrival will coincide with Tito's visit. If that should be the case, you can be pretty sure Greek security will concentrate its manpower on making sure the Good Marshall gets home safely and they won't be worrying about a few Romanian seamen wandering around Piraeus,' observed Ellis with a smile.

"So it's Tito to the rescue," laughed Wagner. "Now that's a touch of irony."

"We'll take whatever help we can get," responded Ellis in an amused tone before adding more seriously, "Jack, it's a little early to predict how this thing is going to play out but the thought that we may have a chance to build a network of agents from among crew members of Satellite ships has a lot of appeal to me. It could become a pretty interesting niche . . . a chance to develop a specialized group of agents whose normal duties involve repeated trips to and from target countries. That should mean we'd have a chance for regular personal access and easier communications . . . not to mention the possibility of setting up dead drops in different ports of call. But we have to make the first recruitment work and that will depend a lot on how you and your friend Nick make out."

"I'll keep my rabbit's foot handy,"

"I hope it works," laughed Ellis. "By the way, I'm meeting with Chris later this morning. I think I know how he'll react, but I want to make sure he's on board and whether he thinks we need Headquarters' blessing before moving on."

"I guess that's what Chiefs of Station do . . . make the tough decisions," observed Wagner.

"There aren't too many easy days," agreed Ellis. "But before we start putting together the nuts and bolts of attempting a recruitment, there are a couple of key questions we need to answer. Do we go solo or do we let our liaison partners participate? If we go it alone and it blows up in our face, we'll have a lot of awkward explaining to do," said Ellis, as though responding to his own question. "And we have to know what kind of incentives we can put on the table for the agent if he agrees to cooperate. The recruitment itself will be a function of the right set of circumstances, good tradecraft and maybe a little help from your rabbit's foot," concluded Ellis. "I'll let you know how Chris reacts. In the meantime, you can start working on the nuts and bolts . . . how and where to meet, a commo system, and an alternative meeting place if we can't pull this one off. You know the drill."

As Wagner stood up to leave, Ellis looked up and gave him a casual wave, signaling the end of their meeting. He waited for Wagner to step out of his office before returning to finish his report to Headquarters.

****

Wagner stood on the sidewalk outside his office, hesitating long enough to organize his thoughts. It was hot and it was noisy. With a few steps he became part of the flow of pedestrian traffic as he headed toward a nearby kiosk to buy a copy of the European edition of the *New York Herald Tribune*.

He hadn't walked very far before he felt a tug on his arm.

"Remember me?" the boy asked with a wide grin. "You bought my pistachios in the National Garden."

"Sure I do," replied Wagner as the boy joined him stride for stride.

"What's your name?" asked the boy.

"Jack."

"Good. I'll call you Mr. Jack."

"What should I call you?" smiled Wagner.

"Dmitri," responded the boy.

"I'm glad to know you, Dmitri. How old are you?"

The boy held out both hands with splayed fingers.

"Ten years old," acknowledged Wagner as he placed a friendly hand on the boy's shoulder. "Where do you sell your pistachios?"

"Wherever I find customers," laughed the boy. "Want some?"

"Sure. Why not?" responded Wagner as he reached into his pocket for some coins.

"You're one of my good customers," assured the boy, who added, "I know everything that happens in the streets. Sometimes there are riots and you should stay away. I'll make sure you know."

"Thank you. You're a good friend," replied Wagner as he watched the boy disappear in the crowded sidewalk.

CHAPTER EIGHT

Heidi looked up and waved her hand in friendly recognition as Wagner approached her desk. "Hi, Jack. You must feel like you've had a weight lifted off your shoulders now that you're finally settled in your own place. At least you look more relaxed."

"You have the eye of a spy," he laughed. "I am more relaxed. I'm glad to be done with house hunting and squabbling with landlords. I'm ready to come up for air . . . which is why I'm here." He paused and smiled before continuing. "Bob and Kathy Foster want to introduce me to Greek outdoor flicks and I'm meeting them tonight for my indoctrination course."

"It should be fun. What's the movie?"

"I think they said it's 'Executive Suite,' whatever that's about. It really doesn't matter. I'll only be there to soak up the atmosphere." Wagner hesitated before continuing. "I know it is very late to ask and you may already have made other plans but if you're free and willing to give it a try, I'd be very happy if you'd go with me. They also mentioned getting something to eat after the movie."

"I don't have plans and I'd love to go. I know Bob quite well and I've met Kathy on two or three different occasions, so we're not strangers. By the way, from my past experience, you're likely to see a few of your other colleagues there. It's a popular way to spend an evening."

"That's great. I'm glad you can go. You'll be taking part in the training of a neophyte," he added jestingly. "Having you come makes a huge difference. I'll swing by at seven-thirty if that will work for you."

"I'll be waiting."

****

The Fosters were already there when they arrived. "Hello, Heidi. Did you tell Jack that outdoor movies are a summer institution in Greece?" asked Foster with a friendly smile. "Where else can you sit in the moonlight and watch a hit American movie for the equivalent of ten or fifteen cents? Talk about a cheap date," he added whimsically.

"Bob, stop abusing Jack," admonished his wife, shaking her head in amusement.

"I'm used to it, Kathy," responded Wagner good-naturedly.

Once inside, Wagner conceded that there was an ambience that would be hard to replicate. Folding canvas chairs were lined up on a dirt floor facing the screen, which itself was surrounded by a maze of advertisements . . . .from admonitions to "Fly T.A.E.", to posters of sleek-haired men promoting the latest Greek hair oil. More posters of American movie stars in romantic poses filled every other available spot.

Some of the seats already had been claimed before they arrived. People stood in groups chatting and young Greek boys were hustling through the makeshift aisles peddling candy and tonic and pistachios. The atmosphere had the electricity of an impromptu celebration. And Heidi had been right in predicting that some of his colleagues would be in audience.

"If you can't find a seat that you like, nobody cares if you pick one up and move it to a better spot," explained Foster to Wagner as they settled in and waited for the show to begin.

"No, these are great. If we were any closer, we'd be sitting on the stage," replied Wagner as he digested his new surroundings.

When the movie ended and the audience began its slow exit, Foster turned to Wagner. "Are you and Heidi game to follow us back to Kifissia to get something to eat? I'm hungry. Is Calambocas okay with you?"

"Sure. We'll meet you there," replied Wagner, looking at Heidi who nodded agreement. "At least I know where it is. I was one of their regulars before I moved out of the hotel."

Calambocas sat in the center of Kifissia in a neighborhood shared by a number of small tourist shops and smaller restaurants. Horse drawn carriages were lined up in front of its entrance. The moonlit night vibrated with activity. A long string of colored lights hung from the trees and bushes that encircled the restaurant. Many of the nearly 1,000 tables already were filled with patrons who had come out to enjoy the fresh air and eat and talk at that slow Greek pace. From a distance, Wagner could hear the sound of an orchestra playing a mixture of Greek, American and Latin American music. The Fosters, who already had arrived and found a table, beckoned to them as they entered.

"Thought you'd never get here," said Foster as he stood up to greet them. "What are you trying to do, starve your old friend?" he asked with a grin as he held a chair for Heidi. "One thing I've learned in my less than memorable career is that Greeks know how to prepare roast lamb."

"Whatever you recommend," replied Wagner. "It beats those brown bag lunches we used to eat while we sat on the grass next to the Reflecting Pool."

"Ah, but think of all the world's problems we solved in those days," laughed Foster.

As they finished eating, Wagner tossed a scrap of food to a stray cat that was prowling under tables in search of food. Foster looked at his watch as though surprised by the time and shook his head. "It's getting close to my bedtime. It may be the weekend for you but I've got to work tomorrow. The pot is still boiling and it's beginning to look like we can expect the Cyprus demonstrations to begin any day now." He rose and took his wife's hand, "But there is still time for one last dance before we have to leave."

As the Fosters moved toward the dance floor, Wagner turned to Heidi. "Would you like to dance?" he asked.

"Yes. I would," she smiled.

They moved easily together for a few moments before he spoke. "It's been a long time since I've danced."

"Well, you haven't forgotten how," she responded.

He pressed his hand tightly against the small of her back and she moved closer to him. He could feel her hair brush against his face as they finished the dance in silent communication.

A full moon lit the highway on the drive back toward Athens. It was almost midnight and there was little traffic except for an occasional approaching car that would repeatedly flash its headlights on and off, a Greek driving idiosyncrasy that Wagner was not yet able to understand and found hard to tolerate.

As they approached Psyicho, Wagner spoke. "We're getting close to my new home territory. I know it's getting late, but if you're interested and not too tired, I can pull in for a few minutes and show you the result of my real estate transaction."

"Why not? We're here and I'd love to see your new home."

After walking through the interior, Wagner opened a door leading to a wide veranda that overlooked Mt. Hymettus. "I haven't lived here very long but this is my favorite spot. It's where I sit at night. It's peaceful."

"I can understand why."

"If you can stay a few minutes, I'll get us something to drink and we can sit outside and you'll see what I mean."

"It's a beautiful night and that's an appealing offer."

"Brandy or iced tea?"

"If it's not too much trouble, I'd prefer tea."

When he returned with their drinks, they sat quietly watching the moonlight reflecting off the granite shoulders of Mt. Hymettus. After a few minutes, as though by instinctive agreement, they rose and re-entered the house.

Heidi followed Wagner into the kitchen and watched him put the two glasses in the sink before he turned to her and smiled. "It got late awfully fast. You must be tired and I should get you home so you can get some rest." He waited a few seconds before adding, "I don't quite know how to say this and I hope you won't misunderstand my intentions, but it is very late and as you can see, I have plenty of room here and if you would feel comfortable staying, I promise to make your breakfast in the morning."

She hesitated a moment before answering. "I like my eggs over easy," she replied softly.

CHAPTER NINE

BRIDEGROOM stood in the shadow of the cemetery wall, his eyes studying each set of advancing headlights, waiting for the car that would slow down. There was very little traffic and as each car passed, he watched it climb the hill, its lights cutting a path through the shudder-darkened houses and finally disappear. He tapped a rolled newspaper against his thigh, unconscious of its touch.

A few yards away the garish iron gate was closed across the cemetery entrance. The guides and hawkers who hovered around the gate by day were gone. The dead were alone, guarded by ornate marble tombstones that glowed with a dull luminescence in the darkness. The graveyard was like an empty store that had been locked for the night with only a small light left burning inside.

Wagner's car slowed down and pulled up to the curb. As BRIDEGROOM walked toward him, Wagner reached across and pushed open the door on the passenger side.

"Hello, Victor. Get in."

"Good evening, Mr. Rogers." BRIDEGROOM felt his hat being crushed against the roof as he tried to ease his bulk into the seat. He could never understand why Americans insisted on driving small European cars when their own models were so much more comfortable and certainly no more conspicuous.

As soon as he had shut the door, the car jumped forward and immediately headed into the main stream of city traffic. "I want to get out of here and find some place where we can stop and talk without being bothered," said Wagner, pushing the gearshift back and forth as he adjusted his speed to the stuttering line of cars ahead of them. His eyes were fixed on the road. "Do you have the report on Popescu?"

"Yes. I have it."

"Is there anything in it that might change our thinking?" inquired Wagner matter-of-factly.

"No. Nothing has changed since our last meeting. Nick still remembers his friend as serious and reliable, but friendly and easy to talk to. Apparently, he is also very devoted to his family."

"What about his politics?"

"According to Nick, Popescu was very discreet. He listened to discussions but didn't express his own political opinions except to close friends whom he could trust and who shared his views. But Nick swears Popescu detests the Communists and what they are doing to his country," replied BRIDEGROOM.

"Does that mean he feels strongly enough to work with us?" prodded Wagner.

"Nick thinks so but I have never met the man so I have no way of making a judgment." BRIDEGROOM hesitated before adding, "That's a decision that you and your colleagues will have to make."

For several minutes they drove in silence. The traffic began to thin as they neared the highway leading out of the city, past the seaside tavernas and pine-sheltered beaches that flecked the coast. Wagner took one hand off the wheel and pulled a pack of cigarettes out of his shirt pocket. "You don't smoke, do you, Victor?" he asked, offering the package to BRIDEGROOM.

"No thank you." BRIDEGROOM watched Wagner tap the open end of the pack against the steering wheel and draw out one of the protruding cigarettes with his lips The flame from his lighter flashed and snapped out. Wagner took a lung-filling drag and leaned back and relaxed in the driver's seat.

The car was moving freely now, Wagner guiding it with effortless ease. For the moment, he seemed to have retreated into his own thoughts . . . almost as if he were alone. Yet, BRIDEGROOM found the silence neither awkward nor uncomfortable. Wagner did not try to force conversation. It was a characteristic of the American that BRIDEGROOM appreciated.

They had driven several more miles before Wagner spoke. "Victor, how do you feel about a resumption of more normal trade relations between Greece and Romania?" He asked the question as casually as he might have asked for an opinion on the weather.

"The two countries are natural trading partners," replied BRIDEGROOM non-committally.

"Does that mean you favor formalizing trade and diplomatic agreements?"

BRIDEGROOM paused to gather his thoughts before responding. "I think you would have to put me down as ambivalent on that issue. I carry the memory of an unhappy personal experience which clouds my objectivity. I can't change the past but it is hard for me to forget that everything I had spent a lifetime building was taken from me because of my political beliefs. I think you can understand why a sense of anger and resentment still lingers."

"It would be hard for me to imagine how you could feel any differently," replied Wagner quietly. "But that's not why I asked you to meet with me tonight." Wagner braked the car and turned on to a rough dirt road which led to a small beach, slowly maneuvering through rows of stunted pine trees before pulling to a stop on a knoll overlooking the sea. He clicked off the headlights and pushed down on the door handle. "Let's get out and get some fresh air."

"That's a good idea. It's a pretty night," agreed BRIDEGROOM.

Wagner led the way as they moved along a narrow path that opened onto the beach, ducking their heads and pushing aside the low-hanging branches that slapped at their shoulders. When they arrived at an opening, they stopped and Wagner turned to speak to BRIDEGROOM. "There is something that has been troubling me since our meeting with Nick and Tina and your opinion is important to me." BRIDEGROOM nodded acknowledgment and waited for Wagner to continue.

"The only chance we have of recruiting Popescu depends on

Nick. I only have first impressions to go on but I do have some questions about whether he can handle the job. I didn't get the feeling that subtlety is one of his strong suits. What do you think?"

"This may surprise you but I think Nick may be just the right person for the job. To some extent his lack of finesse may be an asset. You know the image he presents. He is a bit clumsy, but non-threatening. He just isn't the kind of person you would expect to be engaged in subterfuge. If Popescu is on the ship, I think Nick will be able to approach him without alarming him or raising suspicions among other crewmembers. Because he is not the kind of man that people take seriously, it would be quite in character for him to walk up to Popescu even if we did not plan it for him," concluded BRIDEGROOM.

"That's a pretty convincing answer and it makes a lot of sense," responded Wagner.

"There is one other point I should make," said BRIDEGROOM.

"What is it?" asked Wagner.

"There is substance beneath that clumsy image. Nick is an intelligent man who can see below the surface. If Popescu is on the ship, I think Nick can deliver him to you."

"Thank you, Victor. Now that we have talked, I feel more comfortable that Nick and I can work together to set up a meeting with Popescu." In a kind of reflex action, Wagner reached down and picked up a small rock that he scaled across the surface of the water before turning to BRIDEGROOM and adding in a relaxed voice, "I guess it's about time for us to call it a night and head back into town."

CHAPTER TEN

Nick rubbed the sweat from his eyes with a swipe of his forearm and replaced his dark glasses. The tiny droplets of perspiration made the short red hairs on his bare arm sparkle. A pack of cigarettes bulged in the breast pocket of his faded brown polo shirt. He waved his giant hand and shouted a raucous insult at a passing friend. But he was concentrating on the increasing activity near the main gate to the dock. He took a sip of beer and glanced at his watch. It was almost time for the ship's crew to appear. Soon they would be crossing the street to drink beer and eat sausage in the tavernas and maybe look for women.

Nick made a quick eyeball survey of his surroundings, grateful for the feverish confusion that filled the air. Rumbling lorries belching clouds of black diesel smoke; boat whistles; pushcarts piled high with oranges; a radio blaring from a coffeehouse; swaying dock cranes dipping their thin necks toward waiting freighters; shouting fishmongers; yelping dogs; broken-down buses farting haltingly over the cobblestones; a butcher flapping an apron at horseflies in an outdoor meat stall; and just behind him, a yell of triumph and a hand cracking down on a backgammon board.

He turned his head toward the sound, but now his attention was caught by new activity at the main gate. He took a large swallow of beer and poured the remainder of the bottle into his glass. He was marking time, waiting for the crew to begin drifting out of the dock area. He had watched them the day before and he knew most of them would return to the same bars they had gone to the first day. His friend, Alex, would be among them. They had exchanged nods of friendly recognition when their eyes first met on the previous day, which Nick knew was a silent signal that they would meet in person today. Where and how they would meet remained unanswered questions.

Nick had heard that some members of the crew were trying to make contact with members of the local Greek/Romanian community they had known in the Old Country before the war. Today they would wait in the bars and hope their friends would show up. Some of the others would hurry off to pharmacies to buy scarce medicines to take back to sell on the black market. Whatever they do, the more they move around the easier it will be for me . . . and for Alex, thought Nick.

He knew that somewhere on the opposite side of the street Alex was preparing to join other members of the crew in finding their way through the crowded neighborhood. But he was growing impatient waiting for something to happen. He drained his glass and pushed his chair back from the table. He began to edge his way between the tables and onto the sidewalk.

Nick moved in the direction of the Black Cat Bar, walking very slowly, oblivious of the shoving, pushing crowd that surged past him. He kept his eyes riveted on the gate until he saw the first of the seamen leave. Finally he spotted Alex's familiar figure walking unobtrusively with two other crewmembers.

The big fellow stepped toward the curb and pulled out a cigarette. He was in no hurry. Alex would need time to get settled in the bar before he could join him. Nick stood leaning against a lamppost, trying to pick out the police surveillants who were certain to be recording the movements of the crew. He had spent enough time on the waterfront to recognize their clandestine efforts as readily as he might recognize the gait of an old friend. And he knew that to them his was just another familiar face simultaneously noted and forgotten. He took a final drag on his cigarette and let it drop into the gutter where it lay smoking on a mound of street dust and discarded wrappers.

The sun was boring down from overhead, melting the tar in the streets so that it went soft like a sponge when Nick stepped off the curb toward the Black Cat. He pushed his way through a group of sweating laborers drinking soda in front of a sidewalk kiosk. He was still walking slowly, stopping from time to time to look in a store window, observing the hands on a yellow-faced clock hanging indifferently in the clutter of a pawnshop . . . 11:08.

Finally, he jammed his shoulder against the scarred wooden door and shoved it open. A few people looked up from their drinks at the quick slash of sunlight that burst across the floor. He took a few steps inside and hesitated, waiting for his eyes to adjust to the dimness.

The room was filled with the smell of stale smoke, beer and frying grease. The ceiling and walls were a grimy yellow like the color of decaying newsprint. On one side of the room a badly scratched piano squatted unattended on a raised dance platform. On the other side, a bartender was filling a tray with drinks for a waiter who was wiping his hands on a filthy apron. There was one light illuminating the assorted liquor bottles behind the bar and a few weak bulbs glowed feebly from outlets along the walls.

Only about half the tables were filled, mostly with sailors. A few whores were sprinkled among them. Nick recognized some of the crew from the ship . . . then the local security . . . and finally Alex, sitting at a table with two crewmates. During the few seconds that he stood inside the door, he classified every face in the room. There was no sign of danger.

Popescu had not looked up when he came through the door, yet Nick knew he was aware of his presence. Nick calmly mopped his forehead with a perspiration-soaked handkerchief. With an easy movement, he stuffed the handkerchief into his pocket and started toward the bar, confidently pushing chairs out of his path, a man obviously at ease in his surroundings. He almost passed Popescu's table before he stopped, then stepped back in surprise.

"Hey, Alex!" Nick slammed his giant hand on his friend's shoulder and nearly spun him around. Popescu stared up with a look of genuine shock at the exuberance of Nick's greeting. He started to stand up, a reflex courtesy, but the gentle pressure on Nick's grip on his shoulder forced him back into his seat.

Nick slid into the chair beside him, his gold teeth sparkling with pleasure.

Before Popescu had a chance to respond, the big fellow was tapping a saltshaker against an empty glass and waving at the waiter. "Over here," he shouted, holding the beer bottle aloft as he made a sweeping gesture to include Popescu's crewmates, who rewarded him with friendly smiles. Nick beamed back a warm feeling of good fellowship.

"By now I thought he must have died," joked Nick, good-naturedly pointing a finger toward Popescu. "The last time I saw him he was a boy. Now, look at him. He's an old man," he continued to the amusement of Popescu's companions.

"He hasn't changed. He's as insulting as ever," explained Popescu to his crewmates who were now thoroughly enjoying the exchange between the two old friends.

"A lot of years ago we worked together," explained Popescu in a more serious tone. "I never thought we'd meet again." He turned to Nick. "It's good to see you," he said with the obvious approval of his shipmates.

"How long will you be in port?" asked Nick casually, as though whatever the answer, it would be of little consequence to him.

"We leave in two days," replied one of Popescu's shipmates who seemed to be warming to Nick's personality.

"That's good news," responded Nick. "Maybe there will be time for me to give you my personal tour before you leave. I'll show you every good bar so you'll know where to go the next time you come back," said Nick, speaking directly to Popescu. He paused for a moment before looking at the other two crewmembers and asking, as though as an afterthought, "Would there be a problem with that?"

The two men looked at each other as though deciding which one should reply. "No, I don't think there should be a problem," replied the crewman who seemed to have formed a quick bond with Nick. He then turned to his partner and asked, "What do you think?" The other crewman shook his head from side to side, expressing a measure of uncertainty, but not objecting.

Now that they had established a weak consensus, the first crewman turned to Nick to explain their situation. "You probably know that we have certain rules when we go ashore." Nick nodded his understanding and the crewman continued his explanation. "One of the rules is that we travel in pairs . . . sometimes even three or four crewmembers go ashore together." The crewman stroked his chin and smiled before going on. "Of course, that's how we go ashore and that's how we return to the ship. But sometimes we have informal agreements to separate so we can be alone on special occasions, like meeting an old friend. What's wrong with that?" he asked, throwing up his hands to emphasize his point.

"You're right," agreed Nick. "Is there a law against friendship?"

The crewman looked across the table at Popescu. "We have almost four hours before we have to go back to the ship. If you want to visit with your friend, we'll be here when you get back. Just be on time."

Nick beamed his approval at the offer. "Are you sure it will be all right?" he asked as though seeking further confirmation. "I guarantee I won't kidnap him," he added jokingly.

"It's up to Alex," replied the crewman affably.

Before responding, Popescu slowly scanned the room, checking each face as he weighed the risk he would be taking if he decided to walk out the door with Nick. Finally, he turned to the others and shrugged, "Why not?"

"Bravo" said Nick appreciatively as he reached into his pocket and left enough drachmas on the table to pay for another round of drinks. "I'll make sure he's back with time to spare," assured Nick as he and Popescu stood up and turned to leave.

※※※※

The concierge was dozing, hands clasped prayerfully across his wine-swollen stomach. He was breathing heavily, forcing tiny bubbles of saliva to glisten in the corners of his mouth. His face was covered with black stubble and his lower jaw drooped open against his chest. But he heard the door jam shut and slowly opened his eyes.

The package Wagner carried was wrapped in a newspaper and

tied with white string. He smiled and walked across the entrance hall toward the fat one. "Sorry to wake you. It's a good time to sleep. It's very hot outside."

"That's not a problem. But you should learn to take a siesta yourself," responded the concierge as he eased himself upright.

"One of these days I will." Wagner put the package down on a small table and took out his cigarettes. He tapped the end of the pack and offered it to the concierge. "Later on I am expecting visitors," he said casually. "Two men. You may recognize one of them. He was with me when I rented the apartment, so he'll know how to find me. I don't expect any other visitors, but if anyone else should show up, I would rather not be home." As Wagner spoke, he reached across and slipped a bill into the concierge's shirt pocket.

"Don't worry about anything. I understand. I'll take care of it," replied the concierge.

"Thank you," said Wagner as he picked up his parcel and began mounting the short flight of stairs that led to the first landing. He closed the door and tested the bolt to make certain it was locked. Then he walked across the room and dropped the package on the end of a faded blue sofa.

By any standards the apartment was drab. A heavy mahogany buffet stood against one wall. The wall itself was conspicuously bare except for a large gold-framed photograph of the Parthenon which had been hung there to conceal one of several microphones. The only other furnishings in the room were two straight-backed chairs and a badly scratched coffee table placed strategically in front of the sofa. A pair of nondescript curtains, obviously in an advanced state of decay, hung lifelessly across the shutter-covered window. The room had the cool gloomy scent of a cheap funeral parlor. But the apartment had the advantage of location, far enough away from the busy port area but still within reasonable walking distance. That was an observation Nick had made when they cased the area together two days earlier.

Wagner walked over to the window and looked out through a crack between two of the wooden slats. The sunbaked street was almost empty. His eyes scanned the windows of the building on the other side of the street. In the apartment directly opposite his the red folding door shutters leading to a small balcony were closed. Behind them, the occupants would be in bed . . . sleeping or making afternoon love. But in the apartment just above, the shutters were slightly ajar, just enough to give Reedy a clear view of the street and the safe house.

Alone in the quiet of the early afternoon, Wagner was acutely aware that at least for the moment, he had become a bit player in Popescu's recruitment. He didn't like being left out of the action but he understood that his present role of watchful waiting was a tacit acceptance of reality. The success of the recruitment depended on Nick, whose competence he had questioned only a few days earlier. But BRIDEGROOM had been right about Nick. After spending two days together exploring the streets and neighborhoods of Piraeus while they planned and weighed the best approach to Popescu, Wagner had come to recognize that beyond Nick's loutish façade there was a crafty, perceptive compatriot whose judgment he could trust.

They both knew that even if a meeting with Popescu could be arranged, there would be limited time to convince him to accept recruitment and to provide him with a workable means of communication. They had chosen the safehouse both because of its proximity to the port area and because the neighborhood where it was located had a well-deserved reputation for doing a thriving brothel business . . . a fact that provided a perfect cover story if Popescu should ever be asked to explain his absence from shipmates.

Wagner returned to the sofa and picked up the package he had left there. He smiled as he unwrapped it, his unspoken compliment to his colleagues in Technical Services who, on short notice, had contrived a dry writing system that he could teach Popescu in a matter of minutes. Wagner checked his watch. It was almost 1:00 PM. By now the crew should be ashore and with luck, Nick should be with Popescu. Whether Nick succeeded in separating Popescu from his shipmates is the unanswered question. Now only a knock on the safe house door would provide the answer. There was nothing left to do but wait.

****

Nick led the way out of the Black Cat Bar and onto a sidewalk jammed with foot traffic . . . crowds of people jostling for position and often pushing in opposite directions to reach their destinations. He knew the crowds would shrink as the siesta hours approached but he embraced the temporary chaos, which provided a shield of anonymity for those, like him, who preferred to remain unseen.

Popescu kept pace a step or two behind Nick, who with a quick nod of his head, pointed the right direction. He was headed for the safe house, but only after first taking full advantage of the crowd cover before moving onto the less busy side streets. It was oppressively hot. When they finally emerged from the crowds, Nick stopped, looked at his friend with a mischievous grin, put his arm on Popescu's shoulder and said, "It's good to see you, old friend, but it is hot and I am thirsty and we need to talk. Let's find a place to sit down and cool off."

This wasn't Nick's first visit to this coffeehouse. He had been here at the same hour on the previous day to check on customer traffic and determine the likelihood of finding an empty table where he could have a private conversation with Popescu. He also knew that if their conversation went well, it would take only a few minutes to walk to the safe house where Wagner would be waiting.

Only a few tables were occupied when they stepped inside. They had no trouble finding a place where they could talk privately. The relative quiet of the coffeehouse was interrupted only by the steady drone of an aged floor fan straining to circulate the dead air that filled the room. They ordered cold drinks and began to reconnect their lives.

They had talked for several minutes before Popescu leaned toward Nick with a quizzical smile. "Let me ask you. How did you know I would be on the ship?"

"That's a good question and it makes it easier for me to explain why I wanted to meet you alone." Nick hesitated before continuing. He knew that his next few words would determine Popescu's decision but he was not sure what those words would be. He looked directly at his friend as he spoke. "Alex, you know me too well. You know I am not a fancy talker. If I have something to say, I say it." Popescu gave him a friendly nod of understanding. "So I will speak from the heart. All I ask is that you listen. If you have a problem with what I tell you, I will understand and we will still be friends."

Nick reached up and tugged at his earlobe as he thought about what to say next. "You asked me how I knew you were on that ship. The answer is because I have a job monitoring all the ship traffic in the area, including yours. I recognized you as the radio operator."

Popescu smiled. "Who do you work for?"

Nick waited before replying, aware that his answer would determine Popescu's decision either to cooperate or to retreat. "I work for an American," he answered.

"Are you in the spy business?" asked Popescu matter-of-factly.

"I'm not a spy. I'm just an old radioman," laughed Nick.

"How about your American friend?" asked Popescu.

"He's working for the same things we want," replied Nick.

"Is that why you wanted to meet me alone?"

"Yes," answered Nick.

"Nick, you just didn't want to tell me a story about your friend. What do you want me to do?"

"If you're willing, I want you to meet the American."

"When and where?" asked Popescu without showing emotion.

"Now. He's waiting nearby. We can be there in a few minutes," replied Nick.

"And you say you're not a spy?" laughed Popescu.

"Whatever you want to think," replied Nick with a grin.

"I've come this far with you. Let's go and see what your American friend has to say," said Popescu calmly.

****

Wagner heard the knock and opened the door, still not sure who would be standing on the other side.

"Hello, Mr. Rogers," said Nick with the satisfied look of a

man who had just beaten some long odds. "I've brought my old friend, Alex, to meet you."

"I'm glad you could make it, Nick and it's a pleasure to welcome you, Alex," responded Wagner, extending his hand to Popescu. "I'm not sure it's any cooler inside but come on in. At least I can offer you a cold drink," said Wagner speaking in a relaxed voice as he turned to Popescu. "Nick has told me about your long friendship, so I'm very glad to meet you in person."

Except for nodding his head to silently acknowledge Wagner's warm reception, Popescu remained quiet but Wagner quickly sensed that he was focused on weighing the implications of his meeting with an American, including the extent to which he could trust his safety with him. But Wagner was more pleased than disturbed by Popescu's calm, calculating approach to their meeting. This was not a man who, left on his own, would act impulsively, thought Wagner. Popescu's demeanor reflected quiet self-confidence without a hint of arrogance. Wagner liked what he saw.

Wagner motioned toward the sofa. "Why don't you sit down and I'll get us some cold drinks. Any preferences . . . beer or lemonade?"

"Anything cold will do," replied Popescu with a friendly smile.

When Wagner returned with the drinks, it was Nick who spoke first. "Mr. Rogers, Alex and I stopped on our way from the port. He asked me how I knew he would be on the ship and I explained my work of tracking shipping traffic. He asked me who I worked for and I told him an American. He asked me if I was in the spy business and I told him I was just a radioman but I wanted him to meet you because I thought you both had the same goals. Alex agreed to meet you and now you know everything."

"Thank you, Nick," replied Wagner with growing respect for the wisdom of the big man's straightforward approach in a sensitive situation. "It makes it a lot easier to know where we're starting from," said Wagner as he turned to face Popescu. "I hope that we can speak to each other honestly and without any kind of pretense. I know we share a lot in common and I hope we can work together but in the end, you will make that decision.

I just said that we should speak openly, so let me tell you from the start that I work for the American Government."

"That does not surprise me," replied Popescu. "Tell me what you have in mind and why you think I should cooperate."

"Nick has told me about your devotion to your family and your love of your country. He also told me that you are unhappy with the loss of personal and political freedom in your country and the suffocating influence of the Russians."

"That's true," agreed Popescu.

"What I'm offering is a chance to help change that by restoring freedom of choice and hopefully provide new opportunities for your two sons and all their friends. I'm not suggesting that what you and I might accomplish will change the world. Two or three years ago I might have thought that there was a possibility of mounting an uprising and throwing the Russians out by force. But that would have been wishful thinking."

"And so? What do you propose?" asked Popescu.

Wagner waited before answering in a calm and deliberate voice. "The Russians are going to lose because the world around them is getting smaller. It will be harder and harder for them to build barriers to keep people locked in and equally hard to keep other people from entering. Conditions are changing. You understand this and so do I. A new kind of revolution is taking place . . . perhaps not as dramatic . . . but in the long run, I think it will be a lot more effective. Your country and the other countries of Eastern Europe are slowly learning that they can turn away from the Russians, make independent decisions. They are beginning to understand that the Russians need them more than they need the Russians. The weight of their collective judgment will force the Communists to make concessions and in the end, their influence will wane. When that happens, we'll begin to see more freedom of travel, more trade and more opportunity for young people like your sons. If the Russians want to continue to exert their political influence and build a sustainable economy, they are going to have to adapt to that reality." Wagner looked directly at Popescu as he continued to speak. "If we keep the pressure on them, we can speed up the process of change and the time when your countrymen can begin to experience the freedom of choice. You can help to apply that pressure," he concluded.

"You'll have to tell me how," replied Popescu quietly.

"If we are going to succeed in using our economic and political power to put pressure on the Russians, we need to know where and how to apply that pressure to get the results we all want. To be effective we need to know what's happening inside the Soviet Bloc. But that information is hard to get. The Russians rule by force and intimidation. Newspapers are controlled. Movement by Westerners is restricted and Government officials are paid political puppets. So we turn to people like you who share our goals and who live and work inside the Soviet controlled countries." Wagner delivered his message with a calm conviction that somehow lent a faint ring of logic to even the most flagrant clichés.

Popescu and Nick were seated on the sofa that faced Wagner. Popescu's eyes had been focused like lasers on Wagner while he made his recruitment pitch but his expression remained unchanged, providing no hint of whether or not Wagner's message had been compelling enough to convince him to risk his neck.

Even before he responded, Wagner knew intuitively that Popescu was not about to let anyone he did not know and trust impose his agenda on him. His privacy and ability to make independent personal decisions were freedoms he would not compromise. They were the keys to his survival, which Wagner understood. Wagner put a value on Popescu's seeming willingness to go it alone. It would be a useful trait for an agent operating in relative isolation inside Romania.

"I don't disagree with what you say but I'm just an ordinary seaman. I don't see how I could be of much help to you," replied Popescu quietly.

"You don't give yourself enough credit," interjected Nick as he laid a friendly hand on Popescu's shoulder.

"Nick is right. You are much more than just an ordinary seaman. I understand why you may under estimate the important role you could play if you decide to work with us in freeing your country from Soviet control. You have the rare advantage of mobility. Your home base is a principal Black Sea port city and your work as a seaman means you will be making regular visits to other major ports in our region. Your mobility also means that we should not have any trouble establishing secure communication systems, including plans for possible future personal meetings," concluded Wagner.

Popescu waited before responding, carefully measuring the implications of Wagner's words. "You made no mention of the risks involved." He held up his hand as Wagner was about to answer. "I have no fear of taking personal risks, but do I have the right to risk the safety of my family?"

"You are of course right. There are risks involved. But they are minimal. There is a risk in your meeting with me now or meeting with Nick. Life is filled with risks and with deciding which risks are worth taking." Wagner watched as Popescu leaned toward him, listening intently to each word of his argument. For just a moment, Wagner hesitated and looked hard at the man he was facing. Popescu's rugged build reflected years of demanding physical work and was complemented by a tough chiseled face that was weathered by time and the sea. There was nothing soft about Popescu.

"I can tell you that there is nothing to be gained by gambling with someone's life. But I can also tell you that although we can't eliminate risk, we can reduce it to the point where it is almost a non-factor," continued Wagner. "I would have less confidence in you if you didn't raise these questions. Without mutual trust, there would be no point in our discussion, but I don't think that is the case. We have too much in common, including our goals and our values."

"And if I agree to cooperate, what will you do to protect the security of my family?" prodded Popescu.

"I have already said that there is nothing to be gained by gambling with your safety. We need your eyes, your brain and your insight. You will not be asked to perform any overt action that would attract attention or look suspicious . . . nothing that would endanger the security of your family. You will be a silent observer who will report what you see . . . unusual port activity, food or material shortages, political rumors, rationing of specific products, subtle changes in Russian influence and control and, of course, any unusual military or naval activity," Wagner paused, silently inviting Popescu to ask questions, before continuing his response. "I think we both understand that once we begin working together, there will always be unexpected events that will occupy our attention. But I hope you will see that there is little danger to you or your family in the work I have described."

Popescu relaxed and leaned back on the sofa before replying. "If all you're asking me to do is to report what I observe, then I agree there is little risk." He looked at Wagner with a questioning smile before adding, "But you haven't explained how I can transmit my observations to you without risking exposure."

"If I were in your position, I would ask the same question," acknowledged Wagner calmly. "If there is a risk of detection, it's usually because of a weakness in communications. But because you make regular visits to foreign ports, we have a built-in safety net that reduces any risk to almost zero. It means we won't have to rely on using the Romanian postal system with all the dangers of internal censorship. We will use mail but only when you are in a foreign port. But mail isn't our only option. There are other methods of communicating that we can develop once we begin working together," said Wagner, before adding with an inquisitive smile, "I realize that all this depends on whether you agree that by working together we can make a positive difference."

Popescu looked introspectively at the young American case officer before he replied. "It is hard to explain the sense of frustration . . . call it helplessness . . . a person feels to wake up every day knowing their life will be governed by a combination of evil and incompetence and to have no power to change things. So it is not a hard decision to agree to work with you. My only concern is the safety of my family which you have done your best to address."

"I know it was not an easy decision but I don't think you will ever regret making it. And there is nothing more important to us than protecting the safety of your family and you."

"I trust you," responded Popescu quietly.

"I know we share the same goals and values. I'm looking forward to working with you, Alex," said Wagner as Nick nodded his approval. "But now we have a lot to accomplish. How much time do we have?" asked Wagner, addressing both men.

"Maybe an hour," answered Nick. "Alex has two friends waiting for him so they can go back to the ship together and I promised we would return in plenty of time."

Wagner stood up and walked across the room to where he had left the unwrapped package he had brought with him. As he removed the contents, he looked back at Popescu who was lighting his first cigarette since arriving. "I said we were not going to take the risk of using the Romanian postal system, but you will need a safe means of getting messages to us so, at least in the beginning, letters posted from outside the country to a secure mailing address should give us that link," said Wagner as he eased himself back into the chair facing Nick and Popescu. "This is a mailing address for you to use," continued Wagner as he handed a slip of paper to Popescu. "Try to memorize it as quickly as possible and then destroy it. Whenever you use this address, you'll need to write a short personal cover letter to make it look authentic. Just assume that you are writing to an ailing distant relative. A few words inquiring about his health, along with a comment or two about your family, will be all you need to write. Just be sure to leave as much unused space as possible so that you have enough room for your report to us."

Wagner held a man's belt in his hand as he spoke. "You're going to need a way to send us information that can't be compromised. That's what this belt is for," he said as he handed the belt to Popescu, who uncoiled it, carefully scrutinizing every detail.

"I can see that you managed to acquire it inside the country and that it has been worn before," he observed.

"An ordinary belt normally is not a conspicuous article of clothing, particularly when it is well-worn. We'll exchange it for the one you're wearing now. That will eliminate the worry

. . . and the risk . . . of trying to conceal a communications system," responded Wagner. "Here, let me show you how to use it." Wagner took the belt back from Popescu and laid a letter-size paper on the coffee table between them. He took the buckle end of the belt and gripped the pointed clasp between his fingers. "This will be your pen. The metal buckle has been impregnated with a substance that will let you write messages that will be invisible to everyone except us. We have the developer," he added with a reassuring smile.

Wagner handed the belt back to Popescu. "Why don't you try it? Don't press down too hard or you'll leave an impression on the paper. And be careful the paper you use is not too coarse or you could disturb the fibers. I don't think there is any real chance of risk but it is better for us to be cautious in everything we do together."

Popescu used the implement to write a few lines and then held up the paper to examine it for any impressions he might have left. "It is easy to use and I agree with you that we do nothing to arouse suspicion."

"We will not send you any messages inside Romania, but it is important that you are able read any messages we may send to you by other means that we may arrange over time. The leather in your belt has also been impregnated with a chemical that can be activated on contact with water. If you should ever receive a message from us, just dip some portion of the strap in a small glass of water and hold it there for about thirty seconds. Then brush a light coat of the liquid wherever there is no writing and the message will appear," explained Wagner.

"Let's see if your Communist friends can figure that out," laughed Nick as he gave Popescu a playful nudge.

"But for now, we have to decide how and where and when we can meet again," said Wagner, aware that time was running out before Popescu had to return to his ship. "Do you know which port you will visit next?"

"No. There is a chance we might come back to a Greek port, either here or Patras or Volos. Istanbul is another possibility," replied Popescu.

"Nick will be tracking your trips, so we will know when and

86

where you'll be going. But we need to agree on how we can safely meet you, even if it's only long enough to make contact and arrange a new meeting. If you come back to Greece, Nick will find you. But if you visit another friendly port, we will be watching as you go ashore." Popescu listened without emotion as Wagner described plans for a possible future meeting.

"Until we are able to establish specific places to meet, we'll try to make contact in front of the main Post Office in any new port you visit. Post offices are local landmarks we both can find. Just buy a postcard and mail a greeting to the mailing address I gave you or to your family. That should be enough to explain why you are there and may give us a chance to make personal contact. When we see you leave your ship, we'll keep you within sight and try to determine whether you are being followed by someone from your ship, or anyone else." Wagner stopped and picked up his cold drink. "It's not getting any cooler," he observed with a wry smile before continuing his instructions.

"Once we know you are off the ship, we'll have someone waiting at the Post Office for you to appear. We know there are no guarantees that you will be able to get there but if you succeed, he will approach you, pretending to be a tourist looking for directions. He will have a map of the city in his hand and will unfold it and ask if you can help him find his way. Your response will be that you also are visiting the city and suggest he go inside the Post Office for directions. If it appears that you are not being followed, you will have a chance to exchange information, using the map as a prop while you talk, just in case you are being observed. Try to arrange a future meeting," instructed Wagner, before adding, "but don't take any unnecessary risks. If you have any reason to think that you are under surveillance, your response to our man should simply be, 'I'm sorry, but I can't help you.' He will break off the meeting immediately. In the beginning we need to be careful and move slowly until we are comfortable that we have established a secure routine."

"How will your man recognize me?" asked Popescu matter-of-factly.

"We are going to need some photographs. I have brought a

camera and will get some close-ups of you before you leave," replied Wagner.

"I'm sorry that we don't have more time," said Wagner as he checked his watch, "but it is important for you to get back to your friends before they begin to worry about you." Wagner hesitated for a few seconds before stepping toward Popescu and placing a friendly hand on his shoulder. "Alex, there is one last thing I want you to understand."

"What is it?" asked Popescu who was now standing facing Wagner.

"I want you to know that there is nothing more important to us than assuring the safety of you and your family. Although I know we have just met, you have earned my respect for your courage and commitment to your country's freedom." Wagner paused and added, "And you have not asked for anything in return." Popescu shrugged self-consciously at Wagner's words. "But commitments work in both directions. We have a commitment to protect your family's safety but you are taking risks and we also think our commitment should recognize those risks by providing your family with a small measure of financial security. We intend to establish a ten thousand dollar escrow account for you and your family that will be available on the second anniversary of our working relationship." Before Popescu could respond, Wagner continued, "I also know that you will have incidental expenses, like postage and postal cards, because of your work with us. Those should not be your responsibility. We will accrue one hundred dollars each month to cover those expenses and will pay you in local currencies each time we make contact. But we will have to be careful how those payments are made. We don't want them to attract attention," concluded Wagner.

Popescu extended his hand to Wagner. "You are very generous and you are right. I expected nothing and asked for nothing in exchange for my work with you. But your offer to provide my family with some hope of financial security removes a great source of worry for me," smiled Popescu, before adding, "Of course I realize it is good news that I cannot share with my family at this time."

Wagner turned toward Nick, who had been watching the proceedings with a look of quiet satisfaction. "Nick, this meeting would never have happened without your help. Alex trusted you enough to risk coming here and meeting with me. I know that together we will make a positive difference. I wish we had more time and I know we have a lot of unfinished business that will have to wait until our next meeting, but it's almost time for you to leave." Wagner started across the room. "Let me get my camera so we can take a few shots before you and Nick start back to rejoin your friends,' said Wagner, addressing Popescu directly. Then, almost by reflex, he cautioned," and be sure to keep an eye out for anyone who might be getting too close."

"Don't worry. I have eyes in the back of my head," assured Nick with a broad grin.

When he finally closed the door behind Nick and Popescu, Wagner walked back to the window and looked at the building across the street. Reedy was still keeping his silent vigil. It was only after the two men appeared on the street below that Reedy disappeared from sight, transformed into an unseen escort as they headed back to the Black Cat. Wagner watched for a few minutes before turning back into the room to collect his belongings. That's one I owe Tom, thought Wagner with a smile.

✻✻✻✻

Ellis read the first cable through twice, unconsciously tapping the eraser end of his pencil against the top of his desk.

OP: WEDDING PARTY
COLLINS (IDEN A) BEST MAN (IDEN B) MET JULY 22. BEST MAN AGREED
RECRUITMENT. MAKES FREQUENT VISITS OUTSIDE COUNTRY. GIVEN S/W.
LIMITED TIME PREVENTED DETAILED DEBRIEFING. ANTICIPATE FUTURE MEETINGS.
DETAILS FOLLOW.

Ellis flipped to the identity cable.

OP: WEDDING PARTY
IDEN A: JOHN WAGNER
IDEN B: ALEX POPESCU

When he was finally satisfied with the wording, he scribbled an "O.K.—H.E." on the top of each sheet of paper and handed them to Reedy who, along with Wagner, was in his office to brief Ellis on their observations of the Popescu recruitment meeting.

"Tom, would you hand these to Heidi and ask her to get them typed and on the way?"

"Priority?"

"No. Routine will do it. Thanks."

As Reedy stepped outside, Ellis walked around and leaned against the front of his desk. "Well, Jack, how did it feel to draw your first blood?" asked Ellis with a smile.

"I haven't thought about it in those terms," laughed Wagner. "I'm just glad Nick was able to get Popescu away from the rest of his crew long enough for us to meet him alone. But we didn't have much time, so there's a lot of unfinished business to take care of before I'd call it a success."

"Jack, we work in an untidy business where loose ends are always part of the package. When we first started talking about this operation, I think we recognized that the odds of isolating Popescu and arranging a recruitment meeting were pretty slim. As far as I'm concerned, we exceeded our original objectives and you and Nick did a hellova job making it happen. So don't sweat the unfinished business. We'll handle it," reasssured Ellis as Reedy re-entered his office.

"You're the only one here who has met Popescu. What did you think of him?" asked Ellis, speaking directly to Wagner.

"I think we may have lucked out. Spend a little time with him and you realize you're talking to a very intelligent guy. He asks questions and he doesn't show his own hand until he's satisfied with the answers. He's self-confident, but not cocky. I think he's tough-minded, someone who can make hard choices without panicking. I got the feeling that once he makes a commitment, you can rely on him to honor it. And if he should get caught in a tight situation, I think he is imaginative and wise enough to improvise on the fly. He's a natural for this business," concluded Wagner.

"I trust your judgment and I hope you're right," responded Ellis with a nod of approval, before turning to Reedy. "How about you, Tom? You sat in the hot seat all day. Did you spot anything out of the ordinary?"

"You're right about the hot seat, except that it felt more like a blast furnace. Of course, Jack wasn't worried about a poor bastard like me, frying in the noonday sun, trying to protect his backside so he could make his sales pitch without being interrupted," joked Reedy with a good-natured nod toward Wagner. "But to answer your original question; I watched Popescu and Nick when they arrived at the safe house. I was a little surprised at how few people were in the street and they all seemed caught up in their personal business. I didn't see anyone paying any attention to the safe house and no one lingered in the area once they had finished whatever they were doing."

"How about on their way back?" interjected Ellis. "Anything unusual there?"

"I stayed with them from the time they left the safe house. I kept my distance but I followed them all the way back to the Black Cat where Popescu's friends were waiting. I didn't see anything that seemed suspicious or out of the ordinary," replied Reedy.

"Somehow that just doesn't seem quite right but it's probably just my natural skepticism. I expected that at least a few of our local friends would be keeping an eye on the crew when they went ashore. Believe me, I'm happy you didn't spot anyone who looked like they might be following them." Ellis then turned to Wagner. "Jack, I know you will be debriefing Nick on every move he made today. Make sure he agrees with Tom that there was no one who might have been watching Popescu and him at any point during the day."

Ellis stepped back around his desk, sat down and tilted back in his chair, slowly rubbing the nape of his neck, quietly releasing the day's tensions and sending an unspoken signal that the meeting was ending. As Wagner and Reedy began to stand, Ellis added a final comment. "By the way, I spoke to Chris and briefed him on your meeting with Popescu. He specifically told me to thank you for a job well done." Ellis smiled. "I agreed with him."

CHAPTER ELEVEN

The cord around the package bit into his fingers. BRIDEGROOM slowed and shifted the bundle to the other hand. As he hesitated, he raised his arm, studied his watch. In the clotted darkness of the narrow side street the dial was barely visible. He tilted his wrist back and forth trying to trap a little light and squinted to read the time. He would not be late.

It was a clear moonless night. The sky was black and muffled sounds of night traffic hung like smoke in the warm Mediterranean air. Just ahead a tree trunk writhed into sudden life and he felt his heart lurch painfully before he recognized the emerging shape of embracing lovers. He quickened his steps but there was no one else in sight.

Why am I here? he thought. Why do I let my actions violate my judgment? Why, after two weeks of careful consideration, after all my business instincts have convinced me that the risks are too great, should I be hurrying to keep an appointment that if detected could ruin everything I have worked so hard to organize? He felt the corner of his mouth turn downward in a wry smile. Man is a curious creature. He deliberates for days, then acts on impulse and pretends he has made a decision.

It had been impulse that sent him to the Soviet Embassy the day Tina gave him the letter from his mother. And this morning, standing with the telephone in his hand, saying nothing. Had that been impulse? ("Arrangements have been made for your package. Bring it tonight at ten.")

He had anticipated that call. The first visit to the Russian Embassy had been a regrettable mistake and now a second visit was out of the question. He would disengage. For two weeks he had planned his reply. Polite thanks and apologies for having troubled them but it would not be necessary to send the medicine after all. Yet, when he replaced the receiver on its cradle, he had been silent.

He could still turn back, ignore the summons. He could retrace his steps, unwind down the narrow streets and alleys, retreat to the comfortable anonymity of his room. Would they call again? Perhaps. But if he did not respond, the episode could finally end.

Even as these thoughts crisscrossed through his mind, he broke his stride only long enough to reaffirm his grip on the precious package in his hand. He was almost to the corner. As he approached the intersection, the light from the boulevard began to seep into the side street, slowly stripping him of the protective cover of darkness. He pulled at the brim of his hat, alert now with apprehension, and turned into the glare of streetlights. Just ahead, another hundred yards, lay the embassy. He passed the tall wrought iron fence and already could make out the black lip of the embassy driveway. Then he noticed the match flicker and a man move out of the shadows of a doorway and begin walking toward him. Instinctively his eyes picked out a second man standing coatless on the other side of the street. The embassy was being watched.

The man walked with the slow deliberate step of a pallbearer. He was thin and his loose-fitting linen suit gave an illusion of height. The shadow of his hat-brim halved his face, but in the narrowing distance, BRIDEGROOM made out the flair of a full moustache above a melted chin.

BRIDEGROOM could taste the rising panic. His neck and arms ached with tension. Do I know this man? His mind leafed frantically through a file of forgotten faces. Does he know me? Should I risk meeting his eyes? Will it seem an act of guilt if I look down or away as we pass?

He felt so conspicuous that the slightest movement of a muscle now seemed to shout for attention. Then as his feet carried him steadily forward, he was stabbed by the realization that the embassy drive lay between them. I must not reach it first, he thought, forcing his steps to slow. We must pass on this side where I am just another shopper on his way home. It will be impossible to enter right under his nose.

With enormous effort he made himself assume the languid pace of an evening stroller, enjoying the night air. Then the man stopped. BRIDEGROOM's impulse was to stop too, like the partner in a ritualistic dance, but he knew he must go forward or flee. Only a few yards lay between them, only a few steps more and the irrevocable decision must be made . . . to go on innocently past the drive and lose perhaps forever this life-line to his mother, or boldly to enter and risk shattering the fragile security he had won for himself and for Tina and Nick.

Abruptly, the man turned and started across the street. Weak with relief, BRIDEGROOM felt his feet carry him to his destination. He was tormented by the desire to turn as he mounted the embassy steps, but he kept his eyes fixed on the entrance.

He reached for the polished brass knocker and felt it thump dully against the door. Then he waited motionless in the semi-darkness, aware that he was being watched by the two men standing across the street. In a moment he heard the snap of the bolt lock and the embassy door swung open in a lazy quarter arc into the foyer. BRIDEGROOM stepped quickly inside and the door was closed behind him.

"Good evening," said the doorkeeper impassively as he reached to take BRIDEGROOM's hat.

"Good evening. My name is Bergarsch. I believe I am expected."

"Yes. Come this way." As they walked silently through the hall toward the room BRIDEGROOM remembered from his previous visit, he became conscious that he had seen the man he was following before. He recognized the powerful peasant shoulders and squat thick neck, the fist of a jaw and the round Slavic head with over-sized ears and straight blonde hair. When they reached the door, his escort turned the knob and pushed it in, standing aside for BRIDEGROOM to enter. "You may go in," he said in a low monotone.

"Thank you." For a split second their eyes met and

BRIDEGROOM knew that this was the same man he had seen wearing the chauffeur's cap in the embassy driveway the afternoon of his first visit.

"Hello once again, Mr. Bergarsch. I see you received my call." The Russian extended his hand cordially toward BRIDEGROOM and led him into the room.

"Yes. Thank you for remembering me. I know that you have many more important things to think about."

"A bargain is a bargain, my friend. And, after all, there is nothing more important than keeping one's word," responded the Russian in a relaxed, almost intimate manner.

They were standing in the center of the room, which appeared unchanged from their last meeting. Dark drapes were pulled across the shuttered windows and the only light came from a single upright floor lamp which glowed comfortably next to one of two overstuffed chairs placed informally near the unlit fireplace.

Since morning when he first began considering tonight's meeting, BRIDEGROOM's mood had alternated between one of self-reproach and of self-justification and for a time he had wondered whether he had lost the ability to make a rational choice. But now that he was here, the doubts disappeared. He was dealing with a situation he could understand. He knew he had risked exposure by coming but that decision was made and done with and as he faced the Russian in the quiet of the embassy room, he felt quite calm. More importantly, he at last was willing to admit what he had known to be true from the beginning . . . the Russian would try to recruit him. BRIDEGROOM waited for the first move.

"You have brought the medicine?" asked the Russian, glancing down at the package in BRIDEGROOM's hand.

"Yes. I have it here."

"Good, let me take it . . . and please sit down and be comfortable," said the Russian gesturing casually toward one of the chairs as he accepted the parcel.

"You are sure I will not be detaining you from your work?' protested BRIDEGOOM politely. "You already have been very kind."

The Russian smiled condescendingly as though he had known what BRIDEGROOM would say before the words were spoken. "Quite the contrary, Mr. Bergarsch. It is you who do me the kindness by coming. We Russians live a rather sheltered life, you know. Not by choice, of course, but there are certain inhibiting local restrictions. You perhaps observed two of them standing across the street as you came in tonight. So now that you are here, please stay and join me in a brandy."

"With pleasure," responded BRIDEGROOM. He walked over to one of the chairs and felt its cushion yield softly under his weight. The Russian put the package of medicine on top of the desk at the far end of the room and began idly leafing through some papers which were lying there.

"It has been a long time since your last visit. As a matter of fact, I was surprised not to hear from you before now." For just a moment the Russian paused and looked at BRIDEGROOM like a tailor measuring him for size. Then he walked to the liquor cabinet and poured two brandies. "But I should realize that when a man is as busy as you, he cannot always find time to do everything he might like." The Russian handed BRIDEGROOM a brandy and sat down.

"I apologize if you have been expecting me to call but since we had made no definite arrangements, I really was not certain how to contact you. I think you will understand why I did not want to risk being seen coming here again unless I knew you would be here and," said BRIDEGROOM speaking more deliberately, "I did not know whom to ask for if I telephoned."

The Russian, who had been watching his brandy rock gently in the bottom of the snifter, looked up and said, "You are a prudent man, Mr. Bergarsch, which must explain your success. And of course you are correct. I should have been more specific but perhaps we both have learned a useful lesson . . . for the next time." He inhaled the aroma of his drink and added lightly, "but what does it matter? The important thing is that you have come."

"Yes, you are right. It is important that I have come. I don't know how I would have been able to get medicine to my mother without your help," replied BRIDEGROOM innocently, as though he believed this was the only reason he had been called to the Russian Embassy. The Russian, who was sitting with his legs crossed, smiled and leaned back in his chair. He wore no garters and the exposed flesh of his thin bony shin had the white lifeless appearance of a fillet of fish.

"You are far too modest, Mr. Bergarsch. I am sure that a man with your enterprise would have found another way." The Russian put down his glass and picked an oval-shaped Turkish cigarette from a small box he had taken from his inside jacket pocket. "But it will not be necessary. Your mother will receive her medicine within two days." He lit the cigarette and took a deep drag. The blue smoke trailed past his face and rushed up through the draught created by the lampshade. The sweet smell of the tobacco began to penetrate BRIDEGROOM's nostrils as he answered.

"That is very good news." His voice conveyed an unmistakable impression of relief and in fact he did experience a strong feeling of satisfaction upon learning that the original purpose of his visit had been achieved. Now he would find out what was to be asked in repayment.

The Russian seemed to sense his pleasure. "How long has it been since you last saw her?" he asked.

How long, thought BRIDEGROOM. "Eight years," he answered hesitantly. Eight years . . . could that be right? His mind searched back. "Bergarsch, you will leave the country by boat tomorrow." Standing in that filthy little office in the Ministry of Interior. The bare light bulb, hanging like a suicide from a cord in the center of the ceiling, the faded brown paint and cracked plaster and the flaccid unshaven face of that swine with the malevolent yellow eyes, throwing the visa across the desk. "You get off easy, Bergarsch. Maybe you know the right people. So now you will be taken home long enough to collect what you will need for your trip. I am sorry to tell you we could not arrange first class accommodations but you can be sure that we'll take good care of anything you leave behind." Then his sarcastic laugh like a phlegm-filled cough.

A cold damp smell of gloom had been in the air as the car headed away from the Ministry through those bleak city streets for that last visit. Strange the things one remembers eight years later. The autumn sky, grey and heavy with rain, had seemed about to descend and suffocate everything beneath it. The steady drone of the engine and the click of the windshield wiper, snapping like a metronome, were the only sounds. A few people hurrying along the sidewalk, past the empty store windows, looking for shelter in doorways.

The black sedan moving like a glistening wet rat, sniffing cautiously around each corner, darting ahead, then slowing to feel its way through another intersection. The city sliding past like a worn film clip. Shops, government buildings, fine houses (his own now the official residence of a Russian economic advisor), soot-stained factories, workers' tenements, ever-narrowing streets and finally a shabby unpainted frame house standing wearily between two taller but equally dilapidated buildings.

The dank smell of an empty hallway. The steep climb toward the second floor and the feel of deep grooves worn in smooth wooden stair treads. A loose handrail to keep balance; a staccato rap on the grey paint-chipped door; a crack of light.

His mother standing in the doorway, a soft glowing inscrutable smile lighting her lifted face, her two hands closing his in affectionate welcome (the hostess greeting a beloved guest, the mother receiving her son for tea after a stroll in the garden). Only a slight movement of her quick black eyes, registering and rejecting the image of his escort, indicating anything unusual had happened, was about to happen.

Drawing him into the room with the selfless grace of one who lives in peace among precious possessions. The sight of the cracked windows and broken plaster and stark furnishings contrasting so sharply with her gentle regality, outraging him, sending the blood pounding in his temples, but her voice saying with soft irony, "You are too much indoors these days, Victor. You lack color," and, understanding her at once. forcing himself to answer lightly, "That will soon be remedied. I leave now for a sunnier climate."

"I know. Everything is ready. But you will stay for tea?"

An involuntary glance in the direction of the gawking officer.

Her eyes following his. "Wait outside until you are called, boy." She had spoken as to a house servant. The man's mouth had moved in noiseless astonished protest (generations of obedience warring with a new sense of authority) but the sight of this imperious white-haired woman had intimidated him into clumsy retreat.

There was a moment as the door clicked shut when the spell might have been broken, when they might have wept in one another's arms, but when he had turned, she was serenely pouring tea and not until he himself, suitcase in hand, was closing the door on her still-smiling porcelain composure, did her face convulse as with a tic in the very instant of its closing. Momentum had carried him to the top of the stairs and his escort, arrogance restored, had hurried him roughly forward.

The Russian had been sitting silently smoking his cigarette, his eyes fixed on BRIDEGROOM. He made no effort to interrupt the elder man's thoughts until finally, like a doctor deciding that he has waited long enough to remove the thermometer from his patient's mouth, he snuffed out his cigarette and said in a quiet voice, "Eight years is a long separation, especially since your mother is ill." He paused and then added more deliberately, "But there are ways to make these separations easier to bear."

The sound of the Russian's voice snapped BRIDEGROOM out of his mood of reflection. He leaned forward, about to interject a reply, but before he could answer, the Russian was again speaking. "You know, Mr. Bergarsch, I have been looking forward to this visit. But, to be quite honest, I was not certain you would keep our appointment tonight." BRIDEGROOM shifted his legs uneasily but the Russian forestalled any reply by limply raising his right hand in a gesture not unlike that of a pastor indifferently pronouncing benediction.

"I can see from your expression that my doubts were not entirely unjustified . . . but please don't be embarrassed. I understand perfectly how you must feel. In fact, I would have less respect for your judgment . . . perhaps even wonder about your motivation . . . if you had no misgivings about coming here. After all, I am quite aware that the past few years have not been particularly pleasant for you and I think if I were in your position, it would be natural to ask myself the same question you must ask, 'Why deal the Russians?'" He looked knowingly at BRIDEGROOM, lifted his glass off the table and sipped some brandy.

"What you have said is true," began BRIDEGROOM, carefully measuring each word. "Although I was not aware that my thoughts were quite so obvious, what is the point in denying that they exist?" He hesitated and then asked almost matter-of-factly, "Why should you want to help me?"

The Russian laughed appreciatively before answering. "My friend, if you are addressing that question to me personally, the answer is simple." Still smiling, he put down his brandy glass, leaned back locking his hands across his belly and continued, "For some reason the police in this country appear to be uncommonly interested in everything we Russians do. Now, we have nothing to hide but naturally, this type of activity discourages people from talking with us. Oh, of course, there are the usual diplomatic receptions, but there the air is filled only with alcohol and the chatter of silly women. And," he continued, bowing his head facetiously, "I do not want to forget our local Party comrades. They are very happy to be seen with us but unfortunately they make extraordinarily dull companions. And so . . . you see . . . if the decision were left to me alone, I would help you if only because it is so refreshing to talk with a man who says exactly what he thinks." As he finished speaking, the Russian opened his hands and let them drop on his lap.

"It is kind of you to say that," replied BRIDEGROOM automatically.

The Russian calmly lit another cigarette, casually examined a strand of loose tobacco which he had picked off his tongue and continued as though there had been no interruption. "But I think you will understand, Mr. Bergarsch, if I tell you that this type of decision is not left to me alone." His tone had suddenly hardened and he looked directly at BRIDEGROOM as he spoke. "When you came to me two weeks ago, you presented me with an unusual dilemma. I wanted to help you. I sympathized with your predicament. And to be quite truthful, I was impressed by your courage. But I have no private channel of communication with your mother. And you can imagine that I could not go to my superiors and say, 'Look here, this gentleman, Bergarsch, has a sick mother and he wants us to send her some medicine.' They would ask, 'Who is Bergarsch and why should we help him?'. You understand my position."

"Of course."

"Unhappily, life is quite unjust. There has to be a reason even for doing good. And so I had to think to myself, how can I justify helping this man. I was able to think of a way."

"Yes?"

"You are able to move freely about the city. I am not. You have friends who are politicians and you know what they are thinking . . . or you can easily find out. You visit the Ministries and you talk to civil servants. You guide the refugee movement. Who knows, you may even know a few Americans. So if occasionally you were able to provide certain types of information, it would make it much easier for me to help your mother."

"And if I should refuse, will you send the medicine?"

"My friend, you are a businessman. You wouldn't consign merchandize to a man before he established his credit. Believe me, I want to help you. I might prefer to do it differently, but there is no other way."

So finally the trap has been set, thought BRIDEGROOM, and now it is my turn to move. Even before the Russian had finished speaking, BRIDEGROOM's mind began sifting the alternatives. He still was not certain what the outcome of this meeting would be but he knew instinctively that he could not afford to lose control of the conversation to the Russian. He had to keep his opponent off balance and now that the Russian had revealed his hand, it would be easier.

"You want me to spy for you?" asked BRIDEGROOM, edging his voice with simulated anger. "I am sorry, but it is impossible. I have not tried to conceal my political feelings. You understood them from the beginning. If now you cannot send the medicine, I accept your decision and apologize for troubling you."

"Please don't misunderstand me," said the Russian in a conciliatory tone. "I am sorry if I have been too blunt but we are both practical men. You have a problem that I can help you with and in exchange there is perhaps some way that you can be of service to me. This is not a question of politics. It is a matter of reaching an accommodation. If we have differences, why not discuss them openly?"

"I have no objection if you think there is anything to discuss," replied BRIDEGROOM coldly.

"Let me put it this way, Mr. Bergarsch. We both know that you have accepted certain risks, possibly jeopardized your future security, by coming here. And you have come only because you want me to send medicine to your mother. Therefore, what is more logical than for me to conclude that her welfare is a matter of great importance to you?"

"You are right. Of course it is risky to come here. But, as you have reminded me several times, I am a realist and there is a limit to the risks I will take. I would like to help her but I do not forget that she is an old woman with not much time. And so I am done with it. I also have my own survival to think about. What . . . to get a few grams of medicine to a sick woman you expect me to dance like a doll on the end of a string? I tell you frankly, your price is too high."

"Ah, my friend, as I should have expected, you do not disappoint me," said the Russian, smiling sardonically. "You present a strong case and I am glad you are able to distinguish between loyalty and sentiment. And so for now, let's dismiss this business of the medicine. It is, after all, a secondary affair which can be easily settled later."

"Oh, I wasn't aware of that," responded BRIDEGROOM with mock surprise.

"Then I apologize for speaking ambiguously," replied the Russian. "I shall try to be more precise and I hope you will consider carefully what I have to say."

"Of course," answered BRIDEGROOM, who again had settled comfortably back in his chair.

"Mr. Bergarsch, you are a man of intelligence, a man who does not hide from the facts as they exist. Although you may not always agree with our policy, I think you understand us. It does not make sense that a man like you would delude himself into believing that we would send this medicine of yours because of our generous nature. No . . . you understand us too well to think that. There had to be a bargain. You knew this . . . and it is interesting that still you came. Call it a businessman's curiosity if you like but whatever your reason, it was something more than a son's concern for his mother that brought you here tonight. Another man might have run away, afraid to become involved, but, my friend, I think you enjoy this little game." He paused and sipped his brandy. "And so do I."

BRIDEGROOM listened attentively, reflecting on each word, aware that the Russian was building up to a new proposal. This man is clever, he thought with grudging admiration, and since he is clever, he also is dangerous. Yet, BRIDEGROOM's feelings of concern were tempered by the amusing notion that under different circumstances and at a different time, this might have been a scene in the well-appointed office of the owner of V.BERGARSCH, LTD., IMPORTERS & EXPORTERS. Two men bent on turning a profit. There was the Russian, leaning forward, brandy glass in hand, vigorously outlining the virtues of his services and here he sat comfortably in his armchair, interested but quite skeptical.

"Before you reject our price as too high," the Russian was saying, "it would be wise to listens to what we propose."

"And what do you propose?"

"Let me explain from the beginning," said the Russian, speaking in the reserved manner of a university lecturer. "As you no doubt can imagine, it is an easy matter to recruit local Communist Party members to our service. For them it is simply a question of dedication to a cause. Now you may challenge the sincerity of their dedication, as I do myself, but it really is of no consequence. What is significant is the fact that nearly all of these Party members have been identified and black-listed by the local police. This in no way diminishes their effectiveness as a disciplined political force, which, as I am sure you are aware, is a constant source of worry and irritation to the rather feeble coalition which now governs this country. However, it does limit the value of individual Party members in other equally important activities." The Russian hesitated. "This is all very elementary and I do hope not too boring," he said with an apologetic smile.

"Not at all."

What I am trying to say, Mr. Bergartsch, is that in my line of work we prefer, with only one exception, to employ people who have not been politically labeled. And that one exception applies to individuals who have been labeled 'anti-Communist,' a designation which I think rather appropriately describes your own feelings. Please don't think I am passing judgment. After all, knowing as I do your past experiences, your feelings seem perfectly reasonable." The Russian leaned back and crossed his legs. "But I suppose you are asking yourself, 'Why, if he understands all these things, does he think we can do business'?"

"I assume you will tell me," replied BRIDEGROOM serenely.

"The answer is really quite simple," responded the Russian. "Let us agree that you have legitimate personal reasons for opposing Communism. Does that prove you have discovered a political system that guarantees individual justice? I think not. Whether or not you like the idea, my friend, the fact remains that you live in an unstable part of the world. Here a man concerns himself not with justice, but with survival; and if he is wise, he will use all his resources to survive as comfortably as possible. A bit too cynical, you say? Perhaps. But I remind you that there are two men standing across the street watching this building. If they should decide that you are a threat to their system, do you for one minute think you would be better treated in their hands than you were in ours? No . . . you are too much of a realist to believe that. You have no illusions. Today you deal only in realities. That is why you are here. That is why we can do business," said the Russian solemnly. Then, looking at BRIDEGROOM's empty glass, he said lightly, "But I am neglecting my duties as a host. Please let me pour you another brandy."

BRIDEGROOM unconsciously cupped his hand over the top of his glass and answered, "No, thank you. I have had quite enough."

"As you like," replied the Russian. Then, slowly, as though

only now deciding to take BRIDEGROOM into his confidence, he added, "You have been very patient. I have talked far too much. But now, Mr. Bergarsch, I shall come directly to the point."

And so at last we complete the final turn of the circle, thought BRIDEGROOM ironically. They began by stealing my business and end by trying to hire me to work in theirs. And strangely I can listen without emotion. How is it possible? Where is the hatred I once felt? Or, after eight years, have I forgotten my reasons for hating? Perhaps hate without the hated is as impossible to sustain as love without the beloved.

"You are in a position to obtain information and I am in a position to pay for it," continued the Russian. His words were spoken in an even unhurried voice that nevertheless conveyed an unmistakable threat, a threat that BRIDEGROOM saw reflected in the Russian's eyes. "This is a straight business proposal, nothing more. I am not interested in influencing your politics, Mr. Bergarsch. On the contrary, I encourage you to continue your anti-Communist activities. This is, after all, a much more credible role for you. As you can see, you are being asked to give up nothing. I do not intrude in your politics or your private life. They are your affair. And," said the Russian with a casual movement of his hand, "there is nothing sinister about what I have suggested. I have found it difficult to get objective reports on certain subjects and I think you can provide them. I naturally expect to compensate you for your time and effort." The Russian studied BRIDEGROOM's face and then added, almost carelessly, "Of course, if you agree to what I propose, I will make it my personal business to see that your mother receives any medicine or other help she may require." He hesitated and then said coldly, "I think, Mr. Bergarsch, it would be unwise to reject such an attractive offer."

"You are very generous and very persuasive," responded BRIDEGROOM. "But, you understand the instincts of a businessman. By nature we are conservative. It is almost a fetish with us to want to know all the details of a new transaction before we make a final commitment. And there are a few particulars that are still unclear."

"Of course I am aware that there may be a few minor points

that will need clarification but the important thing is that we seem close to agreement on the central issue, which is gratifying progress," replied the Russian earnestly. "So now perhaps you will tell me. Just what are these details that are troubling you?"

For a few moments, BRIDEGROOM looked contemplatively at the wall behind the Russian. Then slowly, as though with great effort, he turned his head until their eyes met. "You have suggested that we speak openly with one another. Under the present circumstances, I accept your advice," he said, with a slight nod of acknowledgment, before continuing gravely, "You have asked me to procure information but you haven't described the kind of information you want me to procure. You have talked about the risk I have taken tonight in coming to the Russian Embassy but you haven't explained how this risk would be eliminated if I should agree to meet you regularly. What protection would I be offered if my work for you was exposed? You have described this matter as a business arrangement for which I will be compensated but we have not discussed the manner of payment . . . or the frequency. Finally, you have kindly agreed to send medicine to my mother. How will I know if it is received?" He had spoken rapidly but now he stopped and smiled patronizingly at the Russian. "As you can see, I am neither surprised nor alarmed by what you propose. Surprise, after all, is a prerogative of youth and my youth is far behind me. But you will also understand that I am too old to become an adventurer. No, at my age, one measures each new risk with increasing caution."

"I am glad you have asked these questions and I am certain I can provide satisfactory answers. But your list is so long that I wonder where to begin," responded the Russian with an artificial laugh.

"Wherever you wish."

"You ask what type of work I will expect you to perform. I thought I had made myself clear on that point but apparently I did not. For the present, I must answer your question in general terms. After we have worked together, you will, I think, see the answer for yourself." The Russian lit a cigarette and continued. "I am interested in information, all types of information.

Consequently, you will be expected to exploit each of your contacts in local political and refugee circles and keep me informed on every phase of activity you can learn about. I want to know names, opinions, even rumors. I want to know about refugee morale and what is going on in the ministries. I want to know everything you can find out about American policy and their personnel. If there is talk about trade agreements, international fairs or cultural exchanges, I want to know. Obviously, I am concerned with anything connected with military or security affairs. And, of course, I would expect you to inform me at once of any matter involving Soviet policy regardless of how trivial it may appear to you. In short, Mr. Bergarsch, I want to know everything . . . whether pleasant or unpleasant."

"I am flattered that you think I am important and influential enough to obtain this information but the truth is that you over-estimate my capabilities," replied BRIDEGROOM.

The Russian tapped the ashes off the end of his cigarette and answered tolerantly, "It is good of you to give me your opinion but this is an unusual kind of business and you will find that nothing is exactly as it appears to be. I assure you that I would not make this proposal unless I were convinced of your qualifications. However, there is no reason for you to worry needlessly about your personal security. We do not want you compromised and therefore will take every precaution to guarantee that you are not. You see, Mr. Bergarsch, you occupy a unique position in this community . . . one that in many ways is ideally suited for our work. As the spokesman for a large segment of the refugee population, you have gradually acquired a kind of semi-official status. It has become convenient, almost a matter of habit, for government officials to consult with you whenever there is a new question of refugee policy. They have confidence in you and I have been told that as a result, rather close personal relationships have developed which now extend even to members of Parliament. These are relationships which can be profitably cultivated. It is delicate work but we are prepared to give you unlimited support."

BRIDEGROOM waited for the Russian to finish speaking

before he answered in a tone of unconcealed annoyance. "All right, I am willing to concede that I can be of service to you but I do not understand . . . and you have not yet explained . . . how I can accomplish these assignments except at great personal risk. You talk about guaranteeing my protection. I want to know how."

"Of course there are risks and if you agree to work . . . make no mistake . . . you will agree to accept them. But you seem unable to understand that the risks will be small, very small indeed. We are not beginners in this business, Mr. Bergarsch. You are worried about the danger of being recognized as a regular visitor to this embassy. Good, because I am worried about the same thing. In the future we will find more secure meeting places."

"And what about tonight? What if those two men identify me and I am asked to explain why I came here?"

"Just a minute ago I told you that in this work nothing is exactly as it appears to be. Now I will give you an example of what I meant. If those two men recognize you and you are asked to explain your visit . . . and let's admit that such a thing could happen . . . just tell them the truth." He looked at BRIDEGROOM and laughed. "You seem surprised. I don't blame you. This is a new experience for you. But think about it, my friend. Can you think of a better deception than the truth? Naturally, I am speaking about the truth with certain vital facts omitted. But if tomorrow you were to receive a call from the security police, and they should ask you why you came here tonight, tell them why. You came to deliver the medicine. This is, after all, quite true. And show them the letter from your mother. Unless I am mistaken, they will have seen it anyway. And so, as long as you can justify your visit, what will they say?. 'Mr. Bergarsch, it is a mistake to deal with the Russians. They cannot be trusted. We understand your reason for seeing them but don't go back.' If you follow this advice, as of course you will, the incident will soon be forgotten and no one will suspect you of anything worse than a momentary indiscretion caused by a deep concern for your mother's health. It is really no more complicated than that. But tell me, do you have any reason to think that you may have been recognized? Have you seen either of those men before?"

"No, it was the first time I ever had seen the one who passed me on the sidewalk. The other man was standing in the shadows across the street so it was impossible to tell if I knew him, or if he recognized me."

"Good. Then they probably still have no idea who you are and there is no reason why we should help them find out. When you leave here tonight, walk to the corner. It is a busy intersection with a lot of traffic. Take a taxi to Constitution Square and mingle with the crowd. They will have no way of following you. The poor fellows have no money for taxi rides," added the Russian jokingly. "But remember, even if someday you should be asked about tonight's visit, you will only have to explain that you came to help your mother and they will be satisfied." He pushed himself slowly out of his chair and walked toward the liquor cabinet. "However, there is still another question you want answered."

"There are several questions I would like answered," corrected BRIDEGOOM.

The Russian ignored his remark and asked hospitably, "Are you certain I can't interest you in a little more brandy?"

"Thank you. No."

BRIDEGROOM watched him pick up the brandy bottle and examine the label indifferently. "You know, I have spent so much time talking about what you can do for me, that I haven't told you what I can do for you in return," said the Russian as he poured himself a drink. "In the first place," he said, gesturing nonchalantly toward his desk, "I will see that your medicine is sent without delay. And, so that you will know that your mother has received it, I will arrange to have her send you a personal message through the same channel." The Russian headed back to his chair and as he sat down, he added in a tone of calculated earnestness, "But we should keep in mind that this medicine will not cure her. She will need more help. If you should decide to cooperate, you will make it possible for me to guarantee that she will receive the best medical care available."

This man uses my mother like a stick to beat me into submission, thought BRIDEGROOM angrily. But can I afford to refuse his offer? What will become of her if I do? Then, even as these thoughts flashed through his brain, he heard his own voice responding. "I told you once that I will not agree to your proposal simply to get medicine to my mother." He was leaning close to the Russian now and his words were clipped short and spoken reproachfully. "If there should be a bargain . . . which I am beginning to doubt . . . understand clearly that my mother will play no part in it!"

"I'm afraid that this time it is you who misinterprets my motives," answered the Russian dispassionately. "You stated your position quite precisely and I accepted it without questions. And yet, Mr. Bergarsch, although you may find this difficult to believe, I also appreciate how hard this separation must be for you and I would like to help . . . just as a friend. No . . . I assure you that I do not want our business relationship complicated in any way by this personal problem of yours."

"Under those circumstances, perhaps an agreement is possible. But there is no point in a prolonged discussion of generalities. Let me hear what you have to offer," responded BRIDEGROOM, almost brazenly, sensing that at least momentarily he had wrested the initiative from the Russian.

"Mr friend, the more we talk, the more certain I am that it is right that we should be talking." The Russian was holding his glass almost to the level of his chin, as though he was about to propose a toast. "It is quite uncommon to meet a man who moves so quickly to the heart of a problem. You will find this ability very helpful in your work with us. But . . . to answer your question. In the beginning, you will be paid seventy-five dollars a month, and of course, any expenses."

"Seventy-five dollars," chided BRIDEGROOM in a tone of feigned disbelief. "If that is your offer, I can only conclude that either you overstate your case or you underpay your associates. I hope you will remember that I did not come here looking for work. This conversation is, after all, your idea."

"I am sorry if my offer disappoints you but always there has to be a beginning. It takes time to learn this business and we will move slowly at the start . . . for your protection, of course," said the Russian reassuringly. "After you acquire some experience and your assignments become more important, then naturally we will expect to increase your pay." He waited until BRIDEGROOM seemed about to answer and said, "Before you reply, Mr. Bergarsch, stop and consider for a moment that I have not yet seen even one example of your work. Now we both know that you are in a position to provide useful information. Furthermore, you appear to be unusually qualified to do the job. There is only one question that remains unanswered." He paused and then asked softly, "Can you do the job? Until we learn the answer to that question, my offer will stand as made. I think it is a fair proposal that deserves a fair trial. After all, you can always change your mind."

"Do I understand you correctly? Are you suggesting that we begin on a trial basis and that you are willing to give me the right to dissolve our relationship at any time?"

"Of course," answered the Russian as though amazed that BRIDEGROOM could conceive of any other interpretation of his words. "Is that something you object to?"

"Not at all. I am just rather surprised that you propose such a flexible arrangement," responded BRIDEGROOM with a hint of suspicion in his tone.

"Why is it that people persist in accusing us of being inflexible?" asked the Russian, smiling good-naturedly. "After all, my friend, what is there for me to gain by being unreasonable? I am quite well aware that if you decide not to cooperate, there is no way to force you. So, if I want you to work for me, I have to make concessions . . . make my offer so attractive that you will at least agree to try. Oh, I realize that from your point of view there could be improvements . . . a higher rate of pay, for example. But you are an experienced businessman. How many transactions are there that satisfy both sides in every detail? Very few," said the Russian, answering his own question with a listless wave of his hand. "No, if we finally reach an agreement, it will be because we have looked beyond our minor differences and concentrated on the broad advantages of a formal association. I think perhaps you have already done this and if you have, then you understand how much we have to gain by working together."

When he finished speaking, the Russian stood up, walked over to his desk and slid open the top drawer. "I have something in here for you," he said, looking up at BRIDEGROOM, "and it will please me very much if before you leave here tonight, you will agree to accept it." He had taken a plain white envelope out of the drawer and was unconsciously tapping it against the palm of his hand.

"If that envelope concerns me, then naturally I am curious to know what it contains," responded BRIDEGROOM.

"Of course," answered the Russian affably, pressing against the drawer with his thigh and then moving quickly around the corner of the desk toward BRIDEGROOM. "This is hardly the time for me to keep secrets from you. No," he continued as he slowly eased himself back into his chair, "we can't afford to keep secrets. They spawn miscalculation. And in a matter as significant as this it is important that you do not misjudge my intentions . . . nor I yours. It is much better that we have chosen to speak openly because now we understand each other. But sooner or later everything is said and discussion must give way to decision. I think we have reached that point." For a moment, he paused and looked at the envelope in his hand. Then he extended it toward BRIDEGROOM. "There is one hundred dollars in this envelope . . . seventy-five for your salary and twenty-five to take care of various expenses you will have. If you agree to take it, you will be committing yourself to work for me and to accept my direction. But you have my word, Mr. Bergarsch, that if later on you should change your mind, you will be free to withdraw."

Does he think I am a fool? This man is not making a bargain, he is negotiating a surrender, thought BRIDEGROOM. If I accept that envelope, there will be no turning back. But do I really have a choice? Can I abandon her when she is sick and alone? No, he thought sadly, there is no other way. Slowly he reached out and took the envelope from the Russian but when he spoke, there was no sound in his voice to betray his inner despair. "All right, I am willing to give your proposal a short trial and I will do my best to help you. But I want you to know now . . . before we start . . . that you have not convinced me that it will work. And if it does not work, make no mistake, I will not hesitate to terminate the agreement without notice," said BRIDEGROOM sharply, as though it were he who was dictating the terms.

"You make a hard bargain," responded the Russian placidly, "but how can I object? On the contrary, whatever your conditions, I am very pleased that we have composed our differences and I am quite sure that we will have a long and fruitful partnership." The Russian took another sip of brandy and carefully replaced the glass on the table before turning to face BRIDEGROOM. "But now that we have reached an agreement, there are a few things we should settle at once. It is getting late and I do not want to detain you any longer than is absolutely necessary," he said in a voice that had acquired a sudden tone of authority. "We will meet again as soon as possible . . . I suggest Wednesday night. That will give you two days to prepare your first report. Do you have any objection?"

"I think that depends on what information you expect from me."

"Then there is no problem," responded the Russian as though the matter was decided. "I have told you that in the beginning I will want to find out what you already know. We can proceed from there."

"I know very little," interjected BRIDEGROOM with a shrug as the Russian lit a cigarette.

The Russian paid no attention to BRIDEGROOM's remark and continued his briefing. "I want you to prepare a list with the name of every government official that you know . . . or meet in your work. And for the present, it makes no difference what positions these men hold. However, it is important that you tell me everything that you know about each of them . . . their personality, weaknesses, background, politics, the extent of their influence, and so on. I am sure you understand the kind of thing I am interested in." He took a couple of quick puffs on his cigarette and added, "That is all I am asking you to do before our next meeting. Certainly, there is nothing dangerous or complicated about that assignment."

"No, there is nothing dangerous about it," agreed BRIDEGROOM. My only concern is that I may not be able to produce a list that will have any value for you. Of course I know a few government officials but I have no influence with them."

"Mr. Bergarsch, I am not an unreasonable man. I do not expect miracles. All that I ask is that you do your best. But I think that when you begin to write your report, you will discover that you actually know many more people than you can remember right at this moment. And, if it will make you feel any easier, I really am not too concerned with how much influence you exert today. What matters, my friend, is how much influence you are able to develop in the future." The Russian nodded with a sour smile that seemed to BRIDEGROOM more an expression of digestive pain than of good spirits. "Neither of us can say for certain what the answer will be but now that we have agreed to combine our efforts, I am quite confident that this modest enterprise of ours will be very successful. However, this is a business where small mistakes can be disastrous. So we have to guard against the natural tendency to become careless in our daily routine. It is especially important that we plan our future meetings to assure utmost security. Do you know the Green Park?"

"Yes."

"We will meet there Wednesday evening. I want you to arrive first. Stroll through the gardens. Buy a cold drink. Enjoy yourself. But be certain that no one is following you. At twenty minutes before nine, go to the path that leads into the park from the boulevard. There is a small footbridge over a pond. Wait there for exactly five minutes. If I do not arrive at fifteen minutes before nine, return home and we will repeat the same plan Saturday night, only it will be one-half hour earlier. Is that clear?"

"Quite clear."

"Good," said the Russian, speaking now with the easy assurance of a man doing a job with which he is thoroughly familiar. "Is it customary for you to wear a hat?"

"Yes. Why do you ask?"

"Although it is unlikely, there is always a chance that someone may be watching you when we are scheduled to meet. For example, if you should be recognized tonight, it is remotely possible that the authorities will decide to record your activities for the next few days. I emphasize that this is highly unlikely but it is best to be prepared. Consequently, we will need some method for cancelling a meeting even at the last minute. So, if you suspect that you are being watched, simply take off your hat as a signal and I will pass by without giving any sign of recognition. We will try again on a second night which we shall always have arranged in advance."

"And, if we should fail to meet the second time? Or if there should be an emergency and I should have to see you immediately?"

"In that case . . . " The Russian hesitated and began distractedly feeling his pockets until he finally gave up and asked, "Do you have a small notebook?"

"Yes. I have one."

"May I see it, please?" The Russian took it from BRIDEGROOM and quickly thumbed through the pages. "This will do," he said, handing it back. "I am going to give you a telephone number. Memorize it but use it only in an emergency. Until you are certain of the number, you may keep it in your notebook. Then erase it. You have enough entries in your book so that there will be nothing suspicious as long as you write each digit on a separate page. Do you understand?"

"Of course."

"Incidentally, Mr. Bergarsch, this will be the only occasion when you will use your notebook for recording information relating to our work. In the future, each of your reports will be prepared in a single copy which I expect you to keep in a secure place until we meet. Now if that is clear, I will give you the number." The Russian took a last drag on his cigarette and dropped it into the ashtray. Then, speaking slowly and pausing between each digit, he began dictating, "8 . . . 3 . . . 6 . . . 5 . . . 9 . . . 2"

"8 . . . 3 . . . 6 . . . 5 . . . 9 . . . 2," repeated BRIDEGROOM, reading from his notebook.

"That is correct."

"I hope there will be no emergencies which will force me to use this number," said BRIDEGROOM, as he replaced the notebook in his jacket pocket. "But if I should be obliged to use it, whom should I ask for?"

"Of course . . . I apologize, Mr. Bergarsch. We have talked about so many important matters that I have completely forgotten to introduce myself. If you call, ask for 'Mr. Lukas" and identify yourself as 'Charles'. If I am able to answer, we will arrange a time to meet. If I am not, tell whoever answers the telephone the time you want me to meet you. However, we actually will meet one hour later than the time you indicate. I am sure the reason is obvious. It is simply a matter of prudence to assume that the authorities have tapped the line. And for this same reason, you are never to relay any message on the telephone. It is to be used only in emergencies and even then, only to arrange unscheduled meetings. Now, Mr. Bergarsch, unless you have something in particular that you want to discuss, I don't think I should detain you any longer." The Russian placed his hands on the arms of his chair and pushed himself phlegmatically to his feet. "I would like to invite you to stay for a social visit but our two shadowy friends are undoubtedly still patiently waiting for you to leave and we shouldn't disappoint them."

"Isn't there another door that I might use to avoid them?" The tension of the early evening began to return to BRIDEGROOM's muscles as he thought of a second encounter with the two men in the street.

"That is hardly necessary. In fact, it would be quite unwise. You have nothing to hide. You came here with some medicine for your mother and now you are leaving . . . perfectly understandable. On the other hand, if you should be questioned about this visit, I think you would find it rather difficult to explain why a man on an innocent errand of mercy would leave by a side exit. But you have nothing to worry about," continued the Russian confidently as they walked toward the reception hall. "I am quite certain that you have not been recognized and I am equally certain that they will have no means of following you when you leave."

"I hope you are right," responded BRIDEGROOM.

"I know I am," answered the Russian warmly. They had

reached the front entrance and the Russian already had one hand on the knob. "We have accomplished a lot tonight and you will not regret your decision." He paused and then said soberly, "There is just one more thing . . . and again I speak as a friend. When you leave here tonight, I personally will see to it that all arrangements for assisting your mother are completed as quickly as possible. I give you my word that it will be a pleasure to help her but as you know, I would not be able to do this if I did not have the cooperation of my superiors. Oh, don't be concerned . . . there is no question about their approval. However, if they trouble themselves to help in this matter, I am certain they will be very curious to see your information. So it would be extremely embarrassing to me if for any reason you should change your mind about giving my proposal a fair trial. And if they should misunderstand your motives . . . well . . . I cannot guarantee what their reaction might be. Of course, I am sure no harm would come to your mother but her life could be made less pleasant and there is no sense taking that chance."

BRIDEGROOM stopped and for an instant, the two men faced each other in silence, their expressions communicating unspoken thoughts. Then, as though suddenly very weary, BRIDEGROOM took his hat off the table near the entry and adjusted the brim to conceal his forehead. The door swung open and he walked back into the night.

After he had closed the door, the Russian stretched and slowly rubbed the back of his neck with both hands. Then he moved quickly across the hall and re-entered the room where he had met BRIDEGROOM.

"Well, Golnikov, I hope this time you were successful." There was a quality of contempt in the voice. A dark black jacket and tie were thrown carelessly across the back of one of the easy chairs. His collar was open and thick muscular forearms were exposed below sleeves that had been rolled to his elbows. The chauffeur was standing near the liquor cabinet, drink in hand, looking fixedly at the Russian.

CHAPTER TWELVE

"Hey, Mr. Jack, I've been looking for you"

"Yasass, Dmitri. How's business? smiled Wagner.

"You speak Greek already," laughed the young boy approvingly, before adding, "I wanted to see you. Be careful today. There will be a big demonstration and a few people are mad at Americans."

"ENOSIS?" asked Wagner as he pulled a leaflet out of his pocket to show the pistachio boy. "An airplane dropped this over my house this morning."

"I know. But there are some people who want to start trouble . . . maybe throw rocks. So stay inside," warned Wagner's young friend solemnly.

"Efharesto," said Wagner as he put a friendly hand on the young boy's shoulder, before asking, "Did you save any pistachios for me?"

"Vevayeh," laughed the boy, amused by Wagner's beginning attempt to speak a few words of Greek.

As the boy handed Wagner his pistachios and pocketed the payment, he looked up at him and repeated his warning. "Remember what I told you. There are some crazy people who want to start trouble. So be careful."

Wagner was about to turn and enter his office building, but he stopped and smiled at his young friend. "Don't worry about me. I'll be careful. Just be sure you stay in a safe place yourself."

****

Ellis looked up and waved Wagner in as he spotted him standing in his office doorway. "It's almost time for lunch so I only want to hear good news," he joked as Wagner pulled up a chair.

"That eliminates half of what I was going to tell you," responded Wagner with a laugh.

"Is this going to be one of those 'good news, bad news' days?" asked Ellis with a wry smile. " Well, go ahead. Fire away."

"I'll start with the good news," began Wagner. "I've had a chance to talk with Nick about the time he spent with Popescu. He feels certain they were not followed and he said he made it a point to stay alert for any signs of surveillance, both inside the Black Cat and to and from the safe house meeting. He feels equally sure that Popescu's shipmates accepted his reunion with Popescu as a stroke of good luck and nothing more."

"That's re-assuring but we get paid to worry about that kind of thing. I trust your judgment, Jack, and I know you have a lot of confidence in Nick at this point," observed Ellis, before adding, "O.K., you've given me the good news. Let's hear the other half."

"Well, Hank, I'm not sure whether you'll consider this either bad news or good news. I'll just call it a status report and give you my observations and recommendations."

"Fair enough," smiled Ellis.

"I went out to the safe house and met with Kostas. He's the contract agent who's been giving W/T training to the three Romanians we're planning to airdrop back into the country. After meeting him, I understand why so may people are high on him. It doesn't look like he's been given much support but somehow he's managed to hold things together under a pretty tough set of circumstances. Put bluntly, I think we have a potential disaster in the making," said Wagner as he looked across the desk to Ellis, who showed no reaction, other than to motion to him to continue his report.

"While I was at the safe house, Kostas introduced me to his three trainees. After meeting them and spending a little time with them, I came away with the feeling that their only qualification for any kind of operation is that they are three warm bodies. They are uneducated and . . . sorry to sound bigoted . . . peasant types. Not only have they been unable to understand what Kostas is trying to teach them, but there have been some pretty strong indications that they are close to exploding emotionally."

"What does that mean?" asked Ellis calmly.

"There are a couple of situations that Kostas told me about. The first incident was a blow-up in the safe house when one of the agents became so agitated that he went after Kostas with the leg of a table and had to be restrained by the other two." Wagner hesitated before continuing. "Hank, you'd better sit back and relax for the next one. Apart from the obvious security implications, apparently all three of them have had enough extra-curricular activity to manage to contract cases of gonorrhea," concluded Wagner.

"Jesus, Mary and Joseph!" responded Ellis in exasperation. "How long has this been going on?"

"Apparently for a while. Kostas told me he has been taking them to see a Greek doctor for treatment," answered Wagner.

"Did Swasey set that up?"

"I don't know but I assume so. Kostas said the doctor has a Company clearance to take care of this kind of situation," responded Wagner.

"I guess he didn't think it was important enough to mention it to me," said Ellis disdainfully. "O.K., I get the picture. You've given me your observations. Now let me hear your recommendation," said Ellis with a half-smile.

"Scrub the operation," replied Wagner. "Frankly, we could drop them with or without parachutes. The end result would be the same. They'd be dead ducks."

"I can't argue with you, Jack. But I want to get over and fill Chris in. I'm sure he'll agree. Fortunately, your Popescu recruitment gives us a little welcome leverage with Headquarters. Maybe you can get working on a draft dispatch. Do you think you can make a convincing case without going into too many gory details?

"I'll give it my best shot," replied Wagner. "By the way, do you have any thoughts about where we can dump those three guys?"

"Ah, that's the big unanswered question," smiled Ellis. "We'll find a way." He looked up as Wagner started to leave. "I assume you got the word that the Ambassador is closing down all American offices at 2:00 o'clock and advising Americans to keep out of the downtown area during the Cyprus demonstration?"

"That's what I heard," replied Wagner. "I'm having lunch with Bob Foster and we're coming back here to get a bird's-eye view of the action from our penthouse perch. Just don't tell the Ambassador," he added with a parting wave.

****

"And so now they have to use old women for their dirty business." Nick spat out the words in disgust as he slammed his huge fist down against the top of the mantel.

"They don't change, Nick. We should know that by now," replied BRIDEGROOM, calmly ignoring the big man's rage.

"But what about your mother?" asked Tina anxiously. "Will he really help her?"

"If I follow his instructions, he will help. He understands very well that there is no control over me without her . . . which of course is the reason she was forced to write the letter."

"Bah!" grunted Nick fiercely. "I would like to crack his Bolshevik neck in my fingers."

"Unfortunately, that would not solve our problems . . . although I agree it is an appealing thought," said BRIDEGROOM with a half smile.

"What does it mean for us, Victor?"

Tina asked the question that he had been repeating in his own mind since his meeting with the Russian the previous evening. And now as he spoke, the answer was slowly revealed . . . to Nick and Tina . . . and to himself. "You will not become involved." He raised his hand before Nick could protest and added, "at least, not directly involved. But I am going to need your help and it will not be easy. If we should fail, we lose everything. I am sorry. I should have told you before I went to the Russians. But now I cannot change what has been done."

"It doesn't matter. We understand," said Tina. "What is it that you want us to do?"

"I will meet the Russian again tomorrow night when he expects my first report. It is important that we satisfy him this time."

As BRIDEGROOM explained the details of his assignment, Nick took an orange from a bowl on the table beside him and began slowly to tear off the peel. From time to time, Tina nodded her head in understanding at BRIDEGROOM's words. Then, as BRIDEGROOM finished speaking, Nick broke the orange into halves, laid the two pieces on the table and yanked a grimy handkerchief out of his pocket. "So they've pulled us back into their stinking sewer," he said, wiping the juice from his fingers.

"That, Nick, is what the Russian thinks he has done," replied BRIDEGROOM, savoring the sound of his own words. Then he smiled and added, "but this time he will be disappointed."

"But, Victor, we can't let them harm your mother. She has suffered enough."

For a moment BRIDEGROOM looked at Tina with a mixed feeling of gratitude and admiration . . . wondering at that quality of human spirit that somehow survives the grinding harshness of life and allows someone like Tina to willingly give up her precious little security for an old woman she would never see again. "Please don't worry, Tina. She will be safe enough . . . and she has so little left that they can take away," he said gently.

Nick bit off a chunk of orange and turned impatiently to Tina. "Stop whimpering, woman, and give Victor a chance to tell us his plan."

"Yes, it's time to get on with our work," agreed BRIDEGROOM wryly recalling the Russian's admonition of the previous evening (' . . . this is an unusual kind of business and you will find that nothing is exactly as it appears to be.'). Well, let us hope he doesn't discover how right he was, thought BRIDEGROOM. Before continuing, BRIDEGROOM looked at Nick and Tina but resisted the urge to express his gratitude for their support. Instead he calmly laid out his plan in a voice that reflected none of the emotion that was burning inside him. "The problem is no different from the one we might have had with Mr. Rogers if Popescu had not appeared at just the right moment. Would Rogers have pressed us to activate our phantom agents in Romania that we invented to justify our value and keep Mr. Fletcher satisfied? We were lucky with Popescu so there is no longer any reason for deception in our dealings with the Americans. But it could have been different," he added ruefully.

"Still, the only harm we might have caused the Americans would have been to raise false hopes. I'm glad that didn't occur." BRIDEGROOM hesitated before sharing a last thought. "But I have no concern about inflicting harm on the Russians. In fact, it would be a pleasure." He slowly rubbed his chin as he collected his thoughts before continuing. "No, we will have to prepare reports that look authentic . . . that keep them interested . . . and yet that they can neither confirm nor disprove. It will be difficult and risky. But in the beginning I am sure the Russian will be satisfied with very little and I can always use the excuse that I am inexperienced. They, after all, are the ones who insist that I work for them. And since they give us no choice, what else can we do but accept their money and their help?"

"And give them swill in return," exclaimed Nick, spitting orange seeds into his hand to emphasize his pleasure. "Ah, Victor, if only your mother could know, she would dance for joy."

"She knows Victor would never help the Communists," retorted Tina indignantly defending the old woman's judgment.

"Yes, Tina, I think she will guess what is happening. But remember, things are more complicated now. There is so much more that can go wrong. If the Russians should find out about the Americans . . . or the Americans should find out about the Russians . . . "

"Or either of them find out about us," interjected Nick with a laugh.

"Then there will be trouble," responded BRIDEGROOM. "So we will have to be very careful about selecting names for the Russian. He will have ways of checking our information and you can be sure he will take great pains to examine our first report. I will give him the names of some refugees and a few Government officials I have met. When he finds that what I tell him about them is accurate, why should he question two or three names of the list that he won't be able to verify?"

"So we will invent a few more phantom agents, eh? This time for the Russian," grinned Nick.

"Yes. But this time it will not be so easy. The Americans were obliged to accept our word. As long as we were able to prepare letters that looked as though they had come from the Old Country, they were satisfied. The Russian is in a different position. There is always the danger that he will want to meet one of our imaginary agents. And if that should happen, we will have to be prepared with convincing reasons why it cannot be arranged. The important thing is that we anticipate these problems."

"How much information do you intend to give him and what do you want us to prepare?" asked Tina, the earlier tone of anxiety now completely gone from her voice.

"I will give him a few names . . . but only as much background on them as I think is absolutely necessary. There is no point in making our reports too complete. He will only press harder. But if we give him a little at a time and force him to ask questions, we will know better what he is after and it will be easier for us to move in the direction that we choose. I think tomorrow night I should include the names of two fictitious agents. We can always add more later. We have enough experience in this business to understand that the Russian will expect me to organize a network for him. And he will want my agents strategically placed. So we will begin with someone in the military and someone else in the political field. That means we will have to create people who seem to have access to useful information and at the same time not be prominent enough for the Russians to trace. That is what I want you and Nick to work on," said BRIDEGROOM crossing his legs and leaning back in his chair.

Nick, who was still standing beside the fireplace, exchanged a glance with Tina. Then he shuffled across the room and dropped heavily onto the sofa. "I meet a lot of soldiers in the tavernas. They like wine and they like to talk," he said thoughtfully.

"It would be easy, Victor . . . that is . . . if you think a soldier would interest the Russians?" added Tina, obviously pleased with Nick's idea.

"Of course he would probably prefer a general but I think we may be able to interest him in a dedicated young corporal," responded BRIDEGROOM in a tone that conveyed an unspoken compliment. "Furthermore, a low-ranking soldier will be much more practical from our point of view. It will be a simple matter to collect information for our reports and impossible for the Russians to verify our soldier friend's identity."

"But what if the Russian wants to meet him?" asked Nick.

"In that case, we will tell the Russian our informant is afraid. After all, it is possible to be a Communist sympathizer and still not want to be shot for treason."

"What a pity," said Nick with a sly grin, "the Russian will have to be satisfied to take information from a soldier who is a coward."

"I would prefer to think of our informants as cautious rather than cowardly," replied BRIDEGROOM lightly, "but I leave that matter to you and Tina. The important thing is that you develop a background for this soldier by tomorrow," continued BRIDEGROOM, his voice becoming serious. "You know what soldiers are like, Nick . . . how they act. And, Tina, I want you to give this man a family history. He should be young, disillusioned, poorly educated . . . probably from a village. You understand."

"Yes, Victor, of course. But are you going to tell the Russian everything about him in your report?"

"No. I will only indicate that I have met this soldier and that I think he might be persuaded to give information. We'll let the Russian tell us what to do about it."

"Don't worry, Victor. Tina will give you an unhappy soldier with eleven hungry brothers and sisters, an epileptic father and a consumptive mother," said Nick jestingly.

"What do you want us to do about a politician?" asked Tina, paying no attention to Nick's joke.

"We will work on that together and we will have to be very discreet. If we pretend to have an informant who is an active politician, the Russians will insist on knowing who he is and would easily discover that it is a deception. Still . . . there are other ways to feed their appetite for information. I myself know enough about politics to give the Russian as many reports as he asks for. Of course, they would have no real value but as long as I describe them as the private remarks of an unsuspecting cabinet minister or member of Parliament, it would be difficult for him to discount them entirely. But that is not the problem. No, the problem is to produce a man who will interest the Russians because they are convinced he has close ties with Government officials. He would be even more attractive to them if they thought that occasionally he might have access to official files."

"But, Victor, isn't that the reason the Russian has hired you?"

"Yes, Tina, of course," replied BRIDEGROOM as he stood up and took a few strides toward the center of the room. For a moment he hesitated. Then he turned and began speaking in the low dispassionate tone that Nick and Tina had come to associate with matters of importance. "Yet . . . consider our position. From the beginning, we are at a disadvantage. This is not a complaint . . . only a simple historical fact. He uses my mother to force his bargain and can I be sure no harm will come to her if I refuse him? No . . . I think not. But does he expect me to make Communists out of cabinet ministers or discover military secrets or influence policy? It would be impossible. Oh, of course if I chose, I could be helpful to him in many ways. But I have no stomach for it," he said with a quick motion of his hand. "No, Tina, there is only one way to protect ourselves. We will have to convince him that we are cooperating and at the same time, we will have to divert his attention. Remember, he knows I am a leader among the refugees and I also will be obliged to give him the names of people in the Government with whom I am acquainted. If I do nothing, he will press . . . and press . . . and press . . . until I am forced to do what he demands or I am exposed because I refuse. But if I take the initiative and pretend that I am exploiting my contacts and organizing a network, then the ultimate control over what is done will remain in my hands. Of course there is no question that he will be continually asking me to pay more attention to this person or that person, but if I explain that I am devoting all my time and efforts toward working with the agents that you and Nick and I will create .

. . then what can he say?" BRIDEGROOM shrugged and added ironically, "What can he expect from an amateur?"

"And meanwhile they will take care of your mother."

"Yes, Tina," answered BRIDEGROOM thoughtfully, "and if in the end we are discovered, I can only hope that they will treat her no worse than they would have if I had rejected them in the beginning."

"Well, we already have a soldier. Now where do we find a politician?" asked Nick.

"There is no way to fabricate a politician, Nick. If we should try that, our entire operation would collapse in ten minutes. You know that." BRIDEGROOM walked to the end of the room and sat down on the arm of an overstuffed chair so that he faced both Nick and Tina. "However, I am quite friendly with a deputy in the Ministry of Foreign Affairs who spends most of his time working on refugee problems. I am sure the Russians would be interested in knowing more about him but I am not going to reveal this relationship to the Russian. No, there is a better way of handling it." BRIDEGROOM paused and wearily rubbed his eyes. "The second fictitious name on our list will be the friend of the deputy . . . not I. I will have no trouble preparing reports and if someday the Russian insists on meeting this friend of the deputy . . . well . . . there is always Boris."

"Your old friend?" asked Nick.

"Yes. There was a time when we did a lot of business together. He lost everything the same way I did. He has no love for the Communists and nothing left to lose. I have a feeling he would welcome the chance to even the score, at least a little." answered BRIDEGROOM. "These days he lives in Patras. It is a long bus ride but I will pay him a visit and find out whether, if needed, he would accept a role in our continuing drama with the Russians. I think I know the answer," he smiled and then added, "But for now, we have to concentrate on preparing my first report for our new benefactors."

*****

"Jack, this is a beautiful place for a restaurant. How did you find it?" Heidi smiled and raised her wine glass in mock salute as she spoke.

"I can assure you that the 'Chez Lapin' was not a stop on Nick's tour when he introduced me to the side streets and back alleys of Piraeus," laughed Wagner. "No, it was Bob Foster who told me about it this afternoon while we were busy ducking flying missiles that a few of the demonstrators were lobbing in our direction."

"I could hear the crowd noise from my apartment but that's as close as I got to all the action. What did you see?"

Wagner looked out across the harbor before responding. "Well, I'm now convinced that no one can accuse the Greeks of a lack of passion. What started out as a meeting and some fiery student speeches at the University escalated into a full-scale riot. Once it picked up momentum, there were probably four or five thousand people in the streets. I think most of them were there as spectators but there was a hard core of agitators doing their best to stir up trouble. It was easy to spot them from where we were watching."

"Where were you and Bob standing?"

"We were watching from a window on the top floor of our building where we had a clear view of the street below. There was a lot of shouting and a few people carried banners with anti-American slogans. It was calm in the beginning but then the crowd began pushing through a series of police cordons until they made it to Constitution Square before heading back in our direction. At that point, things got a little heated and there was a lot of brawling with police outside the Grande Bretagne, Zonar's and in front of our building. The American Mission building was a target for the rock throwers but apart from a couple of overturned cars, the only damage was a few broken windows. The police had anticipated trouble and had the building very well protected. On the whole, it wasn't bad and the only casualties were a few bruised heads," concluded Wagner with a casual wave.

"Sounds like fun and a great way to end your busy week," joked Heidi.

"Strange as it may seem, as long as you were out of the line of fire, as we were, there were a few comic episodes," smiled Wagner.

"You've piqued my curiosity."

"The fire brigade had their water cannons out to disperse the crowd. But in one case we watched a Greek priest climb over the top of one unit and put it out of commission."

"So much for the separation of Church and State," laughed Heidi.

"I don't think that's a big issue in Greece," responded Wagner with an appreciative smile. "Fortunately, it ended peacefully and there were no serious casualties. So now that we've settled the Cyprus issue, let's enjoy the rest of the evening without worrying about international politics," said Wagner as he reached across the table and gently touched her hand.

Their table was on the edge of a large outdoor dining deck. The restaurant was built high on the side of a Piraeus hill. In the dark water below them tiny waves, tipped white in the moonlight, were washing silently toward the shore. For a few minutes they sat quietly. In the distance they could see the lights of Athens painting the night sky with a soft yellow glow and further on the red landing lights of the airport stood like sentinels waiting to guide the next descending aircraft to a safe landing. A few couples were dancing to the romantic music of Nikos Gounaris.

"He has a beautiful voice," said Heidi softly.

"He is the most popular performer in Greece and has done tours in several other countries, including a fairly recent trip to the States," responded Wagner as he rose and reached for Heidi's hand. "May I have this dance?" he asked with a smile.

She slipped easily into his arms. They danced without speaking until she looked up and their eyes met. "Thank you for a wonderful evening," she said.

Wagner touched her face and held her closer and they went on dancing.

CHAPTER THIRTEEN

The night air hung thick and listless. From time to time there was a muttering of leaves stirring irresolutely against a quickly spent breeze. Beneath the rude wooden bridge the water of the lily pond lay still and black. BRIDEGROOM felt the uneven planks tilt loosely under his feet. He was walking slowly, conscious that there was nothing to do now but wait. With an involuntary gesture he reached inside his jacket and touched the envelope in his pocket. Then he stopped and rested his hands on the railing, casually testing its weather-pitted surface with his fingertips.

From a tavern in a far corner of the park he could hear the faint sounds of orchestra music. It was as though they came from a different world. Around the pond thick rows of hedges stood in shadowed silence along unlit footpaths, forming dark winding corridors where the only sounds were the soft whispers of lovers. Even the occasional report of a backfire or the sudden acceleration of an engine was muted by the tall tree-shrouded wall that surrounded the park, smothering the clamor of traffic on the streets outside.

The smoldering darkness of this section of the park was broken only by the weak yellow glow from a few ineffective hooded lanterns. BRIDEGROOM slowly turned his body so that both ends of the footbridge were in his line of vision. For a moment, almost like a child playing a guessing game, he began wondering from which direction the Russian would appear. Then he saw him . . .

Golnikov was walking toward him with short choppy steps, his arms moving only slightly at his sides. He was hurrying like a man who had just been pushed unexpectedly from behind. But as he came closer, he relaxed his pace and nodded recognition.

"I see my directions were adequate," he said stiffly. His eyes looked past BRIDEGROOM, examining the darkness beyond the bridge.

"They were quite clear. I had no trouble finding my way here. And I am certain that no one was interested that I came," added BRIDEGROOM.

"There is no reason why they should have been . . . if you followed my instructions. But I prefer not to stand here. It is too exposed," he said, speaking in that impatiently nervous tone characteristic of men accustomed to the threat of surveillance.

"Whatever you say," responded BRIDEGROOM, drawing alongside the Russian.

They walked to the end of the bridge and turned into one of the intersecting footpaths that tunneled into the night. Now that they no longer were silhouetted in the light of the bridge, Golnikov slowed almost to a halt. "You brought the report?" he asked.

"Yes."

"Good. Let me have it"

BRIDEGROOM stopped, took out the envelope and handed it to the Russian who quickly slid it into his own inside jacket pocket. Once the transfer of the document was completed, they resumed their leisurely stroll. To a casual passerby they could have been two old friends absorbed in philosophical discussion. BRIDEGROOM moved heavy-footed, his hands clasped thoughtfully behind his back, occasionally turning his head toward his companion to catch a particular point. Beside him Golnikov walked as though in procession, only an infrequent gesture of his hand disturbing the solemnity of his stride.

"This is not the place for me to examine your paper," Golnikov was saying, "although I assume you have prepared what I requested."

"I have done my best," replied BRIDEGROOM, "but of course I am not practiced in this kind of thing."

"It is at least a first step, Mr. Bergarsch . . . true, only a first step . . . nevertheless an essential one." As he spoke these last words, Golnikov lowered his voice until it became almost inaudible. Out of a corner of his eye BRIDEGROOM could see that they were passing two lovers locked in uninhibited embrace on a bench half hidden in the shadows of an overhanging hedge. When they had moved safely out of earshot, Golnikov continued his speech as though there had been no interruption. "Next I want you to write a report describing the refugee community . . . an easy assignment for you, my friend."

"I know something about that subject, of course," replied BRIDEGROOM non-commitally.

"I'm sure you do," responded the Russian with a short nasal laugh, "but perhaps I should point out that I am more interested in your personal analysis of the local refugee movement than I am in a catalogue of its personnel. I want to know who and what holds the refugees together. How are they influenced? But more important . . . how can we influence them?"

"I think you credit the refugees with a greater sense of community and purpose than the facts warrant," answered BRIDEGROOM almost casually.

"An interesting observation . . . and quite possibly an accurate one. However, you overlook one fundamental quality of human nature," said Golnikov, reverting to the pedantic tone that BRIDEGROOM had first observed in their initial meeting. "Men taken as a whole are docile sheep . . . victims of emotional malnutrition. They have neither confidence nor convictions. And so, because they are weak, they yield without a struggle . . . you might say, with a sense of relief . . . to a stronger will. It absolves them of the responsibility of thinking for themselves. Your refugees are no different."

"There are strong arguments to justify your assessment of men but so often have I seen them contradicted by men's actions that I no longer find them convincing," responded BRIDEGROOM.

"Come now, Bergarsch," interrupted Golnikov sarcastically, "does it offend you to think that men carry their principles as lightly as a film of dirt?"

"Hardly. It is simply that I have grown skeptical of absolutes," chided BRIDEGROOM gently. "Oh, I of course concede that most of us shed our ideals as soon as we are required to stand in their defense. But . . . and perhaps this is the whim of an incurable romantic . . . I believe that when men abandon their principles, they do so as individuals and not as dehumanized parts of mass movements. Even then, the surrender is seldom unconditional and to the extent that the individual withholds his surrender, he retains his independence . . . and with it some measure of dignity."

"You are playing with words but I am concerned with practical politics . . . not metaphysics," responded Golnikov making no effort to conceal his annoyance. "Keep in mind, Bergarsch, this is not our first experience with a refugee community. I assure you that if one knows what methods to employ, any group . . . yes, any group . . . can be easily subverted."

By now they had reached a small circular clearance, one of several intersections within the park. From here new paths uncoiled quietly into the dark like probing tentacles. Ahead of them, perhaps another fifty yards, the plume-like tops of pine and eucalyptus brushed against a sky washed with soft tones of pink and white, reflections thrown up by the open kiosks and moth-flecked streetlights that illuminated the wide macadam promenade stretching like a swollen flight-deck along one far edge of the park.

An image of the scene that lay in the distance focused in BRIDEGROOM's mind. Lethargic evening strollers escaping the dead air of over-crowded rooms. A boy peddling an ice cream cart. Homeward-bound laborers cutting hurriedly between busy city blocks. Black-shawled old women. Mustached shoe-shine men squatting like legless beggars, their eyes caressing each passing female rump. A chestnut vendor preparing his fire, spitting into red coals to test their heat. Swaggering soldiers. Prostitutes, their cheap perfumes filling the air like sweet-scented disinfectants, breasts bobbing like loose melons in sheer summer blouses, flinging their tight-skirted taunts in open invitation.

Golnikov, like BRIDEGROOM, also was conscious of the activity that lay ahead and with the slow arching motion of a ship changing direction at sea, swung toward a new path that would return them to their hedge-sheltered sanctuary. They walked a few more steps in silence before Golnikov, as though sensing a loss of rapport with his agent, laughed and said, "But what is the point in argument? Perhaps we will both be happier if we regard our little operation as a scholarly examination of political allegiances. After all, to be a scientist today is quite fashionable. And politics is a science . . . imprecise, of course . . . but nevertheless, a science. So, if we are going to make this study of the refugee community, why not apply the principles of basic research? First we will determine its present mood. I am leaving that in your hands. Then we will inject certain stimuli. This will be my responsibility. And finally we will observe the results. When we view our work in this light, it becomes an extraordinary challenge . . . does it not? And, incidentally, an opportunity for you to demonstrate the fallacy of my thinking."

"If one of your functions is political experimentation, that is your affair. But it is not mine. I have agreed to provide information . . . nothing more," said BRIDEGROOM in a voice laced with irony. Once more he was conscious of the need to resist before the Russian could trap him into the role of agent provocateur. If ultimately that should come, thought BRIDEGROOM, it will be on my terms.

"I was not aware I had requested anything more," responded Golnikov evenly.

"You are quite right, of course. I hope you will forgive me for being overly sensitive," answered BRIDEGROOM. Then, before Golnikov could reply, he added, "But I think you understand how easy it is to arrive at wrong conclusions. Particularly since it is obvious that you will need the close cooperation of someone capable of influencing whatever leadership exists among the refugees. But then, I should remember that you are experienced at this sort of thing."

Golnikov continued his slow mechanical pace without replying. Then he stopped and began to speak, almost casually. "Yes, we are experienced. But would you want to place your security in the hands of amateurs? Obviously not. You have made it very clear that you long ago learned the first rule of survival which is to protect your own self interest. So you resist certain assignments until you are certain you will not be compromised. It is quite a sensible attitude. Why should I object if all you ask is that my arguments be convincing? How can I expect an intelligent man like you to perform your assignments unless you can see the chances of success? For the present, I am asking for a simple report on a few refugees but if some time later I should have a more important request, you can be sure that I will produce strong arguments to support my position, I think you are aware, my friend, that no matter what the request, I always will have at least one argument powerful enough to overcome your lingering doubts."

BRIDEGROOM listened almost wearily, wanting to break off the exchange with the Russian. Is this man capable only of repeating himself, he thought, aware that he had heard this same clumsy threat before and would hear it again. "Certainly I feel much easier knowing that if there should be a weakness in my position, you will quickly point it out to me."

"It is part of my job, Mr. Bergarsch. You see I can't afford to wonder whether you are cooperating. I have to be certain. It is a matter of mutual trust. However, in this instance I will give you plenty of time to prepare your report. Let us say a week. We will meet here again next Wednesday at 9:20. Naturally, you will take the usual precautions."

"And if we fail to meet?"

"You already have instructions for alternate times," he said as though admonishing a child for forgetting his lessons. "And, who knows, I may even have some news of your mother's health. So we both have something to look forward to. Now, unless you have another question . . . goodnight."

"No, there is nothing else. Goodnight"

Golnikov listened to BRIDEGROOM's footsteps empty into silence. A smile set on his lips. He reached into his pocket and touched the envelope, like a heart patient reassuring himself that he had not forgotten his glycerin tablets. He was alone now . . . free for a few minutes to relax and savour the thoughts. So Borakowsky was wrong, he thought sardonically. Bergarsch had shown up and now it is only a matter of patiently leading him into a trap from which there is no escape. He felt a sense of exhilaration as he contemplated the operation. But this is too complex for my peasant friend in his black chauffeur's suit to comprehend. The unwelcome thought of Borakowsky waiting sullenly for his return filled Golnikov with disgust and fear. An involuntary shiver caught his body like a cold chill as he lit a cigarette and sucked the warm smoke into his lungs. Slowly he began walking through the darkened path, hardly noticing the rustling of bushes and the whisper of a man's voice, followed by the playful laughter of a girl. For a few minutes he strolled aimlessly, hearing only the faint sounds of music from the tavern. Finally he came upon a bench hidden among some shrubs and sat down.

The narrow wooden slats pressed into his shoulder-blades as he reclined, legs crossed, one arm flung carelessly along the top rail. With a curious twist of humor he recalled a picture he had seen of an American statesman posing in a similar position on a bench in a New York park and wondered whether he looked as nonchalantly smug and self-satisfied. But even as he played contentedly with this thought, taking quick puffs on his cigarette, his ear caught the soft crunch of approaching steps. He turned toward the sound with the annoyed air of a man whose privacy was being invaded. The moon cast a light through the trees at a point some yards distant where the path curved toward him revealing the long slender legs of a girl walking alone.

Although he could not see her face, the figure was that of a young girl, her round flanks accentuated by a skirt stretched tight as elastic around her thighs. The fact that she was still locked among the shadows gave her body an added sensuality and Golnikov's entire attention suddenly shifted to wondering about the size of her breasts.

As she walked closer, she gave no indication that she noticed him. When she was still at least thirty feet away, she stopped, reached down and slowly slid her hands from her knee to midthigh as she straightened her stocking. As she did, she turned her body slightly as though examining her leg for imperfections.

Golnikov took a deep drag on his cigarette, the fiery tip

glowed like an ignited fuse. Although he had been sitting motionless, the girl seemed to sense his presence and fully aware of his attention, with a movement both deliberate and nonchalant, raised her skirt the full length of her other leg and tightened her garter. Golnikov felt a quick burning sensation in his loins as though it were his own bare thighs she was caressing. Completely consumed by excitement and anticipation, he watched her as she stood looking at her leg with the detached pleasure of a woman admiring a valuable jewel.

Then, with the same easy confidence of someone approaching to ask directions to the nearest bus stop, she walked toward him. "Do you have a match?" she asked in a low voice that carried with it a suggestion of amusement.

"Yes, of course," replied Golnikov fumbling in his pockets as the girl sat down beside him with a movement as provocative as though she were getting into bed. As she did, she crossed her legs, ignoring the fact that her skirt rode far up her thigh revealing the bare white flesh above the top of her nylons. Golnikov's temples began to throb as though he were drunk and only with effort did he restrain himself from leaning down and biting her leg.

He struck the match and the girl bent toward him, her shoulder touching his. He could smell the perfume on her face. In the glow of the match, her dark insolent eyes seemed to be toying with him. As he held the match, he felt the fingers of her right hand close around his wrist to steady the flame. Then she took the lighted cigarette from her mouth and blew out the match so that her breaths seared his cheek. She picked the dead match from his fingers and tossed it to the ground. "American?" she asked.

For a split second Golnikov puzzled over what she meant. Then, like a fantastic joke, it dawned on him. "Yes, how did you know?" he replied, getting a vicarious thrill out of the role he was now so unexpectedly playing.

She shrugged, "There is something about Americans. I knew a captain once. He used to take me out in his car." She shifted the position of her legs, making a token effort to adjust her skirt. "Do you have a car?"

"Yes."

"Good. Someday you can take me for a ride," she said laughing and leaning her head against his shoulder so that her hair touched his mouth. "What time is it?" she asked, straightening up again.

Golnikov pushed up the sleeve of his jacket to look at his watch but before he could read the dial, he felt his hand being drawn close to her face. She peered at the luminous hands and then pressed his wrist close to her ear so that she could hear the watch tick.

On an impulse, Golnikov thrust his other hand into her low cut blouse and excitedly began massaging her bare breasts. "You are just like the captain," she laughed. "Maybe you come from the same city." Then she removed his hand and without releasing her grip, started to get up. "We can find a better place for you to do that," she said.

Her invitation jolted Golnikov into a realization of what was happening to him. He was torn between lust and logic. The lower half of his body seemed to be moving toward her almost by itself but he replied with an awkward formality, "No, I'm sorry. I have other plans."

Once again she eased her body next to his and turned her face toward him. He could feel her moist lips nibbling at his ear as she spoke, "What's the matter? Are you afraid of me?"

Suddenly he was lost. He put his hand behind her head and forced his mouth against hers. She yielded without resistance . . . finally sliding away and standing up. "Are you coming?" she asked.

He stood up and reached out to put his arm around her waist but she moved aside, at the same time taking his hand and leading him through an opening in a tall hedge and past a row of shrubs to a small but concealed clearing of grass. In a frenzy of emotion Golnikov tore off his jacket and kneeled down to lay it on the ground. Then, without getting up, he felt the soft flesh of her buttock in his hands as he drew her down beside him.

****

Golnikov stood brushing the dirt and pine needles from his clothing while the girl watched with a mocking look of boredom. He felt sick with self-disgust and his mind was whipped with a compelling urge to get away. The smell of her cheap cosmetics almost nauseated him. It is always the same with these whores, he thought, with an anger born of his own weakness and inadequacy. What only a few minutes before had seemed so desirable, he now regarded with a distain one might feel for a dirty animal.

"Are you always in such a big hurry?" she asked, calmly re-applying her makeup. Without replying, Golnikov reached into his pocket and pulled out a few crumpled bills. He pressed them into her hand.

"I'm sure you have other engagements," he said coldly. "Don't let me detain you." Then he turned and groped his way back through an opening in the bushes, the girl's stinging laughter echoing in his ears.

When he reached the path, he began walking swiftly in the direction of his car which he had parked nearby on an almost deserted side street. Now that he was alone, a great swell of tension tore through his body, flooding his brain. He was racked with self-reproach and half stunned by the realization that he had surrendered control of his emotions so easily. But even as he fought to re-assert his sense of command, he was seized by a sudden new fear. What if she were a police agent who had been following me all evening, he thought. If she were clever enough, she might have seen me take the envelope from Bergarsch. The thought struck him like a hammer and he grabbed for his pocket. The report was gone!

He began slapping himself wildly as though he were trying to destroy an insect loose inside his clothing . . . his panic increasing with every movement of his hands. Frantically, he searched the contents of each of his pockets. And in a final act of desperation, he yanked off his jacket and shook it like a dust cloth, vainly hoping to see the envelope fall to the ground.

Was it lost or stolen? Where? By whom? Each new thought was more terrifying than the previous. If she were an agent, did she steal it . . . and now how will they use it? Publish it and expose our operations? Soon there will be elections. The Royalists will use it to ruin us. Instinctively, he turned and began half walking, half running back through the park, trying to retrace his steps, his eyes devouring the ground in the desperate hope of spotting the envelope.

But what can I tell Borakowsky? That Bergarsch did not show up? No! If the report is published, he will find out what happened and it will be the end. There is only one hope left . . . one last chance. It could have fallen out when I took off my jacket. That has to be it! He began running faster until he came to the bench where he had been sitting. Without stopping, he plunged through the bushes, the brambles catching his trousers, scratching his hands. Then he felt himself stumble and heard a wail of protest, followed by fierce obscenities. In an instant he was being pushed and battered by a half-clothed, half-crazed man with enormous white eyes that seemed ready to spring from their sockets.

Oblivious of the blows that were falling on him, Golnikov shouted, "I lost something!" somehow expecting this would explain everything and calm his nearly berserk antagonist. A girl on the ground let out a cry and pulled down her dress. "You won't have anything left to lose when I finish with you, you lout!" The enraged man continued to pommel the Russian with his fists. Golnikov raised his arms in a defensive motion and as he did, realized he had blundered into the wrong clearing.

Slowly he began backing away. trying to disengage, his arms curled over the top of his head for protection. By now the blows were landing less frequently and were much less punishing. Yet, with a final unexpected gesture of fury and frustration, his gasping adversary doubled both fists and slammed them down like a mallet on Golnikov's head, nearly toppling him into the bushes. Golnikov fell backward, fighting to retain his balance. At the same time, the bug-eyed man thrust his face toward him and spat, shouting one last damning obscenity.

Golnikov stumbled out onto the path which, in spite of the commotion, remained deserted. As he strove to orient himself, his anxiety mounted and he began to imagine someone else finding the envelope before he could return to the spot where he had met the girl. He made no effort to straighten his clothes which by now were in complete disarray. Instead, with a sense of urgency close to anguish, he rushed along the path toward the first intersection. He stopped and looked. Then he saw the light near the bend in the path and the bench swallowed in shadows.

For a moment he hesitated, haunted by a growing fear that the envelope would not be there . . . almost not daring to look. An unpleasant image of Borakowsky clouded his brain as he started toward the bench, slowly at first; then with quickening stride he began to run until the sharp thorns of bushes were again clutching at him and he burst through to the clearing.

The moon had slid behind a cloud leaving the clearing in cave-like darkness. Golnikov bent over like an old woman but it was impossible to see anything, so he got down on his knees and began to grope with his hands, moving first in one direction, then another. He lit a match and held it close to the hard-packed grass until it scorched his fingers. He lit another. As he did, a blinding beam of light flashed in his face.

"Hey! What are you trying to do?" In spite of the authority of the question, the voice was uncertain, as though the speaker was not sure of his right to intrude.

While Golnikov struggled to his feet, the man with the flashlight walked toward him. As he came closer, Govnikov realized that it was a young Gendarme, probably not twenty years old, who must have noticed the glow of his match and stopped to investigate. Certainly he is not looking for trouble, thought Golnikov with a sense of relief. "I was here earlier in the day and I think I dropped a letter that contained some rather personal references I wouldn't want anyone else to see. You know what I mean," replied Golnikov with a hesitant laugh that he hoped would convey the idea that he was sharing a private confidence with the young soldier.

The gendarme grinned sympathetically as he listened to the explanation. "It is hard sometimes to avoid these things . . . but what can we do?" he asked with a shrug that implied he was speaking for harassed men in general. Then he flashed his light in a wide arc on the ground. "Where do you think you dropped it?" Together Golnikov and the gendarme began combing the area for BRIDEGROOM's missing report.

No sooner had they begun their search when they were startled by the approaching sound of loud joking voices. "What?...Does he need a light to find his way in?" said one. This was followed by raucous laughter before a second man, scarcely able to control his merriment, responded. "Let's go in and hold it for him."

The gendarme quickly swung his light around catching two blinking and obviously tipsy youths coming toward them through the hedges. They were momentarily blinded by the light and stood immobilized before one of them regained his drunken composure and gaily asked, "Hey, do you need any help? It looks like you're having trouble finding something." Again his companion burst into uncontrolled laughter.

The gendarme, his light held steady at his waist, moved menacingly toward the intruders, intending to convey an impression of confidence that in truth he did not feel. Golnikov watched from a distance. It was as though he had been cast into the center of a fantastic burlesque. How was it possible that his destiny should have come to rest so uncertainly in the hands of two drunkards and a simpleton soldier?

Until this moment, in spite of his panic, he had clung to the belief that he had not lost all measure of control. But now he listened to the rise and fall of three voices with that sense of drifting detachment one experiences during the initial stages of anesthesia . . . the real and the unreal were becoming inextricably confused.

The gendarme pumped his hand excitedly as he talked so that his flashlight cut quick jagged slashes in the darkness. From time to time one of the youths would interrupt to ask a question. But as the discussion progressed, it became quite amiable and when someone jokingly asked, "What did he say he was doing in there, reading his mail?' the gendarme joined in the subdued laughter. After several minutes of muffled but increasingly jovial conversation, the gendarme turned toward Golnikov with the new arrivals following at his heels.

"They want to help us look," he announced cheerfully.

The bizarre events of the last hour had by now put Golnikov in a frame of mind in which he was quite willing to accept any development, no matter how unusual, as normal. "That's very kind of you," he replied, nodding politely to the drunken volunteers, his outwardly calm manner concealing a still desperate urge to get on with the search for the document.

"At your service," responded one of the youths, making a clumsy effort to click his heels and salute, much to the amusement of his companion.

"Let's try over here," said Golnikov to the gendarme. "Shine your light in this area."

While Golnikov and the gendarme began a methodical search on one side of the clearing, the two youths started kicking at bushes and scuffing the grass in a kind of wild interpretive dance. Finally, one of them got down on his hands and knees, put his nose to the ground and began making loud sniffing noises.

"What in the devil are you doing, Georgi?" asked the other in a tone that suggested he was waiting for an excuse to explode into a new fit of laughter.

"It's too dark to see it. Maybe I can smell it. Hey, what kind of perfume did she use?" he shouted at Golnikov.

Before anyone could reply, the second youth, his body shaking with mirth, lowered his head and charged like a bull toward his crawling companion, butting him the underbelly with enough force to send him sprawling across the grass and under a bush. Both of them ended in a laughing heap on the ground.

The surprised gendarme whirled around, his light exposing the two tangled forms lying on their backs. Almost at the same instant one of the youths reached up and plucked something out of the bush above his head.

"What's this?" he shouted, slowly drawing the envelope across his nostrils as though savoring the aroma of an expensive cigar. "No wonder I couldn't smell it . . . no perfume!"

"That's it! That's it!" Golnikov shot across the clearing and grabbed the envelope from the startled youth. For an instant he stood as though mesmerized. The folded pages of BRIDEGROOM's report bulged in his hand and he fingered the unbroken seal of the envelope like a set of prayer beads. The gendarme quickly observed what had happened and beaming like a proud father, hurried to his drunken assistants and tugged them to their feet. "Bravo, Georgi, bravo!"

The youth acknowledged the gendarme's congratulations by bowing deeply at the waist as Golnikov, now recovered from the shock of events and buoyant with goodwill, thumped him on the back. "Yes, bravo! Good work! You've saved me a lot of trouble." With that he dug into his pocket and pulled out a wad of bills which he was in the habit of carrying whenever he went to a meeting with an agent. "Here. Take this. Enjoy yourselves," he said, thrusting the money at the gendarme.

"No, no, please. It was nothing," responded the soldier holding up his hands in polite but unconvincing protest.

Georgi's good-humored companion had been silent since the discovery but the possibility of Golnikov's reward going unclaimed because of perverted protocol was too much for him. Like a striking cobra, one of his arms slithered around Golnikov's shoulder and held him in a firm grip while his free hand shot out in a fang-like movement and snapped up the money. "Ah, here is a man who knows how to express his gratitude so that we can understand it," he said as he squeezed Golnikov's shoulder and waved the money like a flag above his head.

"It is my pleasure. You have solved a big problem for me," replied Golnikov, forcing a tone of congeniality while he tried unsuccessfully to unlock himself from the uncomfortable clutches of his long-armed friend who insisted on breathing cheap alcohol in his face. "Now go and have a good time," he added as he finally nudged himself free.

"I'll bet you could tell us how," commented Georgi while his friends laughed knowingly.

"I'm sure you won't need my help," answered Golnikov. He offered his hand to each of them. "Good night. Thank you." He turned and started back toward his car . . . and Borakowsky. Behind him he could hear the three men laughing and counting his money.

CHAPTER FOURTEEN

There already were hints in the air that the seasons were about to change. When Wagner arrived in Athens a few months earlier, there was an almost palpable feeling that the entire city was moving outdoors . . . eager to stroll and dine and bathe in the summer sun. Now the reverse seemed to be occurring, thought Wagner as he walked to work past the now familiar landmarks surrounding Constitution Square.

He glanced up at the wall clock as he headed across the lobby toward the elevators. There was a lot to discuss at this morning's meeting with Ellis and he wanted to be on time. He knew he was running a little behind schedule because of an unexpected traffic stop. He and other drivers had waited as an open touring car with King Paul at the wheel and Haile Selassie in the passenger seat sped by on their way to the summer palace as part of Selassie's five-day goodwill visit.

Heidi looked up and smiled as he approached. "No formal announcement needed," she said with a friendly wave of her hand. "He's expecting you."

"Come on in and sit down, Jack. I heard you might have some good news," said Ellis who was nursing a cup of tea. "I'd offer you a cup of this stuff but I wouldn't inflict it on a good friend," he laughed before switching tone and asking, "What's been happening?"

"We finally got our first message from Popescu and it looks good," replied Wagner.

"Every once in awhile something works and makes the effort

seem worthwhile. Congratulations," said Ellis approvingly. "What did he have to say . . . anything interesting?"

"There was nothing earth-shaking but I was encouraged by what he did send. Considering that his only training was concentrated in a relatively few minutes and under less than perfect circumstances, his S/W technique was flawless and the cover message in his letter wouldn't attract a censor's attention. That all tends to confirm my impression that he is a very smart guy and a quick learner," said Wagner before continuing.

"We told him that we wanted him to report what he saw with his eyes and heard with his ears and that is pretty much what he sent in the limited writing space he had to work with. But the most encouraging part of his message was that he expects to re-visit Greece soon, possibly Volos, which will give us another crack at a personal meeting," concluded Wagner.

"That's encouraging. I assume your man, Nick, will be able to keep track of his ship?" questioned Ellis.

"I don't think that will be a problem but I'll be seeing him soon. I don't want to share too many details with him but he knows we're hoping for another meeting," replied Wagner.

"Just keep me posted," said Ellis as he pushed aside his teacup and casually leaned toward Wagner, hands clasped and elbows resting comfortably on his desk. "There are a couple of other items that I think will interest you."

"You've got my attention," smiled Wagner.

"The first is to tell you that we finally have found a place for those three dysfunctional agents that Kostas has been baby-sitting."

"That's a relief. How did you pull that off?" asked Wagner with obvious pleasure.

"Frankly, we got some help from the Army. I don't know if you've met Roger Marcorelle. He's an Army Colonel on temporary assignment with us. He happened to be in Chris' office when Chris and I were discussing our problem and he stepped right in, asked a few questions and offered to help. The net result is that he arranged a transfer of all three agents to the Army. Don't ask me how he managed to pull it off or what they intend to do with them. I have no idea. But it solves a huge problem."

"Couldn't be better news, Hank. I know I'll be talking with Roger to work out the logistics and I'll certainly make it a point to thank him for his help," said Wagner before asking, "Do you have any idea when, where and how we're going to arrange the transfer?"

"No details yet but the general plan is to put them on a M.A.T.'s flight to Wiesbaden where they'll be met and turned over to the Army," replied Ellis.

"I assume Kostas will be their escort and make the turnover. Is it too early to let him know what's being planned?"

"No. I think you should give him a 'heads-up' but tell him not to say anything to the agents . . . just keep them on the normal training routine until you, he and Roger have worked out the transfer details. Then the three of you can decide the best way to tell the agents without triggering an explosion."

"Kostas is going to be a very happy man when he gets the news," said Wagner, who paused and then asked, "You mentioned that you had a couple of items to discuss. What's the second?"

"This won't be a major revelation to you . . . we can call it an official confirmation. But I am obliged to give it to you on a need-to-know basis."

Wagner nodded his head but made no reply as he began filling his pipe.

"A few months ago we were able to bug two rooms in the Russian Embassy. It wasn't easy but somehow it got done," continued Ellis.

"Who handled it? Lagonakis?" inquired Wagner, asking the question almost as a matter of form.

"Yes. John was in charge but it was more than a one-man show. I don't have to tell you that it is one thing to make an installation and another thing to make it work. We ran into our share of problems at the start . . . including trying to locate an appropriate listening post," explained Ellis.

"I assume that's been squared away?" questioned Wagner.

"Finally . . . which brings us to the main point. Now that we have worked out the technical kinks and have our translators organized on a reasonably efficient schedule, we're beginning to pick up some provocative pieces of conversation. I don't want to exaggerate their value, but from a C.E. standpoint it's pretty useful material."

"What are you getting?"

"Well, for example, we felt right along that we knew who their key operators were. Borakowsky's an old hand. We've met him before in Teheran . . . Rome . . . Beirut. You name it. But now there is no doubt about who is in charge . . . he is."

"But no big surprises?"

"Not really. We've always felt that the Second Secretary, Golnikov, was KGB and we've found out we guessed right on that one, too," continued Ellis matter-of-factly. "Essentially Soviet operations here are the same as everywhere else. One way or another half their staff is involved either in direct intelligence or political action." He hesitated a minute and then added wryly, "I suppose that really isn't too much different from our own embassy set up, is it?"

"There is a resemblance," replied Wagner, thoroughly enjoying the allusion.

"Well, so much for meaningless digression," laughed Ellis. "The reason I'm telling you all this is that I think in a round-about way there is something BRIDEGROOM may be able to help us with."

"I thought I wasn't supposed to get any surprises," responded Wagner with increasing interest.

"It is only an idea, Jack. Nothing I expect you to pursue right off . . . certainly not until after we get those three agents resettled and you have a chance to set up another meeting with Popescu. But I'm mentioning it now to give you a little time to figure out an approach."

"Just tell me what you have in mind."

"Fair enough. This is strictly a hunch so I'm not expecting miracles. What it all boils down to is this. The reception on those tapes is reasonably good but they are not philharmonic recordings and they leave a lot to imagination. Beyond that, the Russians are not stupid. They are very conscious of their own internal security and they don't say too much that would make things easy for us. Either that or we bugged the wrong rooms," said Ellis lightly. "However, we do get the impression that they have a special interest in the émigré community."

"That's a little hard to fathom."

"At first glance, it probably doesn't seem to make much sense. But look at it this way. We know they are trying to extend their influence as wide and as fast as they can in this part of the world. And we also know they are using their Satellites, especially trade missions, as part of their plan. The sooner they can build up local support for burying the hatchet and restoring normal trade, the sooner they will get an economic toehold and as far as they are concerned, that is a necessary first step to expanding their political influence.

Historically the émigré community has fought the resumption of pre-war relations, at least until they get some kind of compensation for the property they lost and some assurance for the safety of the families they had to leave behind. In the past they have been able to make themselves heard. But time takes its toll and their protests are getting fainter. In fact, there is growing sentiment among the emigres for letting bygones be bygones. The Soviets are smart enough to want to take advantage of that sentiment. What bothers us is that they seem to have found themselves someone in the émigré community who is willing to argue their case for them. We'd like to know who he is."

"And you think BRIDEGROOM may be able to identify him?"

"Probably not . . . but it's worth a try."

"How much can I tell BRIDEGROOM about all this?"

"About the bugging operation . . . nothing. No, all that I am suggesting is that when you are talking with him you try to guide his thinking a little. Talk about trade negotiations. Make him understand that the Russians are not interested in economic exchange. They are interested in using trade as a wedge for political action. If the émigré community acts as though it wants to forget the past, then the Russians will have one less obstacle to overcome. BRIDEGROOM will understand the psychology of the situation. And I think he will also understand our reasons for thinking that the Russians will be working hard to find a sympathetic spokesman from within the émigré community." Ellis stood up to signal the end of the discussion. "I think BRIDEGROOM will understand why we might have an interest and with luck, he may help us identify the man we're after."

Wagner already was on his feet and the two men walked together slowly toward the door. "If anyone knows what's going on in the émigré community, it will be BRIDEGROOM," responded Wagner.

Ellis put his hand on Wagner's shoulder. "Just remember to take things one at a time. Right now we'll concentrate on getting those agents transferred to the Army and trying to set up another meeting with Popescu. We'll worry about the refugee community later."

✳✳✳✳

"You haven't changed, Victor." Boris stretched his long thin fingers out on the table and contemplated BRIDEGROOM with a beakish smile of admiration. "You still manage to make an outrageous proposal sound logical. Ten years ago . . . perhaps even five . . . I would not have hesitated. Even now, I am tempted. But, sadly, I have grown old and I am much too slow for your game." As he spoke he tilted his head and squinted into the mid-morning sun cascading off the bay. He was hatless and the upper part of his head bulged out above his narrow cheeks like the dome of an oversized light bulb. The dry glare gave his skin a drawn and brittle appearance so that the bones of his face seemed ready to break through like the protruding contents of a package that has been wrapped too tightly.

"Are you afraid?" It was clear from his tone that BRIDEGROOM was trying only to establish a point of information and not to embarrass his friend.

"Aren't you?" responded Boris calmly.

"Of course. I also have lived too long to be fearless. Furthermore, I have never trusted anyone who pretended to be." For a moment, he gazed pensively toward the water as if he were asking himself whether he really believed what he just had said. Not far away workers were unloading cargo from a freighter and piling it on the dock. A few crewmen moved phlegmatically across the deck, while others leaned against the ship's railing and stared blankly into the dust-coated streets of this small port city where with luck they would spend three or four hours drinking wine later in the day. Down on the shore a young boy waded in up to his knees and stood skimming flat stones across the water as though he were trying to hit one of the caravan of caiques that slid incessantly to and from the horizon. Farther out in the bay the gray hull of an anchored American cruiser lay still as a scar on the blue surface.

When BRIDEGROOM turned back, Boris' eyes were examining him with a mocking serenity as though they were reading his private thoughts. "Well, since we agree that fear is not necessarily incapacitating, it seems that what you really are asking is whether I am willing to take a major risk for a reward which, when I take the time to analyze it, has not been very clearly defined." Boris laughed as though he had just told an amusing joke.

"I had hoped my approach would be somewhat more subtle but . . . alas . . . I had forgotten how well you know me," replied BRIDEGROOM with a good-natured shrug. "You are right, of course. The plan I am suggesting is the purest form of speculation. If we succeed, our success may be nothing more than an illusion. And if we fail . . . "

"We will soon know that our failure is quite real."

"Yes . . . this is not like the old days, Boris . . . when we could share gambles together, assuming risks, but always knowing in advance the precise profit we could expect if we succeeded. Now I can promise you nothing except an equal share of whatever may or may not fall our way." BRIDEGROOM slowly lifted his coffee cup and waited for a reply.

Six months had elapsed since BRIDEGROOM last had talked with Boris. And several more hours had passed since Boris had responded to his knock and stood framed in the doorway of his small rented room. But even now BRIDEGROOM had difficulty adjusting to the startling change in his appearance. There was an almost cadaverous look about his old friend; yet Boris had brushed aside any mention of a possible recurrence of tuberculosis. Now BRIDEGROOM watched him slowly making his decision, aware that he was turning the proposal one side and then the other in his mind, painstakingly searching for each hidden weakness. And so although it was true that his physical appearance was markedly different, his manner remained unchanged from that of the hard-headed businessman BRIDEGROOM had known and often worked with before the war.

"Victor, I know I am correct in assuming that you would not be here unless you were sure of me."

"If I could not trust you . . . then who?" replied BRIDEGROOM quietly.

"I do not mean trust. For us, that is beyond discussion. I mean you must have been certain I would join the conspiracy.

"No, Boris, in that you are wrong. I was not sure . . . I still am not sure," answered BRIDEGROOM, his voice half asking.

Boris' arm hung down by his side and his fingers were unconsciously kneading the neck of a scrawny street cat that had come out of one of the waterfront coffee houses and rubbed against his leg to beg for food. "I will do it . . . but before we go any further, I have one question I would like you to answer," said Boris calmly.

BRIDEGROOM leaned forward, his hands folded in his lap, inviting Boris to speak.

"Until now you have been successful with your operation with the Americans . . . why did you risk that achievement with this elaborate scheme to deceive the Russians?"

"It is a question I ask myself and if I could find the answer, I would give it to you. The obvious response is to say that I was overwhelmed with a sense of duty to help my mother by the only means available. That is true but it is also too easy. I knew from the start that they would try to control me and if I resisted, they would use my mother's security as a threat. Although sentiment influenced my decision, it is only part of the answer. Strange as it may seem, I thought I could outwit them and in that way exact a small measure of revenge for the harm they have done to me and to so many others."

"A noble objective," smiled Boris.

"But now I have discovered that I may have mis-calculated and that I can't do it alone . . . and so I turn to an old friend, asking for help," responded BRIDEGROOM quietly.

"I am honored to be asked and I am impressed by your resourcefulness. How many men your age begin a second career in the world of international intrigue?" replied Boris whimsically. "Tell me about it."

BRIDEGROOM picked up his coffee cup and looked at Boris with a smile that conveyed both amusement and gratitude before he responded. "It is really quite simple. Espionage is nothing more than an illegitimate form of the legitimate theatre. We are all play-acting . . . that is, most of us are. The only difference is that we take our roles so seriously that we become what we pretend to be. Think about it . . . there are thousands of people around the world all caught up by some improbable chain of circumstances in this curious intrigue. Important men in London and Washington and Moscow and little men following other little men through dark streets, watching in cafes . . . like that cat at your feet, each one looking for scraps. It becomes a world apart. The search for information becomes an end in itself. Out of all this activity I suppose someone somewhere learns something about someone else's intentions. But in my position it is impossible to judge. I know only what I see. I know men take risks . . . get hurt . . . and that they get paid. I am interested in being paid and as long as my friends think I am on the trail of something important, they will continue to pay. I know what they expect . . . perhaps hope for would be more accurate . . . and I make it my business not to discourage them."

As he finished speaking, BRIDEGROOM tapped a spoon against the side of his cup to attract a slumbering waiter. "Another coffee, Boris?"

"Yes, thank you," answered Boris as though lost in his own thoughts. For a few minutes he said nothing more. BRIDEGROOM watched him slowly break off a crust of bread and hold it out for the cat to eat. When he turned back to BRIDEGROOM, his voice was quiet. "I have little enough left to lose. When Maria and my son . . . "

He closed his eyes feeling the familiar stab of pain he experienced each time he dared release the memory of a young boy killed in the war and a grieving wife who followed him to his grave. Then with an impatient movement of his hand, he said, "But that is over. Now I would like to know why you think your Russian friend is going to insist on meeting your mythical informant?" Boris smiled as he posed the question. "Why now?"

"Call it instinct. But I have been at this business long enough to sense when my clients are no longer satisfied with empty promises and demand to see something concrete . . . either a person, or a document, or valuable information they can verify. We have been lucky in our dealings with the Americans. For awhile we satisfied them by producing forged letters from non-existing agents inside the country." BRIDEGROOM paused and smiled before adding, "Among his other talents, Nick is an expert forger. But then a real person of value appeared and now we can deal honestly with them. To be truthful, I'm glad of that because I respect their good intentions.

Dealing with the Russian is a different matter. His hand is always on my throat and I can feel his grip tighten, figuratively speaking of course, whenever his appetite for information has not been satisfied," said BRIDEGROOM with a sardonic wave of his hand. "His growing frustration is becoming obvious and I know it is just a matter of time before he will demand to see some tangible evidence to support my fairy tales. A meeting with a live informant might assuage his doubts. You see, Boris, espionage is an exercise on infinite patience. Squeeze a handful of sand and what do you end up with?...an empty hand. But they never give up hoping it will not be empty. As long as I fill their hand, they will keep squeezing . . . and hoping. But if their hand is empty too long, they will become impatient. Then they will begin to give me instructions which I may find impossible to satisfy. If that happens, my work will end with all the consequences that might be involved. But if they believe that this time I almost succeeded in leading them to an informant who could provide valuable information, then they will go on hoping that tomorrow or the next day there will be a new chance. It is not important whether tomorrow ever arrives. They will wait. That is why I need your help."

"And if you are wrong and he doesn't ask to see your informant?" asked Boris with an impish smile.

"Then we will have been prepared. What else can I say?" responded BRIDEGROOM.

"And if we do have a meeting, what then?" asked Boris.

"There are two possibilities. The first is that simply by showing up, he will feel re-assured and satisfied. But it is more likely that if there is a meeting, he will have questions."

"Have you thought about the answers?" asked Boris with a touch of skepticism in his voice.

"Yes, but if you agree to join in my conspiracy, we will need time together to agree on the best strategy. Boris, you are the only person I know who has the talent to carry it off."

"I shall try not to disappoint you," smiled Boris. "After all, I had given up all hope of being rehabilitated and now you come and convince me that I can make myself useful again. It is a comforting thought for an old man."

BRIDEGROOM laughed and raised his coffee cup. "To the future success of two old men."

Boris acknowledged the toast and as he replaced his cup on the table, he asked, "When do we begin?"

"Can you come back with me tonight?"

CHAPTER FIFTEEN

"Golnikov, how many months have I been waiting . . . waiting patiently . . . while you have spent your time humoring our friend Bergarsch . . . 'being subtle' as you call it?" Borakowsky spat out the words in an insolent monotone. He was standing with his back turned to Golnikov, slowly rocking back and forth on the balls of his feet, staring into the empty fireplace. His over-developed shoulders bulged like stuffing inside his shiny black chauffeur's uniform so that one might have expected his jacket to rip apart at the seams if he raised his arms. For a moment he said nothing more. Then his hand shot out and slammed down on the mantel and he whirled around to face Golnikov. "Well, we have waited long enough. Do you understand? Long enough! Now we will begin to do things my way."

Golnikov watched the performance with a mixture of fear and fascination. It was useless to reply. The issue was closed. Borakowsky would give the orders now. Last night's meeting with Bergarsch had assured that. Golnikov understood well. There is no margin for miscalculation in this work. And when you discover that one of your informants is working for the British, what else can you call it, but a colossal blunder?

"Do you think, Golnikov, that we can trust any of Bergarsch's agents? What about the Army corporal who gives military information? Who does he work for . . . the Chinese?" asked Borakowsky derisively. "Maybe we should start from the beginning again. Only this time . . . not so polite. You understand? You won't have to worry about hurting our friend Bergarsch's feelings. No,..this time he will take orders."

Golnikov uncrossed his legs, leaned forward in his chair and began to reply. "What happened was unfortunate . . . "

"Unfortunate! Is that what you call it?" interrupted Borakowsky, his voice quivering with rage. "I am certain Moscow will be happy to know you send your regrets . . . but I remind you they will want an explanation as well."

"What is there to tell them?" asked Golnikov, calmly refusing to be intimidated. "Only that Bergarsch has been getting political information for us through the friend of a Government Deputy and now he has learned that the friend is a British agent."

"Oh, that's all, eh? That's very nice," said Borakowsky stepping closer to Golnikov. Then he thrust his face forward and asked angrily, "And Bergarsch . . . what about him? Does the agent know he works for us? And you . . . have you considered your own position?"

"My situation has not changed. I never met the British agent. He has no idea Bergarsch works for us."

"He thinks Bergarsch collects information for a hobby?" snarled Borakowsky arrogantly.

"No. But he thinks Bergarsch is working a deal with some of the Deputies and that the information is helping Bergarsch put pressure on them. Bergarsch has convinced him that some official money intended for the refugees is sticking in the pockets of the Deputies . . . .and he assumes Bergarsch keeps his share."

"You think that is what we should tell Moscow?"

"Yes."

Borakowsky moved over and stood looking down at Golnikov. "Then you are stupid as well as careless," he said, turning away in disgust.

For a minute, neither man spoke. Golnikov nonchalantly puffed on a cigarette, outwardly unperturbed by Borakowsky's abuse. But inwardly he was seized by a strong sense of loathing for this fat-lipped brute whom he well knew was his inferior in every respect . . . except rank.

Borakowsky finally broke the silence in a voice still filled with venom. "Golnikov, why don't you stop . . . take your time . . . think a little. Think about your job. Ask yourself, 'do I like it here?'. If you do, then maybe you should think about how they will react in Moscow when they find out Bergarsch has been using their money to pay an informant who now turns out to be a British agent."

"I know how they will react. And if I think about it . . . how will that change anything?" asked Golnikov almost unconsciously hoping that Borakowsksy would provide an answer. He knew that once the truth was disclosed to Moscow, the operation would be terminated. He also understood they would demand an accounting . . . would fix responsibility. Then it would be only a matter of time before he would be recalled. And what about Borakowsky? How could he dissociate himself from what had happened?

The same unpleasant thought was locked in Borakowsky's mind as he sat down to face Golnikov. "How can you change the past?" he asked smugly. "The answer is simple . . . you can't. But what is it that you want to change? Bergarsch is cooperating. Do you want to change that? Of course not. No, your only problem is to get rid of this informant of Bergarsch who is causing all the embarrassment. But how can you make him disappear so everyone will be satisfied? And how can you make him disappear so we can be sure he will not compromise our future activities with Bergarsch?" Borakowsky posed the questions with the easy assurance of one who already knew the answers.

"Perhaps I can arrange to have him shot," responded Golnikov sarcastically.

A half smile crossed Borakowsky's lips as he replied in a condescending voice. "Please forgive me, Golnikov. You have much more imagination than I have given you credit for. You are quite right. There is only one answer to our problem. Bergarsch's informant will have to be killed.

At first Golnikov assumed the remark was another of Borakowsky's clumsy attempts at ridicule. But the ruthless expression in his eyes told Golnikov differently. A shudder of horror passed through his body. "You must be joking," he said defiantly.

"You think so, Golnikov?" Borakowsky hesitated while he loosened his tie. Then he added coldly, "Well . . . you are wrong. I am not joking. If Bergarsch's friend wants to play the dangerous game, then he has to be willing to pay the price."

"But we are not even sure he is a British agent."

"Bergarsch thinks so?"

"Yes."

"And Bergarsch tells you he thinks this is why his informant will not give us the reports we ask for?"

"He suspects that is the reason. He is not sure," responded Golnikov plaintively.

"What is it that you want, Golnikov . . . a written confession? Or maybe you are just too soft to do a man's work."

Golnikov snuffed out his cigarette and for a few seconds closed his eyes in meditation. When he finally spoke, it was in the weary tone of a man already reconciled to the knowledge that his listener was incapable of comprehending the meaning of what he was about to say. Yet, he felt an overwhelming need to at least attempt to explain his position to Borakowsky, almost a kind of catharsis. "Whatever the reason . . . call it personal weakness if you like . . . the role of executioner does not appeal to me. Nor do I regard the fact that a man enjoys plotting murder as a sign of strength . . . especially when the victim may be innocent."

Golnikov's remarks seemed to amuse Borakowsky who put back his head and laughed, exposing the metal fillings in his teeth. "Oh, I didn't mean to worry you, Golnikov. I know you are much too noble . . . much too sensitive . . . to become an assassin. I would not think of forcing you to live with a dirty conscience," he smirked. Then his eyes narrowed and the ominous tone returned to his voice. "But not everyone can afford your ideals. And if some men have no objection to crushing a skull . . . well, think about it . . . that's good for you. It keeps you clean but we still get the job done."

Borakowsky stooped and plucked a cigarette out of a black lacquer box that was lying on the table in front of the sofa.

He seemed in no hurry to continue the conversation. When he spoke, his face was enveloped in a cloud of smoke as he pointed his cigarette at Golnikov. "There is one small favor that I will have to ask from you."

"What is it?" asked Golnikov suspiciously.

"Now don't be alarmed," responded Borakowsky with mocking innocence. "You know there are people we can use when there are unpleasant jobs to be done. I wouldn't consider wasting your talent on that kind of things. But . . . after all . . . one of the reasons you were sent here to work with me was because you have friends in Moscow who recognize your great imagination. Now, that is what I need . . . your imagination."

"I am at your disposal," replied Golnikov acidly.

"I knew I could count on you. You see, Bertgarsch's friend is going to have an accident.

"What kind of accident?"

"A fatal accident," smiled Borakowsky. "He is going to be run over by a lorry when he is crossing the street. The only question is . . . what street and what time. That is what I am leaving to your imagination to work out for us.."

"So, I will not be the assassin . . . only the assassin's accomplice."

"I am sorry you feel that way, Golnikov. But be reasonable. Who else is there who could make the proper arrangements?" asked Borakowsky cynically. Then, as though suddenly tired of playing games with Golnikov, his manner changed and his voice hardened. "Don't make the mistake of thinking you have a choice. A courier leaves for Moscow on Friday. He will carry your report describing the accident in his pouch. Do you understand?"

"I understand . . . but will Bergarsch?"

"What difference does it make whether he understands or not?" snapped Borakowsky.

"You order me to arrange for Bergarsch's informant to cross a certain street at a certain time. All right . . . I understand. But I cannot get him there without Bergarsch's help."

"Tell me something, Golnikov. Who is in charge . . . you or Bergarsch?" Borakowsky ground his cigarette into an ashtray before turning back to Golnikov.. "I told you we will begin to do things my way . . . and we will begin now. Bergarsch has no objection to taking your money? No. And his mother . . . has he forgotten her? No. Well then, it is time he learned to take orders. Do you hear? I said take orders!" Borakowsky fairly shouted the last sentence.

"And if his informant refuses to appear?"

"That would be a sad mistake. You see, Golnikov, I am planning on an accident. So there will be an accident." Borakowsky put both hands on the table and pushed himself to his feet, where he stood looking down at Golnikov. "And Bergarsch would be wise to cooperate. Because if he does not arrange for his friend to meet him, we will have no choice."

"No choice?"

"That's right, Golnikov . . . no choice. If his friend dies, nothing will be changed . . . for you . . . for Bergarsch . . . even for me. But what happens if his friend lives . . . think about it." Bosrakowsky moved around and stood behind the sofa. "How much does he know about Bergarsch? How much does he know about you? You say nothing . . . but are you certain? Remember . . . this is not a very friendly country. We cannot afford unpleasant publicity. So we will take whatever steps are necessary to eliminate the possibility of embarrassment. If Bergarsch's friend dies, the danger dies. But if he lives, who can guarantee that Bergarsch will not be compromised? No . . . we would never be sure. Bergarsch himself would become a liability . . . a liability that we would have to eliminate. And I know how that would distress you." Without taking his eyes off Golnikov, Borakowsky moved slowly, almost menacingly, around the sofa to the center of the room where he stood with his hands clasped behind his back. "So I advise you to see Bergarsch. See him soon. And when you see him, be certain he understands how important it is . . . how important it is to him . . . that he arranges to have his friend appear at the exact minute and at the exact place we order." Borakowsky turned and headed for the door without waiting for Golnikov to reply.

Golnikov heard the door close but he did not move from where he was sitting. He needed a few minutes of quiet to clear his head . . . to bring his discussion with Borakowsky into focus. His brain already had adjusted to Borakowsky's decision to assassinate one of Bergarsch's informants. He found it more difficult to adjust his conscience. And it was not the fact that a man was going to be killed that troubled him. He had been witness to violent death before. But he regarded assassination as an ugly last alternative.

No, Golnikov was distressed because he understood Borakowsky's motives in ordering the informant killed. He had seen him operate before. He knew Borakowsky took sadistic pleasure from the most extreme forms of cruelty . . . that he was almost pathologically jealous of his authority to order an assassination. But Golnikov understood something more. He was aware that Borakowsky's reputation had been declining . . . that he had been in trouble with Moscow until the operation with Bergarsch began. And Borakowsky himself was shrewd enough to perceive that his position was in danger . . . to understand that his blunt style of operating was no longer in fashion. But he was too inflexible . . . or too dull . . . to change and now anything that jeopardized the operation, jeopardized Borakowsky.

So I must help plot the execution of an unsuspecting stranger, a man who probably is innocent, in order to protect Borakowsky's skin, thought Golnikov bitterly. He stood up, walked slowly to his desk and unlocked the file on Bergarsch. After he had rechecked the procedure for setting an emergency meeting, he slid the file back into place and looked at his watch. He would make the call from a public pay station and with luck, would meet Bergarsch after dark. The rest would be up to Bergarsch, his friend . . . and the driver of the lorry.

****

Something about the sight of Nick's grotesque yellow bunions swelling out through the toes of those broken house slippers offended BRIDEGROOM's sense of decorum. He had often been tempted to say something to Nick about it but never had. Now at this stage it seemed an insignificant matter to make an issue of. If anything, BRIDEGROOM was wryly amused at this homely reminder of the gradual change that had taken place in their relationship over the years. No, the shape of Nick's feet was far less important than the fact that he was an expert forger and absolutely trustworthy. Survival takes precedence over refinement, thought BRIDEGROOM resignedly.

He watched the big feet shuffle slowly toward the window, only remotely conscious of the soft chaffing sound Nick's slippers made as they dragged against the grey marble floor of the safe house. Nick stopped and stared out across the veranda . . . propping his hands against the window frames as though the wall would collapse without his support. A badly rolled cigarette dangled loosely from a patch of moisture on his lower lip. "Why now?" he asked, half to himself and half to Tina and BRIDEGROOM.

BRIDEGROOM noticed Tina unclasp her hands and hold them out as if she were expecting him to physically lay the answer to Nick's question in them. "It is hard to say, Nick," responded BRIDEGROOM, nodding reassuringly to Tina as he spoke. He knew the sudden Russian ultimatum to produce the agent had stunned Tina and Nick . . . transforming what before might have seemed like a harmless game into the frightening prospect of a possible direct confrontation with the Soviet KGB.

"There has to be a logical explanation . . . but I have no idea what it can be," continued BRIDEGROOM. "If they had asked to see him earlier . . . before I told them I suspected him of working for the British . . . then I would have understood. But now for the Russian to insist on a meeting with a man who as far as he knows could expose him to British Intelligence . . . does not make sense," said BRIDEGROOM slowly shaking his head.

"Unless he has found out there is no agent," said Tina quietly.

Nick turned back from the window waiting for the reply to the question that had been churning in his own mind. "I can tell you I too have thought of that possibility, Tina. And I still do not discount it," answered BRIDEGROOM pensively. Then, as though mentally reconstructing his meeting with Golnikov, he added, "But I did not get the impression that he was suspicious. I could be wrong, but after a certain number of years, you develop a sense of feel for these things . . . a blind man's instinct for knowing without seeing."

"Then what will happen if your agent doesn't show up to meet the Russian?" asked Nick.

"I would rather not find out," replied BRIDEGROOM gravely. "Without question it would mean the end of our affair with the Russians. What else might it mean?...well . . . there are a number of possibilities."

"They wouldn't harm your mother?" asked Tina anxiously.

"I am afraid we would have to expect her situation to change," answered BRIDEGROOM calmly. Nick muttered an inaudible curse and flung his cigarette into the fireplace as BRIDEGROOM continued to speak. "But sooner or later this was certain to happen. People like to see what they are paying for. Especially Russians. After all, this is not the first time we have talked about the prospect of them demanding proof. It is something we anticipated from the beginning. No . . . I am not surprised at their request. I am only surprised at their timing."

Nick picked a fig out of a dish on the table and put it into his mouth with one bite. "Don't worry about it, Victor," he said, licking his sticky fingers. We managed to keep Rogers happy before Popescu arrived. Now it will be the Russian's turn."

"Maybe you are right. I hope you are. But things are not quite the same. Remember, Nick, the Russian is not Rogers. And this time we do not control the situation. Unfortunately, the situation controls us." For the next few moments BRIDEGROOM said nothing more. He sat with his elbows resting lightly on the arms of his chair. His head was slightly bowed so that the fingers of both hands touched at his brow in almost prayerful meditation.

Slowly his brain sifted the cold ashes of the past few months. The letter from his mother. His visit to the Russian Embassy. Was he a fool to have gone? The recruitment. At that moment . . . was that the time to have refused? Or was there a choice? The Russian demands for information . . . at first general . . . easily satisfied . . . and then more and more specific. The need to invent non-existent informants. Was this his mistake? Perhaps. But what other way was there to account for a source?

The increasing pressure for details he could not provide. Weak excuses . . . not accepted. More demands. Finally . . . the ultimate excuse . . . the ultimate blunder. Tell the Russian you think your informer will not produce details because you have reason to suspect he works for the British. And so . . . here we are, thought BRIDEGOOM.

"Have you spoken to Boris?" asked Tina gently, as though aware she was interrupting a private thought.

"He will be ready to go whenever we need him," asserted Nick, his old buoyancy returning.

BRIDEGROOM leaned back in his chair and looked across the room at Nick who still was standing near the window chewing figs. Then he turned to Tina. "Nick is right. Boris is willing to help. I already have spoken to him."

"Where is he now?' asked Tina.

"I have him staying in a room near Omonia. Under the circumstances, I do not want to risk bringing him here."

"Does he know what he is supposed to say?" asked Nick in a tone that suggested only idle curiosity.

"Do any of us?" replied BRIDEGROOM with an ironic smile. "How do you prepare your answer before you have heard the question?"

"So? What are you going to do?" prodded Nick.

"The only thing we can do. We will try to guess what the Russian is after. Perhaps, as Tina suggested, he just wants to assure himself that we really have an informant. If there is no more to it than that . . . well...we know that at least we can produce a body for him to examine."

"We'll be safe enough as long as he doesn't try to find Boris' pulse," said Nick with a wide grin.

"You don't really think that is all the Russian wants do you, Victor?" asked Tina, without paying any attention to Nick's joke.

"No, I don't," answered BRIDEGROOM, sitting forward and cupping his hands over his knees. "I think that one way or another the Russian wants to get to the bottom of the story I gave him about my informant being a possible British agent." BRIDEGROOM paused and then added sadly, "Looking back, I wonder how I could have made such an inexcusable mistake. But there are times when the pressure becomes strong and you are tired and it is convenient to use the first excuse that comes into your head, without thinking about the consequences."

"Bah," said Nick. "You know you are not God . . . so how can you expect to predict everything?"

"Not everything," laughed BRIDEGROOM. "Only the obvious. And it should have been obvious to me at the time that I was inviting trouble. Almost any excuse would have been better than inventing the story about the British. Now we are forced to crawl from our own flypaper."

"How?" asked Nick.

"By convincing the Russian that our informant has nothing to do with the British." BRIDEGROOM seemed almost to be thinking out loud as he spoke. "Then when the Russian wants to know why we didn't provide the information he asked for, Boris will give him a simple but safe answer. He will tell him that he didn't provide it because he couldn't provide it."

"I don't understand," said Tina.

"Boris will tell the Russian that it is all a big mistake . . . that he didn't know they were interested in the information he has been passing me. In fact, he will tell the Russian that he has no way of getting the detailed information they want."

"What excuse will he use?" asked Nick skeptically.

"He is going to say the whole thing has been a hoax. He will explain that he has been exaggerating the importance of his political contacts simply for my benefit because he knew I wanted information and because I paid him for it. Naturally, he will become contrite and apologize to the Russian . . . and to me. But if the Russian believes the story, what can he do about it?"

"Beautiful! Beautiful!" exclaimed Nick, clutching his head in his hands as though he were about to unscrew it.

"Only if it works," cautioned BRIDEGROOM. "Of course if it should work, we can expect the Russian to question the credibility of all our sources. And so . . . we will have created a few new problems. On the other hand, I warned him from the beginning that I was an amateur . . . and amateurs are notoriously gullible," said BRIDEGROOM ironically.

Nick, who had been listening respectfully, now took a couple of steps toward BRIDEGROOM. The expression on his face was that of someone troubled by a problem he found embarrassing to mention. Finally he spoke. "Victor . . . there is just one thing. The last time I saw Boris he looked very tired and seemed to be a little nervous." Nick hesitated, absent-mindedly picking a particle of food from between his teeth, while BRIDEGROOM sat with half-closed eyes and slowly nodded that he understood what was bothering the big fellow. "Meeting the Russian will be tough. It would be tough for anybody . . . even someone a lot younger than Boris. Do you think he can handle it?"

For a few moments BRIDEGROOM did not answer. Then he looked up at Nick and said quietly, "Only time will tell. And we don't have very long to wait.

CHAPTER SIXTEEN

Even for an autumn night there was an unexpected chill in the air. BRIDEGROOM turned up his collar against a sudden gust of wind that snapped off the water and burst across the deserted street until it crashed like an open palm against the steam-covered windows of smoke-filled coffee houses. For an instant, a frayed awning flapped wildly in front of a darkened store and then, as though exhausted, it fell limp. The only sound that remained was the rhythmic clack of BRIDEGROOM's heels echoing on the pavement.

The wharves and warehouses were still. Three or four freighters slept at their moorings, waiting for morning when crewmen would climb over the decks and dock cranes would dip long necks and feed on the cargo in their holds. In clusters around the dock area unopened crates and piles of newly unloaded lumber loomed stolidly against the night sky.

The sidewalk had narrowed so that from time to time BRIDEGROOM felt his sleeve brush against the heavy chain link fence that surrounded the wharf area. Most of the buildings on the other side of the street were shuttered and dark. Occasionally a car passed, its headlights momentarily unfrocking the shadows before moving out of sight.

BRIDEGROOM had been walking steadily for about ten minutes since getting off the bus but now he could make out his destination only two or three hundred yards away. It was one of the few patches of light in view. He knew Boris already was inside having a brandy at one of the tables. In five minutes he would come out of the bar, cross the street to meet

BRIDEGROOM and the Russian would drive by to pick them up in his car.

There was enough time. BRIDEGROOM slowed his pace. Finally he stopped. Like an actor about to make his entrance on stage, he stood just outside the neat arc of light thrown down by a streetlight and scanned the block. His eyes picked out the solitary figure of a man standing almost motionless near the entrance of the bar. It was difficult to be certain in the dark, but he somehow sensed that the stranger was watching him with equal interest. BRIDGROOM glanced at his watch . . . only two minutes before Boris would come through the door. Slowly he turned again toward the figure in the shadows. There no longer was any doubt. The stranger was staring back.

Even before he could react to the situation, the door to the bar opened and Boris emerged. Like a stunned witness to a crime, BRIDEGROOM stood immobilized as the stranger swung around and stepped toward Boris. His brain suddenly was pounding with fear. He wanted to run across the street and rescue Boris. But rescue him from what? Perhaps the stranger was just asking him for a match. BRIDEGROOM had no way of knowing. He watched the two men talk . . . saw Boris shake his head in refusal and try to walk away. The stranger followed him. Who was he? A Russian? Or a member of the local security police? The possibilities rocketed through BRIDEGROOM's mind. In the confusion and anxiety of the moment, he did not see the blacked-out lorry parked in the shadow of a warehouse further down the street. Nor did he hear the sound of its engine as the driver pressed his foot on the starter.

Boris obviously was disconcerted by this unexpected encounter with the stranger. He was walking rapidly away from the bar as though he had abandoned all thought of meeting BRIDEGROOM. The stranger kept pace for several yards, then stopped abruptly and threw up in his hands in a gesture of frustration. As BRIDEGROOM watched Boris disappear from sight, the stranger spun around and without warning, started across the street toward him.

Before he could decide whether to stay and face it out with

the stranger or to turn and leave, he heard the roar of the engine and saw the truck lurch like a maddened animal out of the dark.

"Look out!" he shouted.

A look of terror flashed on the stranger's face at BRIDEGROOM's warning. Almost at the same instant the lorry tore across their path, blocking him from BRIDEGROOM's view. Then it was over. BRIDEGROOM saw him lying in the street. Suddenly the true purpose of the meeting ripped through his mind with shattering reality. He had a sinking feeling of horror that was close to physical illness. They have used me to arrange a murder, he thought. And the victim would have been Boris if that poor devil in the street had not come along.

Without being conscious that he was running, BRIDEGROOM already was part way to the stranger before he realized the body was moving. Slowly at first, and then like an explosion, the man erupted off the pavement in an arm-waving, screaming rage.

"You eyeless swine! You half man! You miserable piece of afterbirth! May you choke on a whore's tit!"

BRIDEGROOM halted in amazement as the stranger turned toward him, fists still clinched in fury, and asked in an emotion-filled voice, "What was that imbecile of a driver trying to do . . . kill me?"

"It almost looked that way," answered BRIDEGROOM with a sigh of relief. "Are you all right?"

The stranger slowly examined his clothes and his limbs as though to make certain they were all there. "It was close . . . but at least I still have my pants on," he responded with false bravado. Then he took out a cigarette and BRIDEGROOM watched his hand shake as he lit it. "How can I thank you? I'd be dead if you hadn't warned me."

"You don't know how happy I am that you are not hurt. That's all that matters," replied BRIDEGROOM solemnly. "Here . . . let me help you brush off your clothes."

"No, no . . . that's all right. You've done enough." The stranger had a young face . . . the face of a man still in his twenties. If he had been older, he never would have been able to jump out of the way, thought BRIDEGROOM.

But there was one question still unanswered. "Tell me

something," asked BRIDEGROOM. "Were you coming across the street to speak to me?"

The stranger shrugged good-naturedly and laughed. "Yes. I was coming across the street to do you a favor." He hesitated and said, "Who knows . . . maybe I still can. Only this time I will arrange everything for nothing. I owe it to you."

"Arrange what?"

"A nice clean girl to spend the night with," he answered with a suggestive smile.

For a moment, BRIDEGROOM was too surprised to respond. Then he put back his head and roared with laughter. The tension of the evening suddenly seemed to evaporate. He felt almost light-headed. "My friend, at my age the mere suggestion that I could take advantage of your offer is an undeserved compliment." He put his arm around the pimp's shoulder and added with feigned disappointment. "I am flattered but . . . unhappily . . . I must decline. I hope you understand."

"You'll be missing a good time."

"Oh, I know you are right," replied BRIDEGROOM who by now was enjoying himself immensely. "But what do you say?...if you have time, come on . . . let me buy you a drink. I think we both could use one and at least I am sure I am not too old to handle a glass of brandy."

****

BRIDEGROOM knew he had the Russian on the defensive. He had sensed it the moment he pulled open the car door and slid into the front seat. Apart from the usual amenities, the Russian had said nothing. He gave the impression of single-minded concentration on the task of steering his small car through the rain-slicked streets. From time to time, when lights from approaching vehicles flashed against their windshield, BRIDEGROOM caught glimpses of the grim expression which was frozen like a death mask on Golnikov's face. BRIDEGROOM knew what was bothering him.

Finally Golnikov spoke. "Mr. Bergarsch, unless I am mistaken, we have been working together for about six months. Am I right?"

"Yes. Approximately six months."

"Six months is a long time," said Golnikov slowly. "A man . . . even a highly intelligent man like you . . . can forget a lot in six months. Which probably explains why you did not bother to follow the instructions you received when we first began our association."

"Then perhaps you should repeat those instructions," replied BRIDEGROOM curtly.

"You were told that whenever we fail to meet, you are to repeat the same meeting plan the following day one half hour earlier. I gave you no authority to make an emergency telephone call until a second meeting had failed."

"And I made no bargain to help you commit murder," replied BRIDEGROOM angrily.

"What are you talking about?" demanded Golnikov.

"I am talking about the lorry that tried to run down the man you were supposed to meet last night. What . . . did you expect me to invite him back tonight so you could have a second chance?" BRIDEGROOM measured each word, trying to gauge its impact, wondering how far he could press Golnikov. "There are limits to everyone's patience . . . including mine. If you felt he jeopardized your security, why didn't you say so? That is something I can understand. But I want you to know . . . and never forget . . . that I have no intention of becoming the innocent broker in an assassination. Perhaps murder is your business . . . but it is not mine. In any case, unless you want to end everything right now, don't pretend you don't know what happened last night."

"I'm surprised to see you become so emotional, Mr. Bergarsch," answered Golnikov calmly. "I assure you I am not here to pretend anything or to deny anything. I am here to receive your report on what happened."

"What is there to report that you don't already know?" replied BRIDEGROOM dryly. "I had arranged the meeting exactly as you instructed. At ten o'clock he started across the street and then your truck came. I shouted at him and he managed to jump out of the way."

"You shouted at him?" interrupted Golnikov as though not quite willing to believe his ears.

"Is there anything so unusual about warning a man that he is about to be crushed by a truck?"

"On the contrary. You should be commended," responded Golnikov in a voice laced with sarcasm.

"Furthermore, until that moment, I had assumed you wanted to meet the man alive," added BRIDEGROOM caustically.

"And then you changed your mind?"

"Yes."

"So? What did you do?"

"I helped him to his feet."

"And then you warned him that his life was in danger?" said Golnikov in a slow accusing tone.

"That was hardly necessary. The man is not stupid."

Golnikov made no reply. Instead he slowed their speed and turned into an unlighted side street. The car prowled through the dark until Golnikov finally pulled in against the curb and stopped. He left the motor running while he shifted in his seat to face BRIDEGROOM directly for the first time that evening.

When Golnikov spoke, his tone was quiet, almost intimate. "Mr. Bergarsch, I have no intention of embarrassing you, but I have always looked forward to our meetings together. They have provided a pleasure quite unrelated to official business. Perhaps because I regard you as one of those rare individuals who has perfected the art of tactful belligerence. It creates a stimulating challenge." Govnikov paused. Then without warning his manner changed and his voice hardened. "But tonight I do not have time for a contest. I want answers."

"Answers to what?" asked BRIDEGROOM mildly.

"After he recovered, what did your contact do . . . or say? Does he know who you represent?"

"He has no idea who I represent but he knows someone tried to kill him. At first he accused me but I tried to convince him that I knew nothing about it."

"Did he believe you?"

"As far as I could tell . . . yes. But who can say? The main thing is that he was terrified by what happened and he has refused to meet me again."

"Then he suspects you?"

"Not necessarily but he believes his relationship with me was connected to the attempt on his life. It is impossible for me to see him again. He would run if I approached him."

"So . . . will he report what happened?"

"No," replied BRIDEGROOM thoughtfully, "he is too frightened. He is a good source of information but he has no courage."

For a few moments the only sound was that of the rain pelting off the car roof. Golnikov lit a cigarette and took a long drag as though he had forgotten BRIDEGROOM still was in the car. Then he said softly, "For your sake, Mr. Bergarsch, I hope you are right." He leaned across and pushed open the door on BRIDEGROOM's side letting in a rush of cold air. When Golnikov spoke again, his voice was almost drowned out by the sound of rain splattering off the pavement and pouring along the street. "I want to see you again . . . on Saturday. I will pick you up at ten fifteen near the kiosk. I assume you will be there?"

"Yes."

"Then I won't detain you any longer tonight," said Golnikov making a slight gesture with his hand as an invitation for BRIDEGROOM to leave. "Goodnight, Mr. Bergarsch."

As BRIDEGROOM stood watching the Russian's car sputter out of sight, he was only remotely conscious of the rain dripping off the brim of his hat and seeping under his collar. Slowly he turned, hunched his shoulders against the elements and began looking for the nearest bus stop. He was cold and wet . . . yet strangely relaxed. All his instincts told him the Russian had believed his story. The immediate danger had passed.

*****

Golnikov began taking off his coat before he was inside the foyer. He laid it carelessly across the back of a chair, shook the rain from his hat and let it drop on top of the coat. The entrance hall was empty but he could detect the lingering odor of cigarette smoke. He knew Borakowsky was around. Slowly he unfolded his handkerchief and wiped the moisture from his face. Then he walked toward the closed door of the embassy study.

A blue spiral of cigarette smoke floated sluggishly out of the chair but from the rear only the round top of Borakowsky's head was visible. Golnikov closed the door behind him and waited for a few moments before entering the room. There was no sound of movement . . . no signal of recognition. Borakowsky's head remained immobile.

When he finally spoke, his manner was sullen as though he resented the need for conversation. "Well, Golnikov, are you going to give me your report or did your friend forget to show up?"

Golnikov walked past Borakowsky's chair to the liquor cabinet and poured himself a drink before he turned to answer. "He was there," said Golnikov as though there never had been any doubt in his mind.

"Then maybe he told you why he disobeyed your instructions."

"Because he recognizes incompetence," replied Golnikov acidly.

"Oh . . . whose incompetence?" asked Borakowsky menacingly.

Golnikov smiled almost condescendingly. "Our incompetence," he answered as he took a sip of his drink. He watched Borakowsky's huge peasant hands tighten around the arms of the chair . . . saw his eyes narrow with anger. But there was no reply.

"Yes," repeated Golnikov, "our incompetence. Bergarsch was there and his agent was there. But the lorry driver was a bungling fool."

Borakowsky pointed a warning finger. "Be careful what you say, Golnikov, or you may have some regrets."

"What kind of regrets could I have?" asked Golnikov innocently. "I know you are not worried about protecting the driver. He already has done enough damage." Golnikov walked slowly across the room and sat down opposite Borakowsky.

"Let's be realistic. The entire episode was a blunder but certainly you cannot blame yourself . . . or me." His tone carried the double edge or taunt and charity.

"So you think you share no responsibility?" said Borakowsky unpleasantly. "That's a convenient way to look at it."

"Was there something that I should have done that I did not do?" countered Golnikov. He understood how Borakowsky's mind worked and he knew that Borakowsky was struggling to regain leverage in the delicate balance of power that existed between them.

"You have a short memory. Or maybe you prefer to forget that if you had controlled Bergarsh from the beginning, there would be no problem now," snarled Borakowsky. "No . . . Golnikov . . . we were only trying to save your skin."

"All right," said Golnikov wearily, "I am tired of talking about what went wrong. It's over. All that matters is what we do now."

Borakowsky smiled contemptuously and made an expansive gesture with his hand. "What do you suggest? Certainly you must have an answer."

In spite of Borakowsky's outward arrogance, there was something in his manner that conveyed the impression of uneasiness. Golnikov sensed it. He knew Borakowsky was genuinely looking for a way out. "I appreciate your confidence in me," replied Golnikov ironically. "But it really is not a question of having the answer. It is simply a matter of being willing to face facts."

"Why don't you tell me about those facts," snapped Borakowsky.

"In the first place," said Golnikov slowly getting to his feet, "Bergarsch's contact knows someone wants him out of the way. But he doesn't know who. Consequently, I think we are in no real danger of being exposed." He moved in deliberate steps across the rug, motioning pompously with his glass as he spoke. "Secondly, it is important that we consider the psychological impact on the man. Bergarsch has told me that the man is essentially a coward . . . that the attempt on his life had the effect of terrifying him . . . terrifying him to the extent that he refuses even to meet Bergarsch again. In short," continued

Golnikov, setting down his glass and turning to face Borakowsky, "even if the man is a British agent . . . which, incidentally, we never have proven . . . I think it is safe to assume that he has been frightened into permanent silence.

"That may be true," said Borakowsky speaking through cupped hands as he lit another cigarette, "but Moscow has asked for specific information and now the informant has disappeared. What are you going to report . . . that you are sorry?"

"We can report the facts," replied Golnikov sardonically, "but I was under the impression that you wanted to avoid embarrassment." He paused but Borakowsky remained impassive. Then he added, "No . . . there is only one other explanation for us to give Moscow. We will report that our informant has had a heart seizure and died . . . that we have instructed Bergarsch to develop a new source."

Barakowsky sat with his eyes fixed coldly on Golnikov and took a few final drags on his cigarette. Then he crushed the butt in an ashtray, stood up and started toward the door. As he neared the exit, he stopped and looked over his shoulder. "Bring me your report when it is done. And remember, Golnikov, the final responsibility for Bergarsch is yours. Be careful you don't make any more mistakes.

CHAPTER SEVENTEEN

Boris put down his coffee cup and looked up as BRIDEGROOM came through the door and headed quickly toward his table, nodding a friendly recognition as he approached. Boris smiled and motioned toward an empty chair.

"It's good to see you, Boris," said BRIDEGROOM as he waved to the waiter to bring another coffee.

"I understand why," responded Boris wryly.

"Boris, I assure you that what happened the other evening was as much a shock to me as it was to you. I am just grateful the young man pestered you long enough to prevent you from crossing the street."

"He was very annoying but he unwittingly saved my life," agreed Boris, who paused before adding in a troubled voice, "Victor, I think you are playing with fire. Can you escape before you get burned?"

"I don't know," replied BRIDEGROOM solemnly, "but I regret I involved you and put you at risk. Fortunately, our young friend was able to leap out of the way of the lorry. I'm afraid you might not have been so lucky." BRIDEGROOM took a sip of coffee before continuing. "However, it now appears that the Russian is convinced that the young man was in fact the informant that they intended to assassinate. And so, ironically, we accomplished what we set out to do . . . which was to produce a live person to prove that an informant actually existed."

"That must mean I now have the luxury of taking an early retirement from the spy business," said Boris drolly.

"I think that would be a wise decision," responded

BRIDEGROOM with a smile. "You have been a great friend. I wish there was some way I could properly express my thanks."

"You just have," replied Boris. "And I know I can always count on you if I should ever be in need of help."

For a few minutes they sat pensively drinking their coffee, each man lost in his own thoughts. It was BRIDEGROOM who broke the silence. "What are you going to do now?' he asked.

"I am going to return to Patras and pick up where I left off . . . a dull but safe life."

"I'll miss seeing you but I know we will stay in touch," replied BRIDEGOOM softly.

As though they both understood that there was nothing else left to say, they stood up and faced each other before they instinctively embraced. Boris stepped back and for just a moment, rested his hands on BRIDEGROOM's shoulders. "Just be careful. Break away if you can," he whispered.

BRIDEGROOM nodded his head in appreciative understanding, gave Boris one last weary smile and turned to leave.

****

"So now murder is part of their dirty business," snorted Nick as he listened to BRIDEGROOM describe the botched attempt on Boris' life and BRIDEGROOM's subsequent meeting with Golnikov. "And Boris has a pimp to thank that he is still alive," he added, shaking his head in feigned disbelief.

"He was a very lucky man," agreed BRIDEGROOM with a half smile.

"What will they do now, Victor?" asked Tina, her voice reflecting her concern.

"Now we know that they operate with no constraints. They are capable of doing anything," answered BRIDEGROOM calmly. "But their failure to kill the man they thought was my informer may possibly have given them some second thoughts. I got that impression when I met with the Russian last night."

"How will that change things for us?" asked Nick, whose voice now reflected Tina's concern.

"I'm not sure it will change anything. But it may give us a little breathing room while they re-think their approach. In the long run, I expect them to become more demanding and harder to satisfy," replied BRIDEGROOM grimly. "They will be looking for specific information and they will expect proof." BRIDEGROOM paused and slowly rubbed his fingers back and forth across his brow before adding, "And now I am beginning to wonder whether they will try to force me into some kind of political action...perhaps to test me."

"How will you handle it?" asked Nick who was quietly rolling a cigarette.

"I'm not sure but this may be the beginning of the end of my relationship with the Russian," answered BRIDEGROOM before adding, as though thinking out loud, "We may be nearing the time to find out whether he will honor our original agreement that I could end our relationship if it did not work out after a reasonable test of time."

"So now you will find out if he is a man of his word," observed Nick with a skeptical smile.

"We seem to be headed in that direction," responded BRIDEGROOM warily.

"And your mother...what about her?" asked Tina. "Would she be in danger?"

BRIDEGROOM looked directly at Tina as he answered. "Tina, your concern for my mother means much to me. I wish I could tell you that nothing will change for her but I think the opposite is more likely. I don't think they will harm her physically but they will withdraw her medical support and end her ability to communicate with me." He smiled nostalgically before adding quietly, "Everything will be over."

"I'm sorry, Victor." Tina self-consciously brushed a tear from her eye as she spoke.

"Don't be upset, Tina. We'll work things out. We always do," assured BRIDEGROOM as he quickly regained his emotional composure. He then turned his wrist and checked his watch. "I'm afraid I'll have to leave in a few minutes to get back into the city for a meeting with Mr. Rogers. I know he'll ask about Popescu. Is there anything new there, Nick...any idea of when and where his ship might sail next?"

"Nothing yet," replied Nick. "But they should be leaving port soon. You can tell Mr. Rogers I'm watching every day."

BRIDEGROOM pushed himself to his feet with the effort of a man nearly drained of energy and walked slowly toward the door before hesitating and turning back to look at Nick and Tina. "I couldn't manage all that we are doing without your support. Thank you."

He opened the door and was gone.

※※※

BRIDEGROOM recognized Wagner's car as it slowed and pulled up to the curb to let him in. "Good evening, Mr. Rogers," greeted BRIDEGROOM as he ducked his head and squeezed into the passenger side.

"Hello, Victor. Glad to see you again," replied Wagner cordially. "We picked a good night to take a ride. There's a beautiful full moon. Before we go anywhere else, I'd like to drive past the Acropolis. It can be pretty spectacular on a night like this.

"I'd like that very much," responded BRIDEGROOM, pleased to discern a dimension in Wagner's makeup that he hadn't observed before.

Wagner drove a few blocks until he found a parking space with a clear view of the Acropolis in moonlight. Neither man spoke as they looked up at the majesty of the structures on the hill. Wagner had always imagined that under a full moon the marble of the Acropolis would sparkle with bright whiteness. Instead, he watched it glow with a warm blue-gray, the moonlight developing a variety of contrasting shadows and hues as it reflected on the tall pillars of the Parthenon and the stones of other structures, producing an overwhelming sense of permanence and strength.

"It hardly seems like a man-made structure," observed Wagner, finally breaking their silence. "Somehow one gets the feeling that it must be at least as old as the moon and the moonlight."

"I share the same feeling," agreed BRIDEGROOM quietly as Wagner turned the ignition key and they resumed their drive. In a few minutes they were passing the stadium and heading out of the city on the familiar road to Kifissia.

"Is there anything new developing with Popescu?" asked Wagner casually. "Any word yet on when we might get a chance for a second meeting?"

"No. There's nothing new to report. Nick thinks they should be sailing soon and wanted me to make sure you knew he was keeping an eye on things."

Wagner laughed and moved to a new topic. "Have you been keeping track of the Cyprus demonstrations?" he asked as informally as he might have asked for an opinion on the weather.

"Yes. Unfortunately, some of them have turned violent and caused a lot of needless damage and injuries," replied BRIDEGROOM.

"I know what you're talking about. I've watched a couple of demonstrations from a building where I could look down at the action in the streets. You can see how easy it is for a relatively few trouble-makers to manipulate the crowd and turn a peaceful demonstration into a riot. I think they are less concerned about union with Cyprus and more concerned with promoting their own political agenda," concluded Wagner.

"Who do you think they represent?"

"The Cyprus issue is made to order for the Communists. They can take advantage of all the political passion that revolves around union with Cyprus and re-direct it to serve their own purposes. The fact that the United States is not supporting the Greek position allows the Communists to capitalize on an under-current of anti-American sentiment that the American policy has created. Any wedge that can be used to undermine the relationship between Greece and the United States is a plus for their side. The Communists are using a different issue, but the same tactics, to try to gain political control in Italy."

"Do you think the trouble-makers are acting as individuals or are they taking directions?" asked BRIDEGROOM.

"That's a question we'd like to have answered," responded Wagner. "Maybe you can help us."

"I don't understand how," responded BRIDEGROOM hesitantly.

"We know the Russians are working hard to expand their political influence wherever they can. That probably includes trying to establish connections and build support in the émigré community. That may seem a little ironic since we are talking about the same people who, like you, were stripped of their property and pretty much forced out," continued Wagner.

"Then why do you think they would change their views?" asked BRIDEGROOM, uncertain where their discussion was heading.

"It's not that they would change their views. But it is hard to sustain passion over time. It's not that people don't care; it is simply that they grow tired, and when you are tired, it is tempting to compromise . . . to let the worst of the past fade from memory," replied Wagner.

"You may be right," agreed BRIDEGROOM warily.

"If we understand this, so do the Russians," observed Wagner. "So it's logical to think that they will be looking for someone of influence in the refugee community who could become their spokesman in a political crisis."

"Tell me, Mr. Rogers, do you have any reason to suspect that such a person exists?" BRIDEGROOM's quiet voice betrayed none of the fear that clutched at his stomach and his brain, ready to cry out. Has he brought me out here to accuse me...to tell me this is the end? Were the men in front of the Russian Embassy agents of the Americans? His mind raced from point to point like a spark dancing between live wires.

Wagner waited before replying . . . wanting to tell BRIDEGROOM the truth . . . to give him the facts about the bugging operation. But he knew he could not reveal the truth, even to an agent as reliable as BRIDEGROOM. "No, we have no reason to think the Russians have planted someone among the refugees. But we think they will try. So if you have the slightest reason for suspecting anyone, I want you to let me know immediately."

BRIDEGROOM suddenly felt exhausted, as though a plug had been released draining away his emotions. "I will keep on guard, Mr. Rogers. You can be sure of that."

"I know you will," said Wagner as he slowed the car, turned and headed back toward Athens. "That's enough business for today," he added with a smile. "Let's go back and enjoy what's left of the full moon."

CHAPTER EIGHTEEN

Well, Jack, it took a while, but there they go," observed Marcorelle with a satisfied smile as he and Wagner stood on the observation deck and watched Kostas lead his three agents across the tarmac toward the waiting Military Air Transport C-47 which had taxied to a stop a few minutes earlier. Without hesitating, they mounted the steps of the loading platform and entered the plane. They were followed by ten or twelve stragglers from the American Mission heading to Germany for a little rest and relaxation. Among them were four of Wagner's colleagues from the Athens Station.

"It looks like Kostas managed to get them on the plane without any problems," said Wagner as they watched the loading process continue. "I hope things go as well once they're in the air. Those three guys are emotional basket cases. I know Kostas is worried that they may cause trouble during the flight."

"Can he handle them alone?" asked Marcorelle calmly.

"Frankly, I don't think there will be a problem," replied Wagner. "But he won't be alone. Four of our guys are taking advantage of a free ride to Germany to do a little Christmas shopping. They know exactly what's going on and they'll step in if he needs help."

"I think you're probably right about not having any problems," agreed Marcorelle casually. "Those M.A.T.'s flights over the Alps can get a little bumpy. Those guys will probably be more concerned about keeping their stomachs settled than causing a commotion. There's nothing fancy about a ride in a C-47. Their job is to move stuff, including people . . . no frills. In fact, it's so close to the holidays, I wouldn't be surprised if they bring back a load of Christmas trees just to keep the folks in the American Mission happy," he added with a laugh.

"Roger, I don't know how you pulled this off, but finding a home for those three guys was a huge help," said Wagner as they turned to leave. "I hope we can find some way to make it up to you."

"Forget about it, Jack," responded Marcorelle with a dismissive wave of his hand. "This is just a temporary assignment for me but I've made some great friends in the few months I've been working with the Company, so I feel good about having a chance to do something useful."

"I can guarantee you've made my life a lot easier," laughed Wagner, before asking, "If you have time, do you want to grab a cup of coffee before we head back to work?"

"Sounds good to me. I could use one. Lead the way."

✤✤✤✤

Wagner felt a tug at his sleeve and looked down to see Dmitri.

"Hello, Mr. Jack. Where have you been? I've missed you."

"Hi, Dmitri. I've been pretty busy lately," replied Wagner as he tousled his young friend's hair. "I hope you have a few pistachios left for me."

"Right here," grinned Dmitri, handing a bag to Wagner and falling into step with him as Wagner headed to work.

"It's cold this morning," observed Wagner with a smile.

"It's almost Christmas," nodded Dmitri in agreement.

"Tell me, Dmitri. Is there anything special you'd like for Christmas?" asked Wagner casually.

Dmitri slowed his pace before quietly responding. "Nothing for me." He hesitated before adding, " But I wish I could get something for my brother. He's younger."

"How old?"

"Eight years old."

Wagner stopped and turned toward Dmitri. "What would you like to get him?" he asked.

"Some new shoes, but they are too expensive . . . almost three dollars."

"But what about your shoes?" asked Wagner.

"They are not important," replied Dmitri softly.

"They are to me," responded Wagner with a smile. "If you and your brother meet me right here on Saturday at 11:00 o'clock, we'll go to the shoe store together and then we'll have lunch."

"Are you sure, Mr. Jack?" asked Dmitri with a wide grin.

"I'm sure," laughed Wagner as he started to enter his office building, before turning back to Dmitri. "See you Saturday," he added with a reassuring wave.

****

Heidi looked up and smiled as Wagner approached her desk. "Mission accomplished?" she asked in a tone that conveyed both concern and curiosity.

"They're on their way," replied Wagner light-heartedly. "Assuming they land on schedule, Kostas should be just about ready to make the transfer and put an end to a potential operational debacle. He's going to be one happy guy to see the last of those three misfits."

"I'm glad for you and Henry will be relieved to hear the news. I'll let him know you're here," she said as she started to rise.

"Don't forget. We have a bridge match with the Fosters tonight. They take their game very seriously," joked Wagner.

"So do I," responded Heidi. "Don't worry. We'll give them all they can handle," she laughed. "I'm looking forward to the challenge."

"Come on in, Jack," said Ellis who was leaning comfortably back in his swivel chair. "Sounds like you've found yourself a professional bridge partner. Just remember, I saw her first and she's still my secretary," he observed with a wry smile that somehow conveyed his approval of their relationship.

"It didn't take me long to discover that this place is a hotbed of bridge fanatics," replied Wagner.

"Don't forget chess," added Ellis lightly. "But now that we've taken care of all the parlor sports, what's new?" he inquired casually.

"Let me give you the latest news first," began Wagner. "I met Roger Marcorelle at the airport this morning and watched Kostas and his three agents board the M.A.T.'s flight to Wiesbaden. There were no incidents in the boarding process and the flight left on schedule so it shouldn't be long before Kostas is making the formal transfer and we can close the books on that operation," concluded Wagner.

"Chalk one up on the plus side," commented Ellis approvingly. "As soon as we hear from Kostas, we can send the details to Headquarters. That throttles a ticking time bomb that never exploded, thanks in large part to Roger's help."

"Hank, now that we've closed out the operation, where does that leave Kostas?"

"He doesn't know it yet, but we have all the approvals we need to send him to Washington to begin the fast track to U.S. citizenship."

"That's great news. He's earned it."

"When he gets back from Germany, you may be the one to give him the good news. I'll let you know," continued Ellis.

"I'd consider it a privilege," responded Wagner. "He's an exceptional person."

"What else do you have on your docket?' asked Ellis.

"I had a chance to talk to BRIDEGROOM the other night to discuss the possibility that the Russians might be trying to penetrate the émigré community. He was skeptical at first but agreed that it was a possibility and promised to watch for any indication that they may be trolling in that area. I told him to mention anything that looks out of the ordinary, no matter how trivial it might seem. I'm certain he'll keep his eyes open," concluded Wagner.

"There's not much else you can do but at least we know he'll be sniffing around. Maybe he'll surprise us," laughed Ellis, before asking, "How's our friend, Popescu?"

"You must have read my agenda," joked Wagner. "Actually, it looks like his ship will be visiting Istanbul within the next couple of weeks. We don't have fixed dates yet and it may be a short visit but it will give us a chance to see if we can make even a brief contact with him."

Ellis casually rearranged a few papers on his desk before responding to Wagner's report. "What are your plans? Have you given the Istanbul Station a heads-up?", he asked matter-of-factly.

"No. This is new information and I wanted to run it by you before firming up a plan."

"What are your thoughts?"

"If the ship is only going to be in port for a day or two, the chances are slim to none that we can isolate him from the rest of the crew for a one-on-one meeting. We won't have Nick to run interference for us . . . at least, not in Istanbul."

"So where does that leave us?"

"We'll have to find out whether our back-up plan works. That means we have to identify him when the crew goes ashore. And it means he has to break away and find the post office for a possible contact. It would be a lot easier if the ship was coming back to a Greek port," responded Wagner.

"What about you?" asked Ellis.

"I think I should be there. I'm pretty sure I'd be able to spot him when the crew leaves the ship. It would be hard for someone from the Istanbul Station to identify him based only on a photograph."

"I agree," said Ellis.

"If he is able to make it to the post office and it looks secure, then I think I should meet him. He knows me and I think it would re-assure him and it's possible, even in a brief meeting, that we might accomplish something. But if there is any hint of a security problem, then we'll have to use someone else to play the role of a lost tourist." Wagner looked across the desk at Ellis and raised his hands to invite a reply, before adding, "Those are my thoughts at this point."

"Unless the itinerary or time frame changes, we really don't have any other choices and I think you're right to plan on being there," agreed Ellis, who then asked, "What happens if we can't make any contact with him?"

"I suppose the best we can hope for is that he will use our mail drop," answered Wagner.

"Istanbul is in the dark on this operation," began Ellis, "so put together a background report and let them know we'll need their help. I'd like to see it before you send it," concluded Ellis as he stood up signaling the issue was settled and their meeting was over. He followed Wagner through the door to Heidi's desk where he stopped and pointed a finger at the two of them. "Don't be too hard on the Fosters tonight. They're friends of mine," he said with a mischievous smile.

CHAPTER NINETEEN

"I didn't know my reward for getting dealt winning cards last night was going to be an invitation for morning coffee at the Grande Bretagne," laughed Foster. "Kathy and I had a great time. Heidi is no slouch at bridge and we really enjoy her company. You're lucky to have found her for a partner."

"I know I am," smiled Wagner, before asking, "How about Kathy? Have the doctors set a due date yet?"

"About three weeks," responded Foster.

"I get the impression that most of the American wives fly to Tripoli to give birth at the Naval Hospital there," commented Wagner.

"You're right about that but Kathy has opted to stay in Athens and have our baby at the Alexandra Maternity Hospital. We've found a well-regarded Greek obstetrician and have begun the transition from our local Navy doctors who have been handling her pre-natal care. So far, things are going smoothly. By the way, the local Navy doctors are all good friends and Company cleared. They've been great," concluded Foster as a waiter refilled his coffee cup.

"That's good news. It will give Heidi and me a chance to visit the hospital and see Kathy and your new addition," said Wagner, before pausing and asking, "What's happening on the Cyprus front? The demonstrations seem to be heating up."

"It's not getting any better. The U.S. has made it clear we won't support the Greek position at the United Nations and that has created a lot of anti-American passion. You've seen the demonstrations in Athens but there have been some pretty nasty riots in Salonika and Patras with significant property damage and a lot of injuries. I think the majority of informed Greeks understand the American position. But our friends on the far left are having a field day," Foster smiled and sipped his coffee. "I don't think things are going to improve. My guess is that there will be some form of confrontation before this thing is resolved."

"A confrontation between Greece and Turkey?" asked Wagner.

"That's probably how it will play out. We just have to work hard to make sure things don't get completely out of hand," concluded Foster before asking, "How about you? Anything new on your end?"

"Nothing dramatic to report," replied Wagner. "We're still trying to find the activate switch for one promising operation. I have a meeting with Hank a little later on. The political landscape is changing in our area. It's just a matter of time before we'll see trade missions arriving and eventually a resumption of diplomatic relations with Romania. It's hard to say what that will mean for us."

"I think it will mean you will have plenty to keep you busy." Foster pointed to the clock over the entrance to the lobby. "It's almost time for me to punch in for work," he joked. "Thanks for the coffee and say 'hi' to Heidi. Tell her we're ready for a re-match whenever you two finish licking your wounds."

"That should be enough incentive for her," laughed Wagner as they walked toward the door together.

***

"Come on in, Jack. Heidi has already told me you got your head handed to you last night," joshed Ellis as Wagner entered his office.

"You've got it all wrong, Hank. It was no blowout. Bob got lucky with his last hand," responded Wagner. "But I took it like a man and bought him coffee this morning."

"Well, at least he knows you don't bear grudges," laughed Ellis, before casually asking, "Do you have anything else to report besides bridge scores?"

"You wanted to see the draft of the briefing report on Popescu before it gets sent to Istanbul," answered Wagner as he passed it across the desk to Ellis.

Ellis had already begun reading Wagner's report when his telephone began to ring. "Excuse me, Jack." Ellis lifted the receiver and answered, "4-3-7-2."

Wagner listened to Ellis repeat his own telephone number rather than identify himself by name, a security ritual faithfully followed, though no one had ever successfully explained what that particular bit of coyness was supposed to accomplish.

"Hi, Bill . . . sure I've got a minute. What kind of earth-shattering news do you have?" asked Ellis, obviously recognizing the voice on the other end. As he listened, Ellis' expression changed. He looked across at Wagner with a quick movement of his eyes that managed to convey the importance of the message he was hearing. "What?" he asked incredulously. "Right . . . no, you're coming through perfectly. Can you make it over here in a half hour? Good. Jack is here now and I'll round up a few others before you get here. Thanks for the call."

Ellis smiled to himself as he put down the phone. "This is an unpredictable business. You never know what's going to turn up . . . or for that matter . . . when it's going to turn up."

"Who was it?" asked Wagner.

"Tommaney."

"Sounds like he's got something cooking."

"It looks that way," replied Ellis. "You remember the Soviet agent we've been trying to identify?"

"Yes."

"Well, they've picked up a lead on the monitor. Bill thinks he may know when and where the Russians are planning their next meeting with him."

Wagner whistled softly. "Is he coming over?"

"He'll be here at 10:30 to fill us in on the details. If his briefing is as convincing as his telephone double-talk, we'll have to start thinking about setting up a stakeout. I want you here when he comes."

"I wouldn't want to miss it," said Wagner as he got up to leave.

"When you go by Reedy's office, tell him I want him here too."

"Right."

"Oh, Jack, by the way," said Ellis, holding up Wagner's draft report to Istanbul, "I'll look this over and make sure Heidi gets it off in the next pouch. She'll have a copy for your files."

****

Tommaney had prefect teeth that highlighted the triumphant grin he wore as he stood in the doorway of Ellis' office. "Hello, Henry," he said with a good-natured wave. Then he looked slowly around the room at the others. "Now maybe I'll get you bastards off my back," he chided, holding up the soiled manila envelope he had brought with him.

"It's about time you came up with something. We've chased enough of your false alarms," retorted Hegarty with mock disgust.

"Throw that guy out so we can have a serious meeting, will you, Hank," responded Tommaney.

"Come on in and sit down," laughed Ellis, who, like the others, was enjoying the banter.

Tommaney strode into the room, nodding greetings like a candidate for office. He was tall with dark wavy hair and a strikingly handsome face. But when he walked, he bent his head slightly forward as though the ceiling were a few inches too low. After he had settled comfortably in the chair Ellis had reserved for him on his own right, he looked out at the other case officers seated around the room and with a sweeping motion of his hand said, "Gentlemen . . . fire away."

Ellis spoke first. "By now, I think most of you have heard . . . either directly or from scuttlebutt . . . that Bill's section has had the Soviet Embassy bugged for several months. Some of you may also know that this op has produced some first-rate C.E. material. To be specific, we have been able to identify . . . positively identify . . . the Soviet I.S. chief in this country and we have confirmed the identities of several other members of the embassy staff whom we had suspected were involved with espionage. Now none of us are surprised that they are running ops out of the embassy. That's S.O.P. for both sides. But it makes life a little easier when we know what they are doing and which locals they are using." Ellis leaned forward and added matter-of-factly, "That's why we're all here." Then he turned to Tommaney. "Bill, do you want to fill in the details?"

"Sure," agreed Tommaney. "Most of you guys know we've had Ivan plugged in for better than six months." He hesitated for a moment and added wryly, "I'm sure I don't have to mention what an outstanding piece of intelligence work that represents."

"You must have brought in ringers from Washington to do the job for you," gibed one of the other case officers.

"I had hoped that in something as important as this you men would rise above your usual sour grapes attitude. But what else can I expect from a bunch of Philistines?" said Tommaney disapprovingly. Then, as though deciding that the jesting had gone on long enough, he took some papers out of the envelope and said, "Seriously . . . this has been a good operation. I brought a transcript of some of the conversations we've monitored." He turned to Ellis. "I'll leave them with you. You will probably want to review them later with some of these fellows."

"Thanks," replied Ellis, sliding the papers onto his desk.

"Now the transcript I just gave Hank deals primarily with one situation. I think Jack and one or two others here already know at least something about it. Am I right, Hank?"

"Yes. Wagner, Hegarty and Reedy."

"O.K. Well, for four or five months we've been picking up snatches of conversation that indicate the Russians are working a local agent who seems to have some high-level contacts. And we've been able to figure out that he is being run out of the embassy by the Second Secretary, Golnikov. All of this stuff, or course, has been pieced together over a period of time. You know . . . the Russians don't always talk in the rooms we've got bugged and a lot of the time the reception has been so poor that we just couldn't figure out what they were saying. So until now, we haven't had anything really solid to go on. But last night they got a little careless and if we are guessing right, we think we know when and where Golnikov is going to meet his agent.

We're not certain . . . but we think it will be tomorrow afternoon around five o'clock."

"Where?" asked Ellis.

"Green Park."

"Shit. If anyone else starts using that place for meetings, we'll have to start calling in advance to make reservations," laughed Hegarty.

"Is there anything in the transcript to indicate whether they are going to meet inside the park or whether it is going to be a pickup on the outside?" asked Ellis.

"No. We think it was Golnikov talking and he just said he was going to meet the agent 'at the park'," answered Tommaney.

"But was five o'clock specific?" asked Wagner.

"Yes."

"That means it is going to be dusky . . . particularly if the weather is poor," said Ellis.

"We're lucky they are giving us any daylight," responded Tommaney. "If Golnikov were working for me, I'd can him."

"We'll find out how lucky we are tomorrow," replied Ellis casually. He picked up the pages of the transcript and off-handedly scanned them before looking up and adding, "By now I think you've all figured out that we are going to stake out Green Park tomorrow to see if we can identify their agent. We are going to cover the park inside and outside. I've already asked Bill to see what kind of help he can give us with photographic surveillance and I've arranged to have four cars with local plates available so that we can cover all three entrances and rotate a fourth car. We'll have to key in on Golnikov because he is the one we know. You'll all be getting some blown-up shots of Golnikov to study before tomorrow."

"Are we cutting the locals in on this?" asked Reedy.

"No. This is strictly our operation and we don't want it blown," answered Ellis. "That also means we can't afford to act like an invasion force around the park tomorrow. I want the cars rotating, with one car pulling completely out of the area every fifteen minutes. And I only want three men inside the park itself. Jack will be responsible for the taverna on the fringe of the park. Tom, you'll handle the promenade. O,K.?"

"Right," replied Reedy.

"And Heg, you'll cover the interior of the park, including the section near the Imperial Boulevard entrance."

"O.K.," responded Hegarty.

"You'll all be getting maps of the entire neighborhood around the park and Bill's section is going to blow up an aerial photograph of the park itself so that you can familiarize yourselves with the complete layout." Ellis turned to Tommaney. "How long before they will be ready?"

"You should have everything in about an hour."

"Good," Ellis pushed his chair away from his desk and stood up. "All right, that's it for now. You can pick up all the material and photos from Heidi before noon. Look them over. I want to see you all again at three o'clock. And before you go . . . remember to keep this meeting to yourselves."

CHAPTER TWENTY

BRIDEGROOM sat on the edge of his bed fumbling with the buttons on his pajamas. When he finally unsocketed the last button, he reached toward the night table and turned the face of a loudly-ticking alarm clock so he could see it. It was four o'clock. He had been asleep for an hour. Now it was time to get ready. But for a few minutes, he just sat there, slowly rubbing his hand back and forth across the soft flesh of his stomach, re-gathering thoughts that had been eased out of his mind during the short siesta.

Finally he stood up, dropped his pajama tops on the bed and walked across the room to a marble-top bureau. He poured some water from a pitcher into a large glass basin and bent over to wash his face. The cold water seemed to refresh him and he began to move more quickly. He took a shirt off the back of a chair where he had hung it earlier. Then he lifted up his mattress and removed his trousers, slowly examining the crease before he put them back on.

When he finished dressing, he picked up the report he had prepared for Golnikov which was lying on a plain wooden table among an assortment of books and political periodicals. As he re-read the report, he sipped from a half-filled cup of cold coffee that he had abandoned before his siesta. His concentration was only slightly disturbed by the anguished rattle from the motor of an ancient refrigerator which was wheezing like an asthma patient in a nearby corner.

After studying the paper for a few more minutes, he replaced the cup on the table and carefully folded the report. With a sigh of resignation, he slid it into his pocket, wondering how long it would keep the Russian satisfied this time. Then, as though deciding there was no point in further reflection, he stepped into the bathroom, lifted the toilet seat and urinated noisily. On the way out of the bathroom, he reached behind the door and took his topcoat off the hook. He knew it would be cold in Green Park.

＊＊＊＊

One by one Wagner took a last look at each photograph before he slipped it into the folder. But the last look was hardly necessary. He would recognize Golnikov anywhere on sight. And he had memorized the location of every path and bench inside the park and every street and bus stop in the surrounding neighborhood. When he dropped the last photograph into place, he gave the file drawer a gentle push and listened to it skid over the rollers and click shut.

"What's the matter . . . didn't he pay his light bill?"

"No . . . that's not it. He's just trying to accustom his eyes to the dark so when we get to the park, he can upstage us and steal all the glory."

Wagner looked around and saw Hegarty and Reedy standing in his doorway. It was only then that he realized how dark his office had become during the past few minutes. "When are you two guys going to give up that vaudeville routine and begin doing a little serious work around here?" laughed Wagner.

"He's an insulting son-of-a-bitch, isn't he?" retorted Reedy. "Maybe we should make him walk."

"How are you doing, Jack?" asked Hegarty easily as he and Reedy entered the office. "About ready?"

"Just about. How are you planning to get there?"

"Driving part way. Then we'll leave my car and go our separate ways. Thought you might like a lift."

"Sure," replied Wagner. "Just say the word when you're ready."

Reedy looked at his watch. "I suppose it's about that time," he said. The he half pointed toward the window and added, "You know . . . by five o'clock it's going to be murky as hell in that park."

"Well, with a little luck, maybe that Russian agent will turn out to be the Prime Minister which will make our job easy," commented Hegarty wryly.

"Assuming the Russian shows up at all. Which may be a long shot in itself," said Wagner as he walked to the coatrack, "I think the only way we are going to identify the agent is by tailing him after he leaves the park."

"I hope you brought your sneakers, Tom," quipped Hegarty.

"Never go anywhere without them."

"It's nice to know you guys come prepared for emergencies," said Wagner joshingly. "Now what about that ride?"

"We're all set, Jack," said Hegarty, tossing his car keys into the air. "Let's go."

****

Golnikov waited until the young woman in the very tight slacks who had just crossed the street from the American PX pulled out. Then he nosed his car into the space she vacated. The shops had just re-opened but the traffic was unusually heavy. He would have to hurry to be on time.

He glanced into his rearview mirror and waited for a motor scooter to flit past. Then he cautiously opened the car door and stepped out onto the street. After looking carefully both ways, partially to avoid accident but mainly to re-assure himself that he was not being followed, he thrust his hands deeply into his overcoat pockets and disappeared into the crowd on the sidewalk.

Golnikov walked quickly but inconspicuously among the late afternoon shoppers. His wide-brimmed hat was pulled squarely across his forehead and his dark double- breasted overcoat was too big for his frame. He looked more like an under-paid store clerk on an errand for his employer than the Second Secretary of an Embassy.

He walked without hesitation until he reached the entrance to a busy arcade which formed a passageway to the next street.

Then he stopped long enough to take a quick backward glance before turning in. Slowly he picked his way through the knots of people milling about in all directions in front of the shops that lined the enclosure.

When he emerged on the other side, he immediately hailed a cab. "Where to?" asked the driver as Golnikov slid in and slammed the door. Golnikov looked at his watch. He had planned to take a taxi part of the way and later switch to a bus. But now there was not time for an elaborate security routine and furthermore, he felt certain no one had followed him.

He settled back in his seat and reached for a cigarette. "Imperial Boulevard," he said. Then he added, "You can stop near Green Park."

****

Only bent old men with nowhere left to go walked slowly . . . their gnarled hands behind their backs working the beads of their kombaloya as though they were saying rosary. Everyone else moved quickly, using the paths through the park as nothing more than short cuts. It was nearly January, far too cold and too early for thoughts of the transition from coffeehouses and tavernas to sidewalk tables and park benches.

Wagner had been in the park for about ten minutes and had spent that time casing the area around the pavilion. In the beginning, he had worried mainly about the danger of being seen by Golnikov. But now the afternoon sun had withdrawn and left behind a pall of grey and for the first time, he began to consider the possibility that it might be he who would fail to recognize Golnikov. His concern was unnecessary.

It was almost five o'clock when he spotted Golnikov walking rapidly along a path leading toward the glassed-in pavilion. Wagner watched him make his way among the rows of deserted tables, reminders of the summer season past when the warm night air echoed the sound of bazooki music. There was no hesitation in Golnikov's stride as he mounted the few steps to the pavilion and stepped through the door.

Wagner waited until Golnikov was completely out of sight

before he started after him. He moved quickly, tracing Golnikov's route past the empty stage and among the deserted tables. As he approached the door, he heard the sounds of voices and music filtering through the flimsy glass panels that had been installed for temporary protection against cold weather. He knew from the volume of noise that it was crowded inside.

Wagner felt the door stick as he gripped the knob and pulled. Finally it yielded and jerked open. He stepped inside and found himself staring into a haze of blue tobacco smoke which hung like ground fog over the dozens of crowded tables that jammed the floor. The room was swollen with an impossible confusion of noises. Loud political arguments. Scraping chairs. Clinking glasses. Shouting backgammon players slamming table tops. The hum of a hundred conversations. All this accompanied by a three-piece bazooka band.

Wagner stepped back against the wall to let a busboy edge past. As he moved, his eyes scanned the room, searching for Golnikov. For a moment, he felt the sudden grab of panic . . . the fear that he had let him get away. Then he saw him, methodically pushing his way among the tables at the far side of the room, moving slowly in the direction of the only other exit. Is it already over, thought Wagner? Could I have missed the contact? He watched Golnikov steadily working his way toward the door. Golnikov had not been out of his sight more than two or three minutes. But that's enough time to make contact with a live-drop, thought Wagner, suddenly struck with the fearful realization that he had lost control of his assignment.

Wagner began to make his way slowly along the narrow corridor between the wall and the outer-most tables. There was nothing left to do except continue to follow Golnikov and hope he had not met his agent. But as Golnikov neared the door, Wagner saw him stop, nod perfunctory recognition to someone sitting at a corner table, and sit down.

Wagner eased his way through the crowd toward an unoccupied chair at a table not far from where Golnikov was sitting. A wizened old man with a white handle bar mustache looked up but said nothing when he sat down. Wagner ordered a coffee and glanced around the room. There was nothing to indicate that anyone else was even remotely interested in Golnikov's presence.

From where he was sitting, it was impossible to see the face of the other person at Golnikov's table but Wagner decided against the risk of trying to move closer. Golnikov's agent had chosen a table near the wall and both men were sitting at an angle so that only their backs were visible to most people in the room. It was difficult to judge how much they were saying to one another.

A waiter brought Golnikov a drink. Wagner watched him drop a bill on the tray and wave the waiter off when he began to make change. Golnikov slowly picked up his glass and took a sip of the drink. Then he turned and said something to the other man, as though he were asking him a question. The other man nodded, reached for a newspaper which was lying on the table in front of him and handed it to Golnikov.

For several minutes Golnikov held the newspaper in his hand pretending to read while he finished his drink. But Wagner noticed that he didn't unfold it or open it up to look at the inside pages. Finally, Golnikov put down his glass and slid it across the table. Then he leaned toward the other man and spoke to him for just a few seconds. When they had finished talking, Golnikov stood up and casually rebuttoned his overcoat. Without looking back at the other man, Golnikov headed toward the exit. The newspaper was still in his hand when he went through the door.

After Golnikov left, Wagner's first impulse was to move closer so that he could get a clear look at the other man's face. But he knew if he did this, he would risk arousing suspicion and perhaps wreck any chance for an effective surveillance. He decided to wait for the agent to make the first move, knowing that he probably was delaying his own departure only long enough to give Golnikov time to get away from the park. Wagner's guess was right. After a few minutes, the man at the other table pushed back his cuff and looked at his watch. Then, apparently satisfied that he had waited long enough, the man stood up and disappeared through the door.

Almost before the agent was out of sight, Wagner was on his feet moving after him. It was dark now but the paths and scrubs around the pavilion were bathed in a dull glow of light reflecting through the grimy glass panels. Wagner quickly spotted the solitary figure of the agent walking toward the exit that led out to Imperial Boulevard.

The agent walked steadily with Wagner keeping pace about fifty yards behind. The air was cool and clean. It was the kind of night when even the slightest sound seemed to echo with an inexplicable clarity. Wagner's brain was wound tight with anticipation.

As they moved farther away from the pavilion, the path reassumed its characteristic mantle of darkness and the Russian agent became a shadow lost among other shadows. The agent had only a few more yards to go before reaching the sidewalk. Wagner knew that if a car or a cab were waiting, the agent could be gone before there was a chance to follow. Unconsciously Wagner began to walk faster . . . slowly closing the gap between him and the man he was pursuing.

As they neared the boulevard, the undertone of traffic sounds grew stronger like a crescendo of music before the curtain rises. Then, for just an instant, the agent stepped through the brief trough of light that lay between the park and the boulevard. Within a moment, he again had passed out of sight. But during that moment when the agent's figure was in view, Wagner was struck with a disquieting sense of recognition. Somewhere . . . sometime . . . he had seen the same man before.

Wagner hurried after him . . . almost running . . . hoping that one of Ellis's cars would be stationed outside so that he could follow if the man took a taxi. When he reached the archway leading out of the park, he slowed down and stepped cautiously through onto the sidewalk. He spotted the agent almost immediately, walking flat-footedly toward a brightly lit kiosk about thirty yards from the entrance to the park.

Now there was no question of doubt. Wagner was certain he recognized the choppy stride of the Russian agent. But who was he? And where had he seen him before? He racked his brain for the answer. By now the agent had reached the kiosk where he stopped and bought a newspaper. Then he turned slowly and stepped to the curb, waving his hand for a taxi. And for the first time, Wagner saw the agent's face.

It was as though he had just been informed of a death in his family. His brain spun in disbelief. It can't be possible, he thought. He looked again, desperately hoping he had made a mistake. But his eyes had not lied. He watched with stunned detachment as a taxi pulled up and the agent opened the door and stepped inside.

Almost before the taxi had a chance to shift from first gear, Tommaney's car skidded up to the curb. "Hey, Jack, hop in." Wagner reacted to reflex and slid in beside Tommaney. "Was that the guy?"

"Yes," answered Wagner, reaching for a pack of cigarettes that Tommaney had left on the dashboard.

"Well, let's go!"

"Don't bother."

"Why? Do you know him?"

"Yes. I know him."

"Who the hell is he?" asked Tommaney impatiently.

"He's one of my agents," replied Wagner. Then he added bitterly, " . . . BRIDEGROOM."

"Holy Mother of God!" exploded Tommaney in amazement. "That hurts."

"You're damn right it hurts," said Wagner, struggling to sound unperturbed. But even as he remained outwardly calm, his mind was churning crazily with dozens of separate thoughts. Thoughts about himself and his job . . . about his relationship with Ellis. And what about Washington? Where would he stand back there after this? But his brain kept returning to BRIDEGROOM . . . to the incredible fact of BRIDEGROOM's betrayal. He was almost consumed by an overwhelming surge of anger and resentment that he had put his confidence in a man to whom country and ideals and loyalty meant nothing.

Tommaney had swung his car back into the current of traffic and had driven for several blocks in respectful silence. But now as he stopped for a streetlight, he turned and said, "Well, the day's work is done. I suppose we might as well get back to the shop and make our report."

Wagner took a deep drag on his cigarette and slowly exhaled the smoke. "Sure, Bill. Let's get it over with."

CHAPTER TWENTY-ONE

"It looks as though we got our ass fried on this one, huh, Jack?" Paul Christopher was noted for his direct approach, a style that had promoted rather than retarded his quick rise to Chief of Station. Now, still only forty-three, he was mid-way through his second three-year tour and generally conceded to be headed for bigger things in Washington.

"Incinerated is the word," laughed Wagner ruefully.

"Well, I don't like to be taken any more than the next guy. But this isn't the first time it's happened. And you can be damn sure it won't be the last," responded Christopher with characteristic self-assurance as he shoved aside the report he had just finished reading.

Christopher made no attempt to push the blame on to anyone in particular. That was not the way he operated; which probably explained why he commanded strong staff loyalty. Yet, in spite of Christopher's generally sympathetic attitude, Wagner could not escape the feeling that they were all there specifically to pick his chestnuts out of the fire. And things would never be quite the same again. He no longer was one of the golden boys. No one had to explain that to him. He could sense it in the air. Now he had had his flap . . . the flap that he once thought only happened to the other guy. It would take a while to get used to the change.

Like most staff meetings in Christopher's office, this one was small. Besides Christopher and Wagner, only Ellis, Tommaney and the Deputy Chief of Station, Carl Burns, were present. Burns, who was one of those soft, pink-skinned men who at fifty still look like they have never shaved, was sitting in his customary position of rank, doodling on a clipboard as though to avoid looking the others in the eye. The others were sitting in a semi-circle in front of Christopher's desk.

"I suppose," said Christopher stretching back in his chair, "that since we're in this thing up to our necks, the problem is to figure a way to get out of it."

"I'm not too sure we ought to get out of it," answered Ellis casually.

"Why not?" snapped Christopher. "You don't have any doubts that it was BRIDEGROOM that Jack saw with Golnikov, do you?"

"No, I'm absolutely positive it was BRIDEGROOM," interjected Wagner quickly.

"Well, then?" asked Christopher impatiently rubbing a small bald spot on the back of his head.

"Look, Chris," replied Ellis calmly, "at this point we really don't know where we stand with BRIDEGROOM."

"Oh, come on now, Henry," said Burns petulantly. "You can't be serious. You've heard Bill's tapes. Let's face it . . . the Russians own your agent lock, stock and barrel."

"Maybe they do and maybe they don't," said Tommaney stepping in on Ellis' side.

"What's your point, Hank?" asked Christopher skeptically.

"Just this," answered Ellis. "Let's grant that he's working for the Russians. Well . . . who got to him first? Did we? Or did they? Or is he a freelance . . . working for everybody? We simply don't know." Ellis hesitated as though to let what he had just said sink in. Then he continued. "And we shouldn't overlook the possibility that he's a Soviet double agent. And what if he is? It seems to me we ought to give some thought to doubling him back. After all, we're in a position to turn the screws a hellova lot tighter than the Russians. All it would take would be one word from us to the locals and he'd be out of business permanently. I have an idea BRIDEGROOM is smart enough to understand that kind of message."

"O.K., Hank, what do you have in mind?" asked Christopher.

"I think we ought to lay our cards on the table. Let's find out just how much of a hold the Russians have on him. Then if we decide we can play him back against Golnikov, we will at least have managed to salvage something out of the operation."

Christopher stuck his finger inside the back of his collar and slid it slowly along his neck as though he were trying to fish out the right answer. Finally he turned to his deputy. "Carl?" he asked.

Burns, who had been staring at the ceiling as though it were about to collapse, stroked his chin meditatively before answering. "Do you think Washington would go along?"

"Why don't we let Washington worry about that?" snapped Christopher curtly. "Hank, I'm tempted to give you a shot at it," he said, again addressing himself to Ellis. "But the answer has to be no . . . for several reasons. In the first place, we have to know when to cut our losses. And in this business once an agent goes sour, there is only one thing you can do. Get rid of him."

"Amen," said Burns emphatically.

Christopher winced and continued. "Secondly, before we decide to play back an agent against the Russians, we'd better have a pretty good idea of what we expect to get out of it. And to be perfectly blunt, I don't think there is very much in it for us." Ellis was about to break in, but Christopher held up his hand. "Now before you give me an argument, Hank, let me say this. I'll grant you there is always room for improvement. But as things stand . . . and I mean right at this minute . . . our coverage of the Russians isn't too bad. And the kind of operation you're suggesting generally spells problems. Look at it this way. If we decided to use BRIDEGROOM as a double, then we'd have to assign somebody to prepare feed for the Russians just to keep them happy. That could tie a man up that we could use somewhere else. Now in some cases that would be O.K. But in this case, we'd be dealing with an agent who already has gone bad once. How much faith would you want to put in what he told you? I'll tell you I'd have damn little confidence in what he had to say. So let's forget it. We've got headaches enough."

"Here, here," said Burns approvingly.

"I still think that we ought to hold off a final decision until Jack talks to BRIDEGROOM," persisted Ellis.

"I know how you feel, Hank. And you're right to argue your

point. But I want the operation scrubbed," responded Christopher firmly. Then he turned to Wagner. "When do you expect to see him?"

"Tomorrow afternoon."

"Then you're all set?"

"Yes . . . but what about Popescu?"

"Well, what about him?" snapped Christopher. Then, as though regretting the tone he had just used, he added quietly, "Jack, we're going to write off the whole operation . . . that includes Popescu, BRIDEGROOM and all his friends in the safe house. But when you talk to him, see if you can find out just what in hell he's been up to and what his ties are with the Russians. It doesn't make any difference to me what kind of threats you have to use to make him talk. It's all down the chute now anyway so we don't have a thing to lose by talking tough. That's probably the only kind of language he really understands."

"I'm looking forward to it," replied Wagner grimly. Then, turning to Ellis, "Hank, if anybody's got reason for wanting to pull a rabbit out of the hat on this one, I have. But when I think of the screwing he's been giving . . . not only us . . . but all of those poor bastards in the émigré community who have been looking to him for some kind of leadership, then I begin to think we ought to blow him to the local security people and let them do a number on him." Wagner paused and then added ironically, "Of course, I'll admit that's not a completely unbiased recommendation."

"You may be right," replied Ellis with an easy smile, "but I think it would be a good idea to get him off our payroll before we do him in. We don't want to forget that there is a lot he could tell our friends in the local security services that we might not be too happy to have them find out about."

"Well, unless someone else has something to say, as far as I'm concerned the matter is settled," said Christopher as he pushed himself back from this desk and stretched his long legs out in front of him.

"Almost . . . but not quite," broke in Burns reprovingly.

"Well, Carl, what do you have in mind?"

"Washington still doesn't know what's happened."

"O.K. Send them a cable. What's the problem?" asked Christopher impatiently.

Burns forced a laugh as though to indicate that he realized Christopher must have been joking. Then he said, "Chris, you know how Washington will react if we make too big a thing of this."

Christopher straightened up so that one hand was perched on the edge of his desk while the other gripped the arm of his chair as though he were planning to spring at his deputy. "I don't give a bureaucratic goddam how Washington reacts," he growled.

"Now don't misunderstand me . . . we all feel the same way you do." Burns nodded condescendingly toward the others as though certain they would approve of what he was about to say. "But I think we ought to go slow in the way we present this thing to Headquarters. We've got to remember that the middle of the Atlantic separates our point of view from Washington's." He paused to give his words a chance to penetrate. Then he continued, "I've always felt that as soon as someone gets halfway across, they suddenly forget what it's like to be under pressure in the Field. They no longer see Headquarters in terms of a support organization for field operations. Instead, they acquire all of the characteristics of armchair generals. They sit back there waiting for the Field to stub its toe so they can begin to analyze and pick us apart and inflate their own egos by pretending they are still in control. But I suppose that's just human nature," he concluded pompously.

"Well I'll be a sonofabitch," grinned Tommaney, "here we've got a philosopher in our midst and I didn't know it."

"I was simply stating a personal opinion, Bill. I didn't expect everyone to agree with it."

"Hell, Carl, I'm with you all the way," protested Tommaney lightly. "The less they know in Headquarters, the less they bother us."

"All right . . . now that we all understand the Washington psyche, let's get that cable off," commented Christopher dryly as he picked up a desk lighter and lit a cigarette.

"You're the boss, Chris," agreed Burns in the gracious tone of a man who knows he bears no responsibility for decisions . . . right or wrong.

Christopher watched with a wry smile as his deputy sat back and skinned the cellophane from a cigar. Burns was right of course. He possessed that unerring bureaucratic instinct for smelling trouble and for obscuring facts. But no one had to tell Christopher that Washington would be looking for an explanation for what went wrong with WEDDING PARTY. He looked across the desk at Ellis and asked, "Hank, will you and Jack work up a cable?"

"Sure. But I think it might be a good idea to give a little more consideration to Carl's point," answered Ellis with a half smile.

"This is beginning to sound like a conspiracy," replied Christopher good-naturedly.

"Not quite," laughed Ellis. "But no matter how we handle it, this is going to land like a bomb in Headquarters. I'm just suggesting that we restrict the cable to telling them we've terminated the operation and that the details have been pouched. With luck, they may leave us alone for a couple of days . . . long enough for Jack to get things straightened out with BRIDEGROOM.

"That's fair enough," responded Christopher. Then he turned to Tommaney who was slouched down in his seat. "How about you, Bill? You're usually good for an idea or two?"

"I was afraid you weren't going to ask," replied Tommaney with a straight face. "But now that you have . . . " He waited for the expected laugh, "I'll tell you what I'd do. I'd wait until we prepare the quarterly operational review . . . which will be in a couple of weeks . . . and somewhere around page twelve . . . after we tell them how much the rent has gone up on safe houses . . . I'd mention the fact that we decided to cut operational expenses . . . and that's how Headquarters would find out that our little operation is out of business. Now if somebody's got a better idea . . . ?"

"I think you'd better stick to bugging embassies," chided Christopher appreciatively. Then he stood up as though to signal that the meeting was over. "Hank, I'd like to see that cable as soon as you get it drafted."

"It won't take more than ten or fifteen minutes."

"Good." As he spoke, Christopher moved over to join Ellis and Wagner. "By the way, Jack. There is one thing I want you to understand. If I were presented with the same kind of operational situation again . . . the same risks . . . the same potential . . . I'd do exactly what we did. So don't let it bother you."

****

Swasey took a long drag and dropped his cigarette butt into the empty coffee container he was holding. He listened to it sizzle as it hit the dregs on the bottom of the cardboard cup and then he swung his feet off the top of the desk and reached for his phone. This was certain to be a good day.

As he dialed, he pushed at his cuff and glanced at his watch. They've had time enough, he thought. By now everyone in the Front Office has had a crack at it. While he waited for someone to pick up the phone in Cummings' office, he re-read the cable that was lying on his desk and smiled to himself.

STRONG EVIDENCE BRIDEGROOM UNDER
R.I.S. CONTROL. SCRUBBING OP.
POUCHING DETAILS.

"Swasey here," he said jauntily when he heard the phone click off the hook on the other end. "How are you, Tom? Have you seen it yet?" He tapped out another cigarette while he listened to the reply. Then he laughed easily. "I agree. It looks like they want to keep us in the dark. Well, you know how it is when you are in the Field." He flicked on his lighter and moved the flame toward the tip of his cigarette. "No . . . you're absolutely right . . . we can't operate without more information . . . let's get off a cable. Sure . . . I'll be right in."

CHAPTER TWENTY-TWO

There was a sharp chill in the air, the kind that creeps in with dusk. But the scene was familiar. Perhaps someday when this was all over Wagner would wonder why he chose to return to the National Gardens for his last meeting with BRIDEGROOM. Right now the reasons did not seem very important.

He walked in long purposeful strides . . . oblivious of the few idlers sitting on benches near the entrance to the park. At this point, he did not give a damn about surveillance or operational security. For the past two days his brain had been pre-occupied with rehearsing the final speech he was going to make to BRIDEGROOM. After the meeting in Christopher's office, Wagner's first thought had been to work out a quick, clean termination of his agent. But somehow in the interval subtle changes had taken place in his thinking. Initially he had tried only to anticipate BRIDEGROOM's reaction. Then slowly he began to create an actual dialogue. Until now this imaginary conversation had taken on a reality of its own and Wagner found himself locked in a bitter exchange with a straw man. By the time he turned the corner and spotted his agent, Wagner was seething with resentment.

He slowed down when he saw BRIDEGROOM. He had an unsettling feeling that he was looking at the old man on the bench for the first time. BRIDEGROOM's topcoat was buttoned at the neck and his collar was turned up against the late afternoon breeze. He had pushed one of his hands deep into his coat pocket. The other held a newspaper.

BRIDEGROOM was so intent in watching two grey squirrels

chasing each other around a tree that Wagner was almost on top of him before he looked up. "Squirrels are fascinating little creatures . . . sometimes I think they are more interesting than people," observed BRIDEGROOM quietly as he got off the bench.

Wagner glanced down at the squirrels and then back to BRIDEGROOM. "I suppose that might depend on the kind of people you happen to meet," he answered ironically.

BRIDEGROOM smiled the way an old man does when he knows a young man doesn't understand. "Yes, I suppose you are right."

They stood facing each other in the middle of the path. Wagner was bareheaded and his topcoat was unbuttoned so that the wind caught it every once in a while. BRIDEGROOM had turned down his collar as he stood up, as though out of deference to Wagner, but he still looked cold. "Is there something special?" he asked. "I hadn't expected your call."

Wagner knew intuitively that BRIDEGROOM was uneasy about the meeting and it made him feel good. The sense of anger which had been so strong only moments before was gone. Now he looked forward with pleasure to scraping BRIDEGROOM's nerves. "Yes, there is something I want to talk to you about," answered Wagner evenly without taking his eyes off the old man.

"Here?" asked BRIDEGROOM hesitantly.

Wagner unconcernedly scanned the area as though to indicate he saw nothing wrong with where they were. Then he pointed toward a path leading out to a side street. "Well, if you'd prefer, there's a coffee house over there. It might be a little warmer for you."

"Please . . . " protested BRIDEGROOM, "don't be concerned with my comfort. It's just that . . . well . . . we do not usually meet so openly." Wagner already had begun walking and BRIDEGROOM fell into place beside him as he spoke.

"Do you know yet when Popescu's ship will arrive in Istanbul?" asked Wagner, deliberately ignoring BRIDEGROOM's previous comment.

"Not yet," replied BRIDEGROOM in a tone that suggested

he was puzzled by Wagner's quick introduction of the Popescu operation into their conversation. "But I understand that it is important for you to know," he continued.

"Yes, it is important," responded Wagner noncommittally. By now they had reached the sidewalk. Wagner led the way across the narrow street and entered the coffee house. It was almost empty. He found a table and ordered two coffees. Then he laid his coat across the back of an empty chair and turned to BRIDEGROOM. "How do you feel about the Popescu relationship?" asked Wagner, carefully feeling for a reaction.

"I'm not quite sure I understand what you are asking," replied BRIDEGROOM quizzically.

"It will take a lot of time and effort to train Popescu to be a productive agent. Do you think we can trust him?" responded Wagner as he sipped his coffee with his eyes fixed on BRIDEGROOM.

"In what way?" asked BRIDEGROOM, sensing that Wagner was driving toward a particular point.

"We really don't know much about him or his politics," continued Wagner. "How can we be sure he's not a plant working for the other side? It won't be the first time that's happened," he added caustically.

"I have never met the man so it is hard for me to give you an answer. Nick knew him several years ago and feels sure that he opposes the Communists. I will point out that Popescu made no overt attempt to contact us. It was Nick who identified him and it was we who sought him out." BRIDEGROOM paused and looking across at Wagner, asked, "You have had a chance to meet him. What do you think?"

"I was impressed," answered Wagner calmly. "But when I think of how hard it is to recruit and train reliable agents inside Satellite Bloc countries, I begin to wonder whether it is time to change our strategy. I wonder whether we have been missing opportunities that are right in front of us."

"I'm afraid that decision is beyond my understanding or experience," said BRIDEGROOM with a smile of deference.

"We've working together a long time," responded Wagner. "By now we should be able to trust each other." As he spoke,

Wagner was examining the thick residue in the bottom of his cup. Then he looked up and motioned to the waiter for two more coffees. "You know, Victor, lately I've been thinking a lot about our operation." Wagner's words sounded much like an afterthought and BRIDEGROOM sat back visibly relaxed as though waiting to share an intimacy. "And I think maybe we've been too conservative."

"In what respect?" asked BRIDEGROOM.

"In the way we've been using you."

"You're not satisfied?"

"Quite the opposite, Victor. Frankly, I think we've under-estimated the full range of your talents."

"That is kind . . . but I am sure, not true," replied BRIDEGROOM with just the slightest trace of suspicion in his voice. "Still . . . if you feel there is something else I can do to help . . . "

"I think there is," responded Wagner, moving his chair so the waiter could deliver their coffee.

As the waiter moved away, BRIDEGROOM leaned toward Wagner, his forearm resting on the table. He said nothing but it was obvious from his expression that he was anticipating something unusual.

Wagner lit a cigarette and tossed the match on the floor. "You know . . . we spend a lot of time worrying about people like Popescu and most of the time nothing ever comes of them. And meanwhile we pass up golden opportunities right here in our own backyard." Wagner emphasized his remarks by tapping the table with the tip of his finger.

"Opportunities here?" asked BRIDEGROOM cautiously.

"Yes," replied Wagner, his eyes searching the face of the old man across the table, hunting for some clue of what was going on in his mind. Does he suspect I know about him, wondered Wagner. But even as he asked himself the question, a new wave of doubt flowed through his brain. How can I really be certain it was he I saw? His throat was dry. He picked up his cup and took a couple of swallows of coffee that had no taste. He knew he either would find out now or never know the truth.

BRIDEGROOM sipped his coffee and waited. But when he

heard Wagner's voice, he set down his cup and listened as though afraid he might miss a word. "Let me ask you something, Victor. Have you ever thought about how many Russians and Satellite Nationals there are here in this country?" Wagner did not wait for a reply. "One hundred? Two hundred? I don't know the answer myself. But I do know there are plenty . . . especially when you add in the trade missions. And almost any one of them could give us more information than ten agents like Popescu . . . if we could find some way to get to them." Wagner took a long drag on his cigarette. " That's where I think you should come in."

"In what way?" asked BRIDEGROOM soberly.

Wagner leaned forward and lowered his voice. "Look, until now we've done everything we could to keep you away from target country personnel because we didn't want you contaminated in the eyes of the local security people and we didn't want to risk your leadership in the émigré community."

"And you think that was wrong?"

"No . . . but situations change."

"And now?"

"Now I think you should try to establish contact with those people . . . try to gain their confidence . . . find out what you can about them. If there is a weak link among them, we want to know who it is and how to get at him." Wagner tried to sound self-assured but his temples were throbbing with tension. The urge to blurt out his accusation and have it done with was becoming almost irresistible. But he knew he had to go on playing the game until the old man stumbled into his trap . . . or escaped.

"You want me to break with my past?" asked BRIDEGROOM incredulously.

"No, of course not," answered Wagner with forced geniality. "I'm just saying that we have to recognize that people's attitudes shift with the passage of time. Things that bothered them last year may not seem very important today. So as long as you keep your contacts casual . . . as though they are part of your normal routine . . . nobody's going to pay much attention."

"Are you including local security in that statement?" asked BRIDEGROOM pessimistically.

"Yes . . . as long as you don't become obvious with what you're doing. Let's not make the mistake of inflating the problem. After all, in your position why isn't it perfectly natural for you to encounter Iron Curtain officials from time to time?" asked Wagner as he picked up his cup and sipped his coffee. Then he smiled and said, "In fact, I'd be a little surprised if you haven't already met a few of them." Wagner paused. He could feel BRIDEGROOM's eyes staring across the table but the old man remained silent. "You do know some of them, don't you?" prodded Wagner gently.

"I have always tried to follow your instructions and avoid contact," responded BRIDEGROOM quietly.

"You mean you never have met any of them?"

BRIDEGROOM shrugged and held out his hands. "I'm sorry," he answered like a man who had committed a blunder.

"That's strange," said Wagner dryly.

"Strange?" repeated BRIDEGROOM.

"Yes. You see . . . the other evening . . . " Wagner tilted his head and looked up at the ceiling as though trying hard to recall an almost forgotten incident. " . . . I think it was Thursday . . . I happened to be in Green Park . . . " He turned and saw a flash of panic in BRIDEGROOM's eyes. " . . . and I decided to have a coffee in the pavilion." Again Wagner waited, coldly appraising the old man on the opposite side of the table. " . . . I saw you there with the Russian . . . Golnikov." Wagner took a deep drag on his cigarette. "It wasn't the first time you've been seen with him."

For an instant, BRIDEGROOM's body went almost limp as though drained of its strength. He lowered his head and wearily rubbed his hand across his forehead. Then with what seemed an enormous physical effort, he pulled himself erect and raised his eyes to meet Wagner's accusing glare. "Then you know . . . " said BRIDEGROOM in a voice that fell soft as an ash.

"Yes, I know," sneered Wagner disgustedly. Until now, in spite of everything that had happened, Wagner had fed on the faint hope that BRIDEGROOM somehow would be miraculously vindicated. But now the enormity of the deception was clear beyond question. It was as though BRIDEGROOM had betrayed him a second time. Wagner was seized with an unreasoned sense of loathing toward the old man. He pushed aside his coffee and leaned across the table to get as close to BRIDEGROOM as possible. Then he whispered threateningly, " . . . and you're all done."

"I suppose you will report me to the police?" responded BRIDEGROOM in a matter-of-fact tone.

Wagner snorted bitterly. "What difference does that make to you?"

"I know you can't understand . . . but there are people who depend on me for . . . "

"What gives you the right to talk about obligations?" snapped Wagner angrily. "You don't know the meaning of the word loyalty. You've sold out . . . sold out your country . . . your friends . . . even your own mother . . . or have you got her working for the Russians, too?" Wagner spat out each word as though he were trying to rid his mouth of a foul taste.

"You said you knew what had happened. But it is obvious you do not." For a moment, BRIDEGROOM hesitated while his eyes carefully studied the younger man's face. Then . . . slowly . . . as though he now understood something that previously had eluded him, he added, "Still . . . how could anyone expect you to know?" There was no rancor in his voice . . . only a wistfulness . . . as though he were speaking to himself.

"Just how much do you think I have to know?" snarled Wagner sarcastically.

"Enough so you know the truth."

"Whose version?"

"Mine."

So you haven't given up yet, thought Wagner warily. A quizzical smile flickered on the corner of his mouth and he made a condescending motion with his hand for BRIDEGROOM to proceed.

"The truth, Mr. Rogers, is that I do not work for the Russians," replied BRIDEGROOM evenly.

Wagner reached for the ashtray and slowly ground out his

cigarette until the butt broke open in his fingers. It was a gesture of utter frustration. "Look . . . let's get something straight," said Wagner pointing menacingly at BRIDEGROOM. "I'm not here to negotiate with you. You've been passing information to the Russians . . . which is enough to land you in front of a firing squad. Right now I want to know what kind of information you've been giving them, how long you've been working for them and who you report to besides Golnikov. And if you take my advice, you'll tell me everything . . . because you're in trouble . . . a lot of trouble."

"The question is not whether I am prepared to tell you the truth. It is whether you are prepared to believe it," answered BRIDEGROOM coolly.

"Why don't you go ahead and try me," responded Wagner sharply.

"If you wish," replied BRIDEGROOM without emotion. But for a few moments he did not speak. Instead, he slowly rubbed his knuckles back and forth across his chin as though trying to decide not so much what to say to the angry young man who sat facing him, but how to say it. Finally he began. "I have been meeting the Russian . . . you already know his name . . . for six months . . . perhaps seven."

"And before then? Who did you see?"

"No one, Mr. Rogers. I saw no one. That is when it began," answered BRIDEGROOM calmly.

Wagner's mind raced to remember the date Ellis first had told him about the microphones in the Russian Embassy. What he says fits, he thought. But what does it prove except that we were right about him? Yet, in spite of BRIDEGROOM's obvious guilt, Wagner began to feel inexplicably uncomfortable in the old man's presence. It was that kind of disquietude a person experiences when they sense someone else possesses an insight they cannot share. Perhaps it was the almost undeniable note of credibility in BRIDEGROOM's response. Whatever it was, the urge to hear the old man was strong. But Wagner's fear of being made a fool was stronger. What the hell am I trying to do, he thought angrily, let the bastard suck me in again?

He pressed his hands against the edge of the table and sat

back and took a hard look at BRIDEGROOM as though to remind himself that he was dealing with a Soviet agent. "You must have your dates mixed up, Victor. Because you can't seriously be trying to tell me you had nothing to do with the Russians until seven months ago."

"But I am."

"That's a little hard to believe," replied Wagner acidly. "A man like you doesn't change overnight. No . . . they may have been keeping you inactive, but you've been on their side a lot longer than seven months."

"I think I know how you must feel. And you are right. Men don't change overnight. But try to understand this." BRIDEGROOM leaned forward, his eyes riveted on Wagner. "I do not deny that I have been seeing the Russians regularly. I felt I had no choice. But work for them?...forget what they did to my country? No, Mr. Rogers . . . never."

"You know, what you say has a familiar ring. We hear it all the time," answered Wagner sarcastically. "You say you had no choice. I think you just mean that you made the wrong one."

"Perhaps," replied BRIDEGROOM in a voice that was almost inaudible. Then he slowly began to unbutton the front of his topcoat which he had not taken off. Without saying anything more, he reached inside his jacket, took out a badly scuffed wallet and laid it open on the table. For a few moments he fumbled through its contents until he found what he was looking for. He unfolded the envelope and carefully withdrew the letter. Then after a moment of hesitation . . . as though wondering if he were violating a confidence . . . he handed it to Wagner. "This is a letter I received from my mother. It changes nothing . . . and it excuses nothing . . . but it may help you understand why I agreed to meet the Russian."

Wagner took the letter and began to read, skeptically at first, as though not willing to believe what his own eyes could see. Yet his brain could not erase the words . . . or their meaning. For just an instant, he glanced across the table at the old man, suppressing an urge to reach out, to offer him help. But he caught himself before he let his instincts override his judgment. Don't fall in love with your agent, he thought ironically as he recalled the classic admonition of seasoned case officers. And they are right. He could have shown me the letter in the first place. And if he were reliable, he would have.

"I'm sorry your mother is having difficulty," said Wagner impassively. "But you haven't helped her with what you have done. Now she's nothing but a pawn in their hands. The Russians have been using the same technique for years to get at people like you. They put pressure on through close relatives they can control. And they keep the pressure on, Victor. You have to keep doing what they tell you." Wagner still was holding the letter in his hand. "If I had seen this in the beginning, I could have helped you. Now it's too late."

"It was too late a long time ago," smiled BRIDEGROOM introspectively. "But I appreciate your concern for my mother."

"I wouldn't be doing what I'm doing if I weren't concerned about your mother and a lot of other people just like her," responded Wagner spontaneously. Then, embarrassed by his own sentimentality, he added sharply, "But we're not here to talk about that. Whatever your reasons, the fact remains that you have been working for the Russians. Now I have to know what you have told them . . . how much they know about us." Wagner paused and then said slowly, "I don't think I have to tell you that the best thing you can do now is to give us the whole story. Because we're going to check out everything you say . . . including this." Wagner folded BRIDEGROOM's letter and slid it into his own jacket pocket. "And if everything doesn't check out, there will be no way to help you." In spite of his words, Wagner's voice was strangely devoid of threat. It was more nearly the injunction of a wise counselor.

"I understand," said BRIDEGROOM quietly. "It is your job. But now at least you know why I acted as I did. And there is nothing left for me to conceal from you. So," he said, with a philosophic shrug, "I shall tell you everything that has happened since I first made up my mind to go to the Soviet Embassy . . . "

BRIDEGROOM began to speak . . . slowly at first, carefully picking his words, occasionally pausing and staring into space beyond Wagner as though struggling to reconstruct a particular event in his mind. Wagner listened in attentive silence, like a priest at a confessional, unconsciously tracing his fingers along the ragged scars that marred the surface of the shabby wooden table. When he looked up, it was only to study the old man's expression or to resolve a flickering doubt. BRIDEGROOM seemed to sense these moments and would stop and painstakingly repeat what he had just said. He omitted nothing . . . except to reveal the roles that Nick and Tina and Boris had played in carrying off the deception with the Russian.

Yet, Wagner knew almost intuitively that something had been left unsaid. And knowing this, it now was only a question of finding the missing pieces and of separating fact from fantasy. He looked across the table into the tired face of the old man sitting opposite him. It was inconceivable to think in terms of this old man outwitting Soviet Intelligence. Certainly they are no more willing to accept notional sources of information than we are, he mused. Then, like a dull pain, a new thought crept into his brain.

"How much do Nick and Tina know about this?" asked Wagner curiously.

"I tried not to involve them," replied BRIDEGROOM.

"But they know?" persisted Wagner.

"Yes."

"You didn't mention that."

"No. I didn't think it was important," answered BRIDEGROOM. Then he added quietly, "And in the beginning it was a personal affair."

"Are you sure that's the only reason?"

"What do you mean?"

"I think you know what I mean."

"Is there something in particular you want me to say, Mr. Rogers?' asked BRIDEGROOM in a voice that was flat and lifeless, the voice of a man grown too weary to keep up a pretense.

"No," replied Wagner disdainfully, sensing BRIDEGROOM's mood, knowing it was over. "I'll say it for you. You had an excellent reason for not mentioning Nick and Tina. You were afraid we might discover that they not only helped you prepare false reports to give to the Russians . . . but that they also fabricated material for you to give to us." Then, as though he felt it was necessary to say something else, he added, "You're a fraud, Victor."

For a moment BRIDEGROOM said nothing but his eyes expressed a particular kind of sadness . . . as if there was something he wanted to tell the younger man but knew the chasm of understanding between them was too great. "So . . . finally we have reached the end," he said with a smile of resignation.

"Is that all that this means to you?...the end of some kind of game you've been playing," glowered Wagner. He bent forward, a chiseled expression of scorn on his face. "Just what kind of man are you, anyway? I might have some respect for you if you really had worked for the Russians . . . then, at least, you'd stand for something. But you don't believe in anything except your own self-interest. We gave you a chance to help free your country from Communism and you made a mockery out of it."

"I envy you, Mr. Rogers. You are a lucky man to have such a certain knowledge of what is right," replied BRIDEGROOM quietly. "But have I really betrayed my country?...I wonder? You see, I am not sure enough of myself to dare measure things in terms of absolutes. And therefore, how can I be certain what the people of my country really want? Or . . . as you might put it . . . of what's good for them?

"You're not seriously trying to tell me that you've been a neutral all along are you, Victor?" chided Wagner.

"Neutral?" repeated BRIDEGROOM slowly shaking his head, " . . . no. But perhaps I should remind you that it was Mr. Fletcher who first came to me . . . not I who approached him. And it was the Russians, using that letter . . . " He pointed toward Wagner's pocket. " . . . who induced me to visit their embassy . . . not I who volunteered my services to them."

"What's that supposed to prove?" asked Wagner suspiciously.

"Only that I was not looking for involvement . . . with either side."

"And that entitles you to absolution?" responded Wagner sharply. Before BRIDEGROOM could reply, he continued, "You know, it's people like you that I'll never to able to understand.

You're perfectly willing to accept the comfort and protection of the Free World but you don't want to accept any of the responsibilities that go with it. You'd rather let somebody else worry about that while you self-righteously suck blood from both sides."

"How should I answer?...by saying I am sorry?...by confessing my sins and asking forgiveness? No . . . Mr. Rogers. I am many things . . . but I am not a hypocrite." BRIDEGROOM spoke in a steady deliberate voice as though he was acutely aware that this would be his last chance to communicate his feelings to Wagner. "You see, we live . . . you and I . . . in two separate worlds. You are strong enough to impose your freedom on others . . . or at least that is how it sometimes appears," he added ironically. "Don't misunderstand me . . . I also believe men have a basic right to be free. But after a lifetime, I have concluded that freedom is an attitude of mind and not a condition of geography."

"Do you expect me to disagree?' asked Wagner.

"No. Of course not," answered BRIDEGROOM slowly. "But you may not find it easy to understand that there are people who question the sincerity of your incantations on behalf of freedom. To them, Mr. Rogers, your struggle with the Soviets is a raw struggle for power, not a contest in ideologies. And like most of the human race . . . they have been the victims of power . . . so they find it hard to cheer the combatants."

"Are you trying to say there is no difference between us and the Russians?" asked Wagner incredulously.

"No. There are differences. But they have become so obscured by bombast that it sometimes seems the only difference is that you do all the wrong things for the right reasons and the Russians do all the wrong things for the wrong reasons."

Wagner listened impassively and even when he leaned forward to reply, there was no mark of emotion in his voice. It was as though he was reciting from memory. "This isn't a popularity contest. And we don't intend to run away from our obligations. There are too many people who depend on us."

"Yes . . . I know," answered BRIDEGOOM calmly. "At times power and principle seem to be natural enemies. But power has its own limits. I suppose that is why it is possible to talk about freedom . . . even promise liberation . . . and yet I wonder if the people should rise up on the streets of Budapest or Bucharest, whether you would join them in their fight for freedom or just stand aside and watch because it would be politically expedient," said BRIDEGROOM, before adding with a sad smile, "Perhaps there will come a day when we will know the answer."

Wagner's eyes flashed with resentment. "There's no point in discussing this any more tonight," he snapped. Wagner didn't move from where he was sitting but it was quite clear the meeting was over.

BRIDEGROOM waited for a moment and then hesitantly pushed back his chair from the table and began to stand up. Wagner watched in silence until the old man was on his feet before he added a carefully measured warning. " . . . But don't get the idea that you're out of this. There's a lot we want to know about Nick and Tina and Popescu."

Almost at once, an expression of apprehension clouded BRIDEGROOM's face. Yet he answered in a firm voice. "They are not responsible for what happened."

"Just be sure you're around when we want you," responded Wagner dryly.

BRIDEGROOM slowly nodded his head. "We'll be ready," he answered softly. For a moment he waited, expecting Wagner to say something . . . to make a last gesture. Instead, Wagner reached into his pocket and pulled out a pipe as though BRIDEGROOM no longer existed.

The old man stood there for a few seconds looking down with a grim smile of contemplation. Then slowly he began to re-button his topcoat. Finally, he turned up his collar and whispered, "Goodbye, Mr. Rogers." He was gone before Wagner finished lighting his pipe.

****

Outside the coffee house the street was deserted. Only the echoing sound of some quick footsteps in the distance snapped the silence. Night already had pushed its way into the city and enveloped the trees and hedges of the Gardens in a veil of darkness.

BRIDEGROOM stepped off the curb and walked with his methodical padding stride back across the street toward the entrance that led into the Gardens . . . the same entrance he and Wagner had used such a short time before.

He had no destination. But he needed to keep moving. It was almost as if his world would stop if he stopped. Sometime he would have to tell Nick and Tina. But not now. Now he needed time to clear his brain . . . to make new plans. But plans for what? To do what? A friend had once described life as a series of ever-narrowing concentric circles. He knew now that the last circle had narrowed so tightly there was no more room to move. He wondered about his mother . . . remembering her with a clarity he had not known since he left home. And what about Nick and Tina? What would become of them? Am I responsible for everything that has happened? And if I am? There was no answer.

If he had looked up, he might have seen him in time. But he was no longer conscious of anything around him. He heard the muffled sound of the gun discharging and felt the bullet hit. For an instant he stood as though frozen. Then he reached toward the burning pain that now tore through his chest. He knew he had been shot but he had the strange sensation that it was someone else's blood seeping through his fingers. He looked around as though wanting to ask a question but as he turned, his body wavered and then slumped to the ground.

Borakowsky stood in the shadows and watched him fall. Then he slowly slid the gun back inside his coat. For a few seconds there was the crunching sound of footsteps hurrying along the path and then . . . nothing.

CHAPTER TWENTY-THREE

"One thing you can be certain of in this business is that there is nothing you can be certain of," observed Christopher philosophically as he got up from his desk and walked across his office to pour himself a second cup of coffee. He stood for a few moments silently framing his thoughts before continuing to address his colleagues who had reclaimed the seats they had occupied only a few days earlier.

"BRIDEGROOM's murder is a game changer and gives us plenty of reason to take a hard second look at some of the assumptions and decisions we made the last time we met here." Christopher walked slowly back to his desk but before sitting down, added with a reflective smile," . . . .and I haven't forgotten that my voice was among the more adamant at that meeting. But based on what we now know, the decision to scuttle everything, including the Popescu operation, may have been a mistake. That's why we're here." He paused and took a sip of coffee before continuing.

"You all know George Prentakis, our liaison man with our Greek counterparts. He has a great working relationship with them and they're the ones responsible for investigating the murder. I've asked him to join us and fill us in on what he's found out so far." Christopher turned to Pentakis and with a casual wave, signaled for him to begin his report. "George, the floor's all yours."

"I'll begin by stating the obvious. It was not a random shooting. BRIDEGROOM was the target. The Greeks have found no evidence anywhere that he had enemies in the émigré community. We know he worked for us and we now know he was working with the Russians. That's who our Greek liaison friends think are responsible," concluded Prentakis, before adding with a knowing shrug, "but I have a feeling it may go down in the books as an 'unsolved crime' because of the political implications."

"I think that's called 'getting away with murder'," remarked Tommaney in a tone laced with sarcasm.

Christopher nodded in agreement before turning to Wagner. "Jack, you've been out to the safe house and talked to your friend, Nick. What did he have to say?"

"He repeated the same story BRIDEGROOM had given me . . . that BRIDEGROOM had no contact with the Russians until he received the letter from his mother. He said BRIDEGROOM's only motive for seeing the Russians was to help his mother get her medicine and that he never intended to provide the Russians with any useful information even after they put the arm on him."

"The road to hell is paved with good intentions," intoned Burns laconically, prompting a predictable groan from his colleagues.

Wagner acknowledged Burn's remark with a smile before continuing. "According to Nick, once BRIDEGROOM understood that any help from the Russians would be on a quid pro quo basis, he concocted the idea of creating notional agents to try to satisfy Golnikov's appetite for information. At one point, BRIDEGROOM made the mistake of suggesting to Golnikov that one of his 'so-called' informants might also be working for the British. That apparently touched a raw nerve with the Russians and Golnikov ordered BRIDEGROOM to arrange for him to meet the phantom agent at a specific time and place in Piraeus."

"Ah, the murky world of intrigue," joked Tommaney.

"You're right about that," laughed Wagner. "But somehow BRIDEGROOM managed to convince one of his old friends, a guy named Boris, to masquerade as the agent and show up at the meeting. As BRIDEGROOM's supposed agent began crossing the street to the designated meeting place, the Russians had a lorry ready to run him down. BRIDEGROOM shouted a warning and the intended victim managed to jump out of the way. At that point, BRIDEGROOM realized that his Russian handlers played for keeps and he confided in Nick and Tina that he wanted to break off his relations with them."

"Easier said than done," observed Ellis wryly.

"I agree with you on that, Hank," agreed Christopher. "Once the Russians began doubting BRIDEGROOM's reliability, they stepped up the pressure on him. He had to feel it and know he was in trouble. He just couldn't find a way out."

"They solved that problem for him," commented Prentakis caustically.

Burns looked up from his clipboard and with an inquisitive glance at Wagner, joined the discussion. "My question is, how did they know he would be in the National Gardens at that particular time?"

"Carl, I think I made it easy for them," answered Wagner, responding directly to Burns. "Once I found out BRIDEGROOM was working with the Russians, I focused all my attention on confronting him and ignored normal security precautions. I chose the wrong time and the wrong meeting place. You know the result."

"Jack, don't misunderstand me. I'm not trying to fix blame. That's not why we're here. I'm just trying to figure out how it all happened," replied Burns, trying to ease the tension.

"I think they just got lucky," observed Tommaney. "They don't have the manpower to put a full-time tail on anyone, and that would have included BRIDEGROOM. But once they decided he might be screwing them, they didn't hesitate to try to knock off one of his phony informants. And all they needed was a little more incriminating evidence and BRIDEGROOM was next in line. My guess is they decided to put a shadow on him whenever they got a chance and they had their suspicions confirmed when they spotted him meeting Jack."

"Bill, are you seriously suggesting that they would authorize one of their people to walk around with a loaded gun and make a seemingly spontaneous decision to commit murder in a public park based only on who he thinks he sees?" asked Burns derisively. "That stretches the imagination."

"I understand your point, Carl," interjected Ellis calmly, "but I don't think the decision to kill BRIDEGROOM was spontaneous. I think that decision already had been made. The place and timing of the murder may well have been simply a matter of pure chance and convenience as Bill has suggested."

"That explanation still seems to defy logic," replied Burns with a casual shrug.

"I agree," answered Ellis, "except that we've run traces on some of their Embassy staff, particularly Borakowsky, that reflect a consistent pattern of unsolved assassinations of trouble-making Russian exiles wherever he's been posted. That hit list includes journalists, politicians and an assortment of out-spoken critics of their regime. You can forget about his official rank in the Embassy. We know he's the guy in charge of their dirty work and he has a reputation of being a mean son-of-a-bitch. Golnikov is just his underling." Ellis hesitated before looking across at Burns and adding with a smile, "For a guy like Borakowsky, killing BRIDEGROOM was all in a day's work."

Christopher, who had been quietly listening to the exchange among his colleagues, put down his coffee cup, leaned forward and entered the conversation, putting an end to the post-mortem. "We've spent enough time sifting through the ashes. Now it's time to decide where we go from here. I know each of us has an opinion on what happened, why it happened and who was responsible. The unanswered question is whether or not there were important elements of the operation that were essentially untainted and should be salvaged."

Christopher paused, both elbows on his desk, his hands clasped under his chin and looked out at his audience with a smile of friendly respect. "I have reached my own conclusions that I want to share with you. I know each of you well enough to know that if you disagree, you won't hesitate to tell me why." Christopher continued his presentation in an unhurried, relaxed voice . . . a college instructor quietly lecturing a group of seminar students.

"In retrospect, I think BRIDEGROOM was telling us the truth about his relationship with the Russians. He had no love for them or for Communism. Like a lot of his contemporaries, he lived by his wits and he developed into an opportunistic paper mill, clever enough to invent fictitious informants who produced just enough useless information to keep his clients interested. It took awhile but the Russians figured him out and once they realized he was also meeting with us, they didn't waste time putting him permanently out of business." Christopher paused before adding half-jokingly, "But we can't accuse BRIDEGROOM of favoritism. Remember, we bit on his story that he had three agents back home in Romania just waiting for us to figure out a way to activate them."

"Still it would be unfair to dismiss him as having been nothing more than an unprincipled con man. He was a very talented guy who made a couple of bad decisions that ended up costing him his life. He was the recognized leader of the émigré community and did a good job keeping us tuned in on what was happening in that area. He introduced us to his old friend, Nick, which resulted in our successful ship monitoring program and more recently, the recruitment of Popescu."

Christopher paused momentarily before continuing. "As far as I'm concerned, any decision we make about reviving the operation depends on whether we have reason to think the Russians became aware of Nick and his relationship with BRIDEGROOM. If the answer is no, I think we can salvage the most significant part of what we are trying to accomplish; the Popescu operation and the potential to expand its scope."

"What's your call on it, Chris?" asked Ellis quietly.

"If we can satisfy ourselves that we can trust Nick going forward, and if we feel comfortable that he wasn't exposed to the Russians, then we'll be missing an operational opportunity if we don't try to capitalize on our Popescu connection. And there's no evidence that either Golnikov or Borakowsky knew Nick even existed. It certainly wouldn't have been in BRIDEGROOM's best interest to arrange an introduction." Christopher hesitated, as though examining his own argument for flaws before continuing.

"That leaves us with the question of whether Nick might have been spotted the day he took Popescu to meet with Jack. We had Tom Reedy watching him from the time of that meeting until the time he saw Popescu return to his ship with his crewmates. Tom has told us he saw nothing to suggest any kind of security compromise. At no time did he spot anyone who indicated they had even the slightest interest in either Nick or Popescu."

"How about you, Jack?" asked Christopher, turning to Wagner. "You met with both of them. Did you notice anything that seemed phony or contrived about their relationship or about Popescu's credibility?"

"No. The more time I spent with Nick and the more I watched him in action, the more impressed I became. He has a natural instinct for this business. I have no reason to doubt his story about his past relationship with Popescu or to think there was anything contrived about their reunion in Piraeus."

"O.K. I'm satisfied," responded Christopher, raising his hand in mock surrender before continuing.

"Here's my proposal. First... we zero in on Nick with a full-blown security check. We need to find out everything we can about his relationship with BRIDEGROOM and we need to find out as much as we can about what he's been doing and who he's been seeing since he arrived in Greece. We know he had an understandable loyalty to BRIDEGROOM. And we know he helped BRIDEGROOM by forging a few letters allegedly from contacts in Romania that BRIDEGROOM passed off to Swasey as genuine. What we don't know is whether they were his only misdemeanors or whether the guy is completely untrustworthy. That's the question we need answered."

"Has he ever been fluttered?" asked Tommaney.

"No, but he will be," responded Christopher. There's a Headquarter's polygraph operator making a circuit run who's scheduled to fly in from Rome within the next day or two. He's going to need help from a competent translator." He looked across at Ellis. "That seems like a perfect assignment for Kostas before we send him off to Washington to get started on his citizenship application. What do you think, Hank?"

"I agree."

"Well, that's settled," responded Christopher as he turned back to Wagner. "Jack, get together with Kostas as soon as you can and give him a complete briefing on what's happened and what we're trying to accomplish. We want to make certain all the right questions get asked. I know polygraphs aren't foolproof but they do have a way of exerting a lot of psychological pressure on some people." Christopher hesitated a moment and stroked his chin before adding, "Make sure you give Nick's girlfriend the same treatment. Her responses could either support Nick's story or raise questions about his credibility."

"What about the safe house?" asked Burns. "With BRIDEGROOM out of the picture, what kind of control will we have over Nick and . . . what's her name?"

"Tina," answered Wagner with a smile.

"Fair question. What do you think, Jack?" asked Christopher.

"I think that as an abundance of caution we should find a new safe house. If, after we complete our due diligence, we decide to go ahead with the operation, we're going to have to introduce some discipline and supervision that obviously didn't exist when we depended on BRIDEGROOM. Kostas won't be in Washington very long and when he comes back, he'll need a place to live. He's a good communicator, not an intimidator. I have a feeling Nick and Tina would welcome his supervision. And he was put to the test with those three agents we just cut loose. Tina and Nick would have natural cover as live-in housekeeper and yardman, so continuing our ship monitoring operation without interruption poses no security problem. At this point we don't know what future role, if any, Nick will play in the Popescu operation. My gut feeling is that we'll find him useful."

"Jack's made his case and it's pretty convincing but this is the time for any new ideas," said Christopher, inviting comment.

"I think establishing some consistent supervision is the key to working with someone as enigmatic as Nick and I like the idea of using Kostas. Count me in favor," responded Ellis.

"Anyone else?" asked Christopher, raising both of his arms in further invitation for comments. "If not, case closed. Decision made. Assuming Nick and Tina make it through our vetting procedures . . . and we'll throw the book at them, we'll move on. That means a new safe house, resumption of ship to shore monitoring, the introduction of Kostas for control purposes and most important of all; the continuing effort to establish permanent contact with Popescu and expand our contacts to include other seamen. Jack, that means you should go ahead and make your plans to travel to Istanbul to see if you can make a second contact." Christopher relaxed and leaned back in his chair. "Any questions?"

"Will Headquarters buy in?" asked Burns.

"That depends on who's doing the selling, laughed Christopher. "That's my job," he added confidently. "But for now, this meeting is adjourned . . . and thanks for all your help."

EPILOGUE

Wagner recognized her determined stride as she approached him from the opposite direction, slowing only when she looked up and saw him wave.

"Hi, Jack. I hope I didn't keep you waiting. I was afraid I might be late."

"You're never late, but if you had been, I would have been here waiting for you."

Heidi smiled and took his arm as they stepped inside Floca's for lunch.

"Actually, I was the one who was worried about being late," he confessed as he held her chair for her.

"I knew you were meeting with Chris this morning. How did it go?"

"It went very well, which is why I thought I might be the one who would be late. Chris has an unquenchable thirst for details. At this point I think he knows every move I made, from the time I got off the plane in Istanbul to the time I got back here."

"Henry told me that you had a really successful trip . . . that you met your agent and got a lot accomplished. He called it a 'home run' so you know how pleased he is. I'll add my congratulations and a welcome home. Somehow it seems as though you have been away longer than just a few days." She hesitated before adding, "I've missed you."

"Sometimes you don't have to be away very long to realize how much you can miss someone. It didn't take a trip to Istanbul for me to realize how lucky I am to look across the table and see you sitting there," responded Wagner.

"Those may be the nicest words ever spoken to me," she said softly. Then, as though embarrassed by her expression of sentiment, she added, "You may not realize it but your recruiting talents have impressed a lot of people who think your career potential is unlimited."

"I hope they're right," smiled Wagner, before hesitating and adding, "It may surprise you, but I'm not sure I want to make a career working for the Agency."

"Are you serious, Jack?" asked Heidi.

"Yes. I know I can do the work and probably do it well. That's not the issue." He paused long enough to pick up and examine his coffee cup before continuing. "I have to decide whether I'm really cut out for this job . . . whether I can live comfortably with myself if I stay."

"Have you always had those doubts?" asked Heidi.

"I think they've probably always been there. They've just been lying dormant. My final meeting with BRIDEGROOM and his murder triggered some serious soul searching. And I had time for a little personal reflection while I was in Istanbul."

He looked at Heidi with a questioning smile as he attempted to describe his feelings. "I've thought a lot about my last meeting with BRIDEGROOM and wish I had the chance to do it over. Resentment and phony toughness don't count for much. I treated him shabbily and I regret it. It wouldn't have changed the outcome if I'd shown a little compassion. And it also occurred to me while I was meeting with Popescu that he might be risking his life by working with us but I was in no danger. It's a simple enough problem. I have to decide whether I can do this work without losing my moral compass."

"I think I understand, Jack. But how do you make that decision?"

"I'll take my time. I still have at least another year on this tour to make a decision. And I have friends that I respect, including Hank and Bob Foster, who seem to have made their choice to stay. I want to talk with them. Meanwhile, I'll give some thought to what my alternatives might be," he concluded before looking across the table and quietly asking, "But what about you? Do you have any long-range plans?"

Heidi hesitated, not sure how to respond to his unexpected question. When she answered, her eyes were focused on him. "Jack, I'm fortunate. I don't have the moral dilemma that you're wrestling with. I don't make the hard decisions. I just record them. I enjoy what I do and I work with wonderful people. Beyond that, I don't have any viable options. So I suppose that means that I'll go on doing what I'm doing."

"What if you had a viable option? Would you consider it?"

"Do you have any suggestions?" she asked with an amused smile.

"What if someone came along, someone like me, someone who was uncertain about what he'd be doing or where he'd be doing it in the near future, but someone who loved you very much? Would you consider that to be a viable option?"

"Jack, are you proposing to me?"

"Yes. I can't imagine my life without you."

"I accept," she smiled. "I don't know if you've noticed, but there is a significant patch on my heart with your name on it."

Wagner stood up, walked around the table, bent down and kissed Heidi on the cheek. "Shall we go back and tell Hank our news?"

"Somehow I have the feeling he is going to approve," she laughed as she rose and felt Wagner's arm around her waist as he led her outside the restaurant.

They had just stepped on to the sidewalk when Wagner felt a familiar tug at his sleeve and heard his voice.

"Hello, Mr. Jack."

"Hi, Dmitri. I'm glad to see you," greeted Wagner as he turned to Heidi. "I've told you about my friend, Dmitri, and now you have a chance to meet him."

Heidi looked down at the young boy who was beaming with pride at their attention. "Dmitri, I've heard so many nice things about you that I'm glad a finally have a chance to meet you."

Wagner put his arm around Dmitri's shoulder. "Dmitri, I want you to meet Heidi. She is a very special person. I will tell you a secret and you will be the first to know." Wagner looked at Heidi who nodded her head in approval of what he was about to say. "Heidi and I are going to be married."

Dmitri smiled with pleasure as he reached out to shake Wagner's hand. As he did, he looked up at Heidi and said, "He's a good man."

"I know," she responded.

Still gripping Wagner's hand, Dmitri looked up at him. "And a very lucky man."

"I know," said Wagner with an appreciative smile.

The young boy again turned to Heidi. "Is it all right if I call you 'Mrs. Jack'?"

"I would like that very much."

"I hope you like pistachios."

"I love pistachios," she replied as she hugged her new young friend before reaching out to take Wagner's hand to lead the way back to work.

CPSIA information can be obtained at www.ICGtesting.com
Printed in the USA
BVOW05s0338120916

461718BV00001B/2/P